THE COMFORTABLE SHOE DIARIES

by

Renée J. Lukas

Bella
BOOKS

2015

Bella Books, Inc.
P.O. Box 10543
Tallahassee, FL 32302

Printed in the United States of America on acid-free paper.

First Bella Books Edition 2015

Editor: Medora MacDougall
Cover Designer: Judith Fellows

ISBN: 978-1-59493-427-8

PUBLISHER'S NOTE

About the Author

Renée J. Lukas is a humorist and cartoonist, as well as a screenwriter and novelist. Her work can be found in all four corners of the United States and points in between. When she's not teaching screenwriting, she loves to overanalyze films. Originally from Tennessee, she now calls Massachusetts home.

For my parents
Richard and Marita,
who always believed in me.

For my sister Jennifer,
my hero and best friend,
who always inspires me.

For Jackie, Cason and Hayden,
Tucker and Hunter,
always follow your dreams.

For Julie and Tony,
for all your encouragement.

And for Beth,
who I'm lucky enough
to share this journey with,
whose love and support
make it all worthwhile.

CHAPTER ONE

"Vǎldemort"

Recently I was diagnosed with chronic anxiety disorder. So I don't just worry; I worry *chronically*. Like everything I do, I try to give it a hundred percent. And once again, I've gone the extra mile.

It's no surprise when you come from a family of neurotics who, before you board a plane, don't wish you a safe trip but instead smile and wave and say, "Call us if you make it!"

But you get used to it, and that becomes your normal. Like happiness. For some people, it's an everyday feeling that is just part of their experience, like blow-drying their hair a certain way. For others like me, it's a fleeting, elusive thing that I might catch for a few moments a day—like a lightning bug in my hands.

This would not be a day for lightning bugs. Today I sat in a strange apartment and watched streaks of rain make different shapes down the window. All at once it hit me—I had lost everything in one month—my job, my relationship of twelve years, my house, my credit score, everything. Again, I gave it a hundred percent.

"I have great dishes from IKEA, so we'll use mine." Debra's voice chirped in the other room, trying to make small talk to keep me from crashing into a sea of despair. She was my best friend who invited me to come live with her after my foreclosure. She was always breaking up with her boyfriend, Kurt, and now that they were on a long break, it seemed like a good time to stay with her. Aside from his guitar in the corner, the bedroom was all set up for me. But it was filled with boxes from a life I didn't recognize—my own.

At forty, I got laid off from my job, declared bankruptcy and was single for the first time since three presidents ago. I'd been "off the market" for so long, I didn't know what to do or how to do it. And magazines like *Cosmo* and *Glamour* weren't going to help me, either, because they were all about pleasing a *man*— how to ask him out, how to tell if he's cheating and how to do that thing he won't tell you that he really wants you to do in bed.

Debra came in. "You wanna have dinner soon?" She had dark hair and big brown eyes filled with concern.

"I'm not really hungry."

"You have to eat," she insisted. "First it's 'I'm not that hungry,' then you're not eating at all, then drinking too much, having blackouts under bridges, then wasting away until you're just another statistic."

I'd never noticed it before. Debra was as dramatic as my sister.

Why does everyone have to shield you from a bad mood? Sometimes you have to just let it crash on you. Feel the shards of glass poking you in the eyes. Feel the pain. Experience the blood and gore and darkness. Then later let the sun come out and sing Disney songs.

Debra wouldn't understand. Someone who broke up with her boyfriend every other week couldn't understand a breakup after twelve years—and everything that went with it. Nor could she understand losing a long-held position in a coveted industry. I'd defined myself by my job as an advertising copywriter. I took pride in every stupid toothpaste jingle or hotel billboard. And Debra Lansing, with her Gucci purses, couldn't possibly understand the humiliation of a layoff, let alone bankruptcy.

"I'm too stubborn to waste away." I resumed my blank stare out the window. It probably was a bit creepy.

"I know what you're going through," she said, sitting on the edge of the bed. "Well, not everything. When I screamed at Kurt, he just ignored me. Can you believe that? All I could hear were his stupid dirty boots clomping down the stairs. Then… nothing." Debra waved her hand dramatically. She'd always wanted to go into theater but settled for a job as a financial analyst instead. She saved her best monologues for her friends.

"Seriously? You and Kurt? You'll take him back in a week. And please give me enough notice, okay?"

Debra stared at me strangely. "You look pale. I mean really pale."

"I am pale."

I wanted to be alone without anyone staring at me, checking on my "condition." I was naturally fair-skinned, and my short hair, which used to be naturally a white-blonde typically found in a Clairol bottle, was now a shade of blonde that looked like it was never washed quite enough. I wasn't about to look in the mirror today. All I'd think about was that I was aging faster than the picture of Dorian Gray and couldn't afford a bottle of hair color now if I wanted it.

"Do you want to be alone?" Debra asked.

"Yeah." My voice cracked.

"Okay," she replied. "But it's not good to be alone for too long. Your head starts getting messed up and crazy."

"You need to quit watching *Dateline*."

She smiled faintly and shut the door, as I inhaled the scent of Chihuahua throughout the apartment. Luckily, Rebel, her four-legged oversized rat, was on the other side of the closed door. After my cat hissed at her, they had an understanding.

I searched my thoughts, trying to figure out where I'd gone wrong. Valerie and I had been together for twelve years, and because we couldn't be legally married in Connecticut there was nothing binding us together except our word that we'd stay committed to each other. I could have stayed angry that I was left with a mortgage that was in my name and that my financial awareness was pitiful enough to make Suze Orman scream at me in front of a live studio audience. But the bigger truth was that we'd been living a lie for a long time and denying it, washing it down with beer at places we didn't even like—Scruggy's Sports Bar & Grill—places where we pretended to understand the rules of baseball.

Valerie was a striking woman who carried herself like she owned the world. I was proud of her accomplishments as a top-notch prosecutor. She and I had bonded with our belief in justice for all people. But the flame had long since died, and we kept marking time with visits to theme parks, family get-togethers, new ornaments on the Christmas tree each year, anything to make us feel like everything was okay. Comfortable.

And it was comfortable. Sometimes, comfortable is not where you want to be, unless you're talking about shoes. Doing things that scare you, that give you those butterflies in your stomach, those are reminders that you're alive. We never talked about the elephant in the room until it was so big the roof was starting to pop off. Finally, we talked about it. When we did, we knew it was over. Breaking up something so comfortable was both frightening and exhilarating.

Dating someone again could feel similar to going skydiving and being next in line out of the hatch with nothing but sky to greet you. I wouldn't know. I'd never been skydiving. But after more than a decade of having someone to spend holidays with, it's very scary. You don't know what's out there.

My friend Penny knew. She lived online. Every other weekend we were taking her to the airport to meet someone she'd had "chemistry" with over the phone. They had all ended thus far in heartbreak—and one restraining order. So I'd gotten a glimpse of what was out there and discovered, through Penny, that online was where all the psychos hung out.

* * *

Later that night, I was tossing back a few beers with Debra when my good friend, Maddie Kimball, banged on the door. Maddie was a stocky, intense woman with a movie star face: dark curled hair and a general bitterness toward the world.

She'd turned forty-nine last year, but she remained a perpetual Peter Pan, still figuring out what she wanted to be when she grew up. Most of the time she was angry at her love life and disappointed when she came back from lesbian cruises without having met the dream woman. Of course, she had very specific criteria for this dream woman—right down to chest and thigh measurements. Maddie was looking for Sophia Loren, Angelina Jolie or anyone with a butt you could set a drink on.

I suddenly realized that Debra and Maddie didn't know each other very well.

When Debra opened the door, Maddie came right in, carrying a six-pack of imported beer. "Is everything closed in Connecticut after eight o'clock?" she asked, popping the top off one. "Maddie." She extended her hand to Debra, who looked slightly afraid.

"Debra Lansing," she said, shaking Maddie's hand.

"We met at the Christmas party last year," Maddie explained, taking a seat. Then she turned to me. "How are you holding up?" Her bright blue eyes searched my face.

"I'll make some crab-stuffed mushrooms!" Debra excitedly ran into the kitchen where she could try out recipes she'd collected online. I knew she was thinking of this as some sort of dinner party. What she was about to witness were lesbians in their natural habitat, and with my friends, it was usually a lot more casual than what Debra probably had in mind.

"Tell me you didn't give all her stuff to charity," Maddie moaned.

"Most of it."

"Shit, you could've made a fortune on eBay!" She took a swig of her drink and scowled in disapproval. "What is it with these women?"

"I told you. It was mutual."

"It's never mutual," Maddie argued. "Somebody always does something. Look at Holly and me."

"What happened to you?" Debra called from the kitchen.

"Oh, you know, it's an age-old story," Maddie said. "Girl meets younger girl doing laundry, is instantly attracted to her underwear, and old granny panties is kicked to the curb."

"That's an age-old story?" Debra smiled, trying to contain her amusement. "Wait a minute, back up. Her underwear?"

"The girl had those skimpy Victoria's Secret panties that are shaped like underwear but don't really cover anything," Maddie explained. "Holly always said I wore granny underwear, and I do. I admit it. They're big, white cotton briefs. I want to be comfortable. If I wear lacy, itchy underwear all day on the off-chance I'm going to get some later, I'll just be scratching so much people will think I have a yeast infection."

I shook my head. "That's what's wrong with lesbians."

"Yeast infections?" Maddie asked.

"No, dummy. Because there's no man, neither one of you initiates sex until it becomes just cuddling. And before you know it, you've cuddled so much you're now watching *House Hunters* every night and no one's touching anyone. It happened to me and Val." Her name left a bitter aftertaste in my mouth. "How about no one says her name again, okay? Let's call her…"

"Văldemort," Maddie declared.

We clinked bottles. It was perfect. Nicknaming her after the villain of *Harry Potter* gave me a strange sense of comfort.

It was true. I had seen every episode of *House Hunters*. It had gotten to the point where I could name the couple before they introduced them. "Oh, that's Kevin and Barb from Minnesota. They're moving to Austin." I sounded like an old person making friends at the local pool.

"So," Debra began carefully, "is it true that lesbians don't have as much sex?"

"You're talking about lesbian bed death," Maddie replied as if she were a lesbian scholar. "It's a myth."

"I don't know," I sighed.

"Okay," Maddie replied. "We're not thinking with our chattahoochies all day, so we might have to work harder to get it going. But once it gets going, it's hot." I could tell she was trying to remember what sex felt like.

Debra, now with her mushrooms in the oven, sat in awe like she was looking at a fascinating museum exhibit.

The doorbell rang, and Rebel barked so hard Debra had to put her in her room. I was relieved. I didn't want to watch her sniffing crotches all night. Dog owners never seemed to notice that.

At the door was Penny Granger. She was a wisp of a blonde, a couple of years younger than I, with long hair and an attractive face. She was a contradiction of lipstick and hiking boots, and she loved to wear T-shirts with peace symbols or messages about how to be more positive. She'd heard the news about me and Văldemort and got away from her computer long enough to come over. I was touched at the show of support.

"Hey!" she called in a slight Southern accent, after introducing herself to Debra. She gave me the hardest hug I'd ever gotten from her.

"I'm glad you came." I smiled. Maybe being alone tonight wasn't the best thing.

Penny handed Debra another six-pack of imported beers, which Debra examined and placed in the fridge. Debra was used to wine-drinking women at her monthly book club where they read romance novels and talked about each other's boyfriends and husbands. Tonight would be an eye-opener for her.

"Now we have a party!" Maddie exclaimed. "We'll get your mind off that bitch." She touched my shoulder.

Just then everything seemed like it would be all right.

"I'd love to," I managed to say. "But don't be so nice or you'll make me cry."

"Too late for that," Debra chimed in. "I'll get boxes of tissues, and we can watch *Terms of Endearment, Love Story, The Way We Were…*"

Maddie covered Debra's mouth. "I'm going to stop you right there, straighty. That's not what lesbians do to forget our exes."

"It's what I do every time I break up with Kurt. It's healthy to embrace your pain."

"It's also healthy to watch movies where the women are hotter than your ex," Maddie explained.

"Yeah," Penny agreed. "You got *Terminator Two*? The one with Linda Hamilton holding that rifle? Mmm!"

We laughed at her. Sometimes Penny seemed more suited to be a princess from an animated movie.

"What?" Penny wailed. "I mean it. She could shoot me any day."

"Me too," I admitted, already feeling better.

Debra stood dumbfounded in the kitchen. "Wow. That's... cool."

"It really works," I said. "You should try it next time you two, you know."

"I told you, there won't be a next time." Debra didn't believe herself.

Maddie hiked up her pants like Don Knotts and took another beer out of the fridge.

"Wow," Debra said. "You girls certainly have plenty to drink." Her nervous giggle either came from awkwardness or judgment.

"That's the plan," I replied. "If the movie doesn't help me forget, the beer will."

Some of us laughed.

And there we were, all gathered around the TV, watching Cinderella go to the ball and find her Prince Charming. It was an odd choice for a group of lesbians. But Debra didn't have any *Terminator* or Jodie Foster movies—not even old *Charlie's Angels* reruns.

"This is so romantic," Penny cooed.

"Yeah," Debra sighed.

"It's crap," Maddie spat. "More Hollywood bullshit that teaches little girls to wait around for a man. What if the girl turns out to be gay?"

"Yeah," I agreed. "Sometimes I'd give anything to see them make one with a Princess Charming."

Maddie thought a second. "Yeah."

"It's a cartoon!" Penny hollered. "Y'all read too much into it."

"Cartoon, music video, it's all the same sexist crap. Why can't Cinderella stop being a victim, tell off her bitch of a stepmother and make Charming prove he's husband material first?" Maddie folded her arms. She really needed her own talk show.

I popped one of Debra's crab-stuffed mushrooms into my mouth. "Damn, this is good. It's a little bite of heaven." I moaned a little too loudly, I guess.

"Are you having an orgasm?" Maddie asked.

"If you tried one of my mushrooms, you'd understand." Debra was quietly offended that Maddie hadn't touched an appetizer yet.

"No thanks," Maddie said flatly. "I'm not interested in touching one of your mushrooms."

"These mushrooms are from a gourmet cuisine website!" Debra huffed.

"I'm just not into them, okay?"

I laughed, but Debra didn't get the joke. She was still upset.

"Will you guys stop!" Penny hollered. "We're supposed to be here for Sydney. It's her night, right?"

Penny had shamed everyone.

"Sorry, kiddo." Maddie gave me a hug.

When the slipper fit Cinderella, there was a collective sigh of relief that we could shut it off.

"It gives me hope," Penny said, tearing up.

"Are you still looking online?" Maddie asked.

"Yeah," Penny answered. "Not everyone on there is bad."

"Oh yes, they are," Maddie exclaimed. "Look at all the nuts you've met at the airport."

"So," Debra said, standing up, "did we get your mind off Valerie?"

"Văldemort," I corrected.

"What happened with y'all?" Penny asked softly.

"We just fell out of love," I responded.

"I never understood that," Maddie said. "If you once loved someone, how can you fall out of it unless you didn't really love them to start with?"

"I did in the beginning," I said defensively. "I know it seems kind of weird. But that's what happened."

"So you guys don't do the club scene?" Debra asked, trying to get me out of the hot seat.

"It's just not fun," Penny said. "The music now is pounding, like listening to a wreckin' ball, so you can't hear what anyone is screaming in your ear."

"The songs suck now too," Maddie said. "It's techno shit. You scream for hours, trying to have a conversation. Then you just go home, crawl into bed, and the only tongue you get is from your dogs."

"Eww," I groaned.

Maddie realized she was talking about herself and saw everyone staring at her. "Well, you'll go home to your computer." She was looking at me and Penny. "A cold, flat comfort in the night."

"Uh, you know, thanks." I stuffed my face with chips.

"Clubs are more occasional for women our age," Maddie told Debra. "I don't know what you do in the straight world, if it's really like *Sex and the City*, where you sit around drinking Cosmos all day. But when lesbians get older, they quit the bars and start having cookouts."

"That's not true," I said. "Is it true?"

Maybe Maddie *was* an authority on lesbians.

"Think of all the friends we've had who have coupled off," Maddie continued. "We never see them anymore unless it's a cookout. Barb and Sally? When did we see them last?"

I thought about it. "Their Fourth of July…cookout."

Everyone laughed.

"Wow." For Debra, it was like taking a class in Lesbians 101.

It felt good to laugh. I laughed until I couldn't breathe. I never wanted the night to end.

CHAPTER TWO

"'C' is for Cookie"

The next morning, I woke to the sounds of dishes clanking in the kitchen. I realized I'd never lived with Debra before. Was she a cheerful early riser who sang in the shower?

Cookie trembled in her cat carrier. She wouldn't come out since we'd moved. She was black and white, a fat cat who was nearing her dotage. She looked like an Oreo, so she was named Cookie. Ironically, I'd gotten her as a Christmas gift for Văldemort. When we split up, Văldemort refused to keep her and threatened to take her back to a shelter. So I had no choice but to keep her out of guilt. Me, who wasn't a cat or animal person, whose throat closed up if I ate dinner near her while she was licking herself, who couldn't pet her without washing my hands—yes, I was the perfect choice to be a cat mother.

It wasn't just my animal issues, either. I did like animals, but from a distance. At least the gorillas at the zoo had a bullet-proof partition between you and them. Unlike Dian Fossey, I wasn't about to go lying in the jungle for an afternoon nap with a family of gorillas. And those movies showing regal horses galloping through the countryside—they never reveal the truth: that in real life, up close, horses smell really bad, the kind of stink you can't even describe, it's so bad. No one ever talks about that. But if you do, people look at you strangely like you must be a heartless person who squishes baby chicks in your spare time. I'm not like that. I feel sorry for dogs and cats locked up at the pound. I can't even watch the commercials with their sad faces. That must mean something.

My Aunt Rita was always sending me emails about the plight of dolphins and the inhumane treatment of chickens locked up all their lives before being slaughtered. I tried to buy cage-free eggs at the store. But I had to tell her I couldn't be a vegan because I don't like beans. That one stumped her.

"You'd need a source of protein," she'd commented over the phone. "Let me get back to you on that."

She never found a solution but kept sending me pictures of abused dogs. I felt terrible and depressed, as if somehow it was my fault.

Honestly, Cookie was a scary cat. She hissed at everyone. And because she wasn't declawed, she scratched everything. Like all animals, Cookie was unpredictable. I was a little scared of her myself. Even though she'd purr on me and all of that, I'd never approach her from behind or she'd think it was a sneak attack and rip my skin off. I always came to her gently, cautiously, from the front, letting her sniff me first, even though she'd known me for ten freaking years, before attempting to pet her. She was psychotic, and my sister Joanne hated but tolerated her. I felt sorry for Cookie, that she couldn't do better in this life than having an owner with OCD, someone who was possibly as neurotic as she was. Maybe that was why she was so mean. If she'd been human, she'd probably tell me off while smoking a cigar, then throw her martini in my face.

On the other hand, maybe we were meant for each other in some weird, cosmic way. In between the hissing and biting, there were those moments of total peace when Cookie slept in my lap. She made a soft rumble like a weak motorcycle starting. But the moment her back leg went up and she dove into her naughty place, I'd throw her off my lap so fast and run to the bathroom to disinfect myself. It was a strained relationship, full of love, disgust, fear and sometimes hate.

But Val's words to me the last time I spoke to her were so strange and eerie, not like the Val I'd known, the one with integrity and a sense of responsibility.

"She's your cat!" I shouted.

"Fine. Then I'll make arrangements to have her taken to the local shelter." This wasn't Val's voice; it was a fembot. Someone had possessed her mind, most likely her new girlfriend. The only way Val would have made sense to me in the end would have been if her head had spun completely around and she'd started to barf up green goo. Then I would have said, "Oh, she's just not in her right mind. She's possessed." But this new version of her was strangely cold and disconnected, as if she'd never known me or the cat she'd held like a baby every night for a decade. I guess that was what she needed to do to start her new life, to sever any connection to the past. But for me, the past gets woven into the tapestry that makes up your whole life. Whether you disconnect from it or try to run miles away from it, it's part of you and makes you who you are today. You can't get around it by changing personalities or not taking phone calls. For me, facing the past was the only way to move forward.

Not that it was comfortable for me to face, either. Thoughts of Val were more like a minefield of cringe-worthy emotions I had to tiptoe around. But I had to come to terms with my role too in order to move on. I was no saint. I'd burned more bridges than I cared to count. But for me, it was better to leave the scabs alone and let the wounds heal rather than to run around trying to pick at them and start some new flaming infection of toxic emotions. I'd save those for my therapist.

Cookie went to her bowl and I heard the tiny sounds of crunching. How strange, I thought. We're in the middle of so much turmoil—I wondered if she sensed it. No matter what was going on, she didn't seem to care as long as she had food and a place to sleep. I marveled at how simple and clear Cookie's priorities were. I prayed she wouldn't get sick and need any expensive treatments. She would have been better off with a lawyer like Val who could afford any kind of drops or pills an older cat might need—not with someone who had just been cut loose from the *Titanic* without a lifeboat. I petted Cookie softly, to let her know things would be all right. I wasn't sure how they would be all right, but I wanted her to believe it.

CHAPTER THREE

"Little Miss Sunshine State"

Still tired, I stumbled out into an apartment that was Martha Stewart clean, not the trashy mess of beer cans I'd last seen.

"Sorry I didn't help clean up," I said.

Debra was scrubbing down the kitchen counter.

"Forget it," she sang.

"I should've helped."

"No," Debra said. "You needed to get some rest. You were exhausted. It was a great night, you know? I learned something about all of you."

"We're gay?"

"Besides that." She flipped a waiting egg in a pan. "You guys are no different from me and my friends. When there's a breakup, everyone understands the pain. Some are better at consoling than others. Some say all the wrong things and make it worse. But you're friends, so you stick together no matter what."

I smiled at her, glad something good came out of the evening. Then I glanced out the big living room window, at the buildings and buzzing streets below. All at once I remembered that I had no job. Except for Debra, I hadn't told my friends about that or the bankruptcy. I was too embarrassed. Suddenly I was a deadbeat. A loser. After all, this kind of thing didn't happen to me. I'd done everything right, having a job, paying my bills. But unemployed? That kind of person was someone I'd heard about on the nightly news, not the someone staring back at me in the mirror. I was in such a deep hole and without a clue how I was going to get out of it. If I didn't do something fast, I'd only sink deeper.

I spent my first unemployed week visiting the unemployment office, where I tried not to make eye contact with anyone, furiously sending résumés with cover letters to companies I used to make fun of explaining why I'd always wanted to work there and yelling at a Congressman on TV who said that people were unemployed because they wanted to be.

I slumped on the bed in the spare room and stared at the ceiling until I saw faces of old, scary men with beards in the paint patterns. They were staring down at me, calling me a loser.

I could hear Debra out in the living room talking softly to someone who I was sure was Kurt, and I knew their reunion would be coming soon. I'd need another place to live fast. Of course this sent my anxiety levels rocketing higher than ever, so I actually took some of the medication my therapist had recommended.

I ran through my options. I couldn't live with Maddie and her seven dogs. Okay, maybe she only had three, but it felt like seven. Her house smelled of dog pee, but she never noticed it. Penny might have been a good choice, but she only had one bedroom. My New Age friend Ariel smoked like a chimney— not good for my asthma. I was running out of ideas.

There was a soft, tentative knock on the door. My heart sank to my knees. I knew what was coming.

"It's open," I called.

Debra entered with a guilty face. "Sydney," she began. "There's something I need to tell you."

"Let me guess. You forgave him again, and I need to move."

She stepped back, indignant and surprised. "No, I was going to say we're out of bread. You mentioned a sandwich for lunch, and I'll have to go get bread."

"Really?"

She put her head down. "Well, that, and yeah, Kurt's moving back. But not right away! Stay as long as you want!"

I sat up, familiar hot flashes fluttering up my spine. Another anxiety attack. "What does he care if I'm here? You guys share a room anyway." I was so low my shoulders hung over my head.

"This is usually his music room. But he'll deal with it."

"Will he?" My eyes filled in spite of myself. The last thing I wanted was to show any emotion. I envisioned Xena and took my warrior princess stance.

"He knows you need to stay a while. It's just…" She trailed off.

I stood up, Xena pumping through my veins. "It's just he's the self-centered kind of guy who doesn't care if you're helping out a friend. The guy you always fight with for being self-centered, and then you take him back even though, oh…he's still self-centered!"

"Please, try to—"

"Save it! You know what? You're not a real friend. Real friends don't let each other down."

I stormed out in a huff, my pride underneath my shoes.

I drove around Connecticut for hours, my eyes blinded with tears. I didn't know where I was going, what I'd be doing. And frankly, I was more terrified than I'd ever been. The last time I was this scared was during a freak seesaw accident in first grade.

I stopped off in Danbury to visit Penny. I must have looked like a mess because her expression was one of horror when she opened the door.

"Aw, hon, come on in." She closed the door behind me and led me straight to the bathroom. "You should take a bath. It'll help you relax. I've got fresh towels in here."

I was crying so hard I couldn't catch my breath. Just seeing a kind face set off the waterworks and there was no stopping them. Everything seemed out of my control.

Sitting in the bathwater, I thought of my dad, how he hated baths. He was very fastidious and said that taking a bath was like lying in your own filth. I missed him.

Then I went over everything that had happened, just like they tell you never to do. It rained the day I got laid off. I remember seeing my boss's lips move, but his words sounded more like the teacher from the *Peanuts* cartoon strip: "Wah, wah, wah…downsizing…wah wah severance package…wah, wah, wah." I shivered at the memory.

My ego was trampled. How dare they fire me. I'd won awards! I wasn't some lazy person hanging out in the breakroom gossiping, someone to be cast out like yesterday's trash. But the bomb dropped on me anyway.

It had rained so hard. I sat in a stairwell afterward and looked out the window. My first thought was that this was the break I'd always wanted. Now I'd have time to be like J.K. Rowling and write that *thing* that was going to put me on the map as a writer. I was getting burned out anyway, I'd told myself. The truth was, it was a good living. And the odds of writing that *thing*—well, my work was once described as more suited to an independent film. No boy wizards or vampire babies. I was screwed.

I'd picked up my journal the first day after getting laid off. All I could write were sad tales of women losing their jobs, stuck in their forties and suddenly, frighteningly, single again. It read more like a Lifetime movie about a midlife crisis. Yeah, audiences would flock to that.

"You okay in there?" Penny knocked on the door.

How sweet, I thought numbly; she's making sure I didn't drown myself.

"Yeah," I called. "For now."

"That's not funny, Syd. Considering your…state of mind."

I had no state of mind. I had no state. Suddenly it occurred to me. Without my job, there wasn't much point in being in Connecticut. Now I truly felt homeless.

The bath helped me escape for a while. I could stare at the bubbles and watch them float and see how long it took before they popped on something. Kind of like life—you're going along, floating higher and higher, but something will always stop and pop you. I realized I could put a negative spin on anything. Just wait until I got to the shampoo.

When I emerged a cleaner version of myself, Penny put a hot cup of tea in my hand. I didn't drink tea, but it was the universal sign of comfort. We sat on the couch.

"Thanks," I said, holding up the mug.

"Ariel got it for me. It's ginger something, supposed to release toxic emotions."

"Of course." I smiled.

Ariel was our bisexual, New Age friend who was big on astrology, Tarot cards and energy fields. Penny broke up with her last girlfriend because Ariel mentioned the girl had negative chakras. I had no idea what chakras were at the time. I thought it was a venereal disease.

"I'm going to have to move out," I finally said. "Debra's taking Kurt back again."

"You're kidding!"

"Nope. Wish I was." I took a sip. "Penny, there's something I haven't told you. I lost my job."

She nodded wisely. "I know."

"You know? How?"

"Debra told us the other night when you went to the bathroom." Penny lowered her eyes. "None of us wanted to say anything until you said something. Then Maddie was all, you know, because you told Debra and not us. But we told her to shut up about it."

"It's nothing personal," I said. "I just felt really bad."

"I know." She patted my leg. "So what's with Debra and Kurt?" I was grateful for her changing the subject.

"Oh, you know. The woman has no sense."

"How many times does she have to get screwed over?"

"I didn't mean that. I meant she has no sense, being straight." I smiled at my weak attempt at a joke.

"Glad you haven't lost your humor." Penny touched my hand.

"My sister's straight. Of course, she's crazy too." I zoned off into the distance when my cell phone rang. Like telepathy, it was Joanne, my sister. I exhaled dramatically. "You mind? It's Joanne."

"No, no." Penny headed outside. "I have a garden full of tomato plants that aren't going to grow themselves."

"Hello?" I said.

"Where is she? I'll come up there and bitch-slap her!" Joanne's raspy voice made my phone tremble. I knew it had been a matter of time before the news reached down to Florida.

"Well, hello to you too."

"How can you be so calm about this!" Her voice hit an octave that could break glass. "That bitch! And when were you going to tell me about this? Next Christmas?"

"No, I just needed some time to figure out where my next paycheck is coming from. I don't really know the answer to that, though."

"How convenient. Suddenly, you're not making any money, and she decides to leave."

"No," I insisted. "Seriously, Jo, it was mutual."

"It's never mutual." She sounded like a rabid dog.

"It was, believe it or not."

"Really?" Joanne persisted. Why was it so hard for everyone to believe? "But you did have a place together. And how convenient, she could just walk out and leave you with everything to deal with. She knew with this economy you'd never sell that dump."

"I happen to like that place."

"Oh please, Syd. The walls were peeling."

There was silence. I was tired of defending myself. Maybe I didn't call her right away because I didn't want to relive it or start to cry and feel stupid again.

"I'm sorry, Syd," she finally said. "But you're my sister. Someone hurts you, they hurt me. And right now, ugh! I could just...ugh!"

"I get it."

"You know how I found out? From Mom."

"I figured."

"Is it because you're up there? Are we not as close as we used to be?"

Joanne was very dramatic, like everyone else in my family. But it was true. I knew things would never be the same since the first time I spoke to her on the phone after she had her first baby, Cabbot. I was telling her about jumping off a cliff, leaving my secure job to become a writer someday, and her response was, "No! We don't eat that! Damn. Cabbie chewed on the plant again. You know I've called Poison Control four times?" From then on I knew it would be a struggle to stay on her radar.

"Sometimes, I guess. I still want to talk to you." I tried to steady my voice.

"If you need anything," she said, "you know you can come down here and stay with us."

"Thanks, I appreciate it."

There was no way I'd move back to Florida. Joanne and her husband Nathan lived in a Stepford Wives enclave in Tampa. Everyone was conservative, had at least two-point-five children and a dog. It was a requirement. And Joanne fit all the requirements. Now I had two nephews, Cabbot and Tayler, and visiting Joanne always reminded me of how broken my life seemed, like pieces of a jigsaw puzzle that would never quite fit together. She had a house that went on for miles with granite countertops, a pool, a garage for two cars and a boat if they should decide to buy one and more than one guest room. I could actually choose which spare room I wanted.

Most of all, Tampa, like the rest of Florida, is hot. Everyone is a little crankier down there because they're so hot. When I used to live there, I would have thoughts of killing someone at least once a day—someone in traffic, in the grocery store parking lot—not real murder, but dark, evil thoughts because I was so hot and irritated. These things just weren't normal.

And we never had seasons, so it was harder marking time and memories. Thanksgiving was eighty degrees and sunny, just like Halloween. Houses were cookie-cutter and so was the weather. There is something unnatural and overly man-made about the whole state. It was originally a swamp that wasn't meant for humans to inhabit. But instead we came and conquered, like everything else, putting up condominiums, ignoring the threat of hurricanes, alligators and sinkholes. And worst of all was the swarm of red ants that attacked me once just because I stopped riding my bike on the sidewalk and put my feet on the ground for a minute. When I looked down, my left leg was red and crawling. I screamed and ripped my pants off right out in the open. But that's another story for my therapist.

All of those were reasons enough not to return. But the real reason was that I didn't want to go back in time. Going back would make me wonder, what was it all for?

Sure, you learn and grow from all your experiences, blah, blah, blah. But returning to the sameness of your youth gives you this sense of running in place, like a hamster on a wheel, never going anywhere. I didn't want that to happen to me. I think that was my real objection to returning to Florida. After all, who are we kidding? The state is more beautiful than a postcard.

"You'd be starting fresh," Joanne insisted. "It's not going backward."

"It is!"

"Is that what you think of me? That *I'm* going nowhere?" There she was again—defensive Joanne, always just under the surface, waiting to burst into the conversation and make it about her.

"This isn't about you," I said calmly.

"I have a very happy life, you know!"

"I'm sure you do! I didn't say you didn't!"

Did she protest too much? It was hard to tell. Joanne always seemed irritated lately. I thought it was because she lived in Florida.

"I'm sorry," she said. "I'm just sick over this." She was a human sponge, absorbing everyone else's stress and pain—so she barely had time for herself.

Her husband, Nathan Hutchins, wasn't around much. When I visited, he would stare blankly at me and try to get along with me because I was Joanne's sister. At least that's how it seemed.

He was no stranger to money; he came from a wealthy Southern family. He grew up in Georgia, where his dad, Owen Hutchins, owned practically all of Augusta. He, in turn, had sold his soul to a business that was doing better than anyone expected, a clothing store chain called *Wholesome Threads*. It was based, he said, on the idea that everyone really wanted to get back to simple values again, the basic beliefs of our founding fathers. Well, some of our founding fathers were adulterers and slave owners. When I joked that he probably didn't want to put those beliefs on any shirt, I got another blank stare.

His stores' shirts had sayings about being proud to be Southern or proud to be a "family man" or "family woman." I thought it was code for discrimination, and the success of his business scared me a little. I do believe that if it wasn't for Joanne, there would be some unwholesome threads in there for sure. My biggest supporter, she insisted there was nothing homophobic in his store or she'd divorce him.

I came out to my sister when I was twelve. The words "I'm gay" sounded too startling, so I revealed my secret by saying that *The Bionic Woman* was more than a TV show to me. It was my reason for living. Correction—Jaime Sommers, a.k.a. Lindsay Wagner, was my reason for living. Then I learned that Joanne had been watching *The Bionic Man* because of Steve Austin. Why would anyone waste their time on Steve Austin running with his collar and chest hair bouncing in slow motion? It made no sense to me. When we realized we'd watched those shows for completely different reasons, we laughed so hard we couldn't stop. It was a laugh that lasted for days.

Joanne never judged me. She never said, "Ew, gross" or "You're going to hell." What she did instead was the most common reaction in our family—guilt. She told me she supported who I was but added, "You know this will kill Mom."

Mom's reaction is one I save for my therapist.

Before we hung up the phone, I said, "Thanks for the offer. But I really do want to get my life back together my way. Can you understand?"

"Yeah, I guess. But you're sure it's nothing you just don't want to tell me because you're afraid it'll hurt my feelings?"

"I'm sure."

"You really like my husband?"

"Yes."

"Then it's the dog? We can keep Sergeant out back while you're here."

Sergeant was their black Labrador, who sometimes bared his fangs at me. Nathan insisted he only did that when he was startled. And I guess every time I reached for the remote control or went to the bathroom, it startled him. Yes, I could just picture them keeping him in the backyard during a classic Florida lightning storm.

"It's not the dog," I lied. It was partially the dog. But the getting-my-life-together part was completely true.

When Joanne was satisfied that my decision not to accept her offer wasn't based on her husband, her dog, her children, her neighborhood or her own personality, she hung up, vowing to work toward legal rights for lesbians.

"I love you," I said. "You're the greatest sister a girl could ever have, you know."

"Same here, Syd." There was a pause. "Don't feel like any of this is your fault. Sometimes bad luck comes in waves."

"I know."

I shut off my phone and stared at it a while. I really missed Joanne. The lump in my throat was swelling.

When Penny offered, I accepted. She'd just gotten a new pullout couch, and I'd be sleeping there. I felt like a refugee, looking for someone to take me in, all the while completely embarrassed. Who wants to be that friend that other friends get together and talk about and worry about? That was a role I really didn't want to play.

Then one night I decided I was ready for another role. I was going to make my big leap back into the dating scene.

CHAPTER FOUR

"Sex Out of the City"

Penny and I spent many nights on our laptops. When I wasn't combing the want ads, I'd post a comment underneath some controversial article and wait for the flurry of responses from anonymous people dumping on me.

"How's it going with the Kansas girl?" I asked.

"Great. She's talking about flying in this weekend." Penny was giddy, typing faster.

"Uh, so, where would you like me to go?" Penny's one-bedroom apartment was small, but there was a basement. It was dank and scary, and if you added a few flying moths you'd have *Silence of the Lambs*.

"It's okay if you're out here on the couch," she buzzed excitedly.

Oh no. Unless I got some earplugs, there was no way.

"Okay," I lied calmly. "You really feel good about this one?"

"Oh, yeah. We have so much in common. We both grew up in Tennessee. We both like country music. And we both think Faith Hill is a hottie."

"Well, you can certainly base a relationship on that." I sounded like a bitter, sarcastic old lady who lives alone, sitting on her porch, rocking away and wondering where she went wrong in life. "I'm really happy for you," I quickly added.

Penny came into the living room and plunked down opposite me. She had a look of dreamy stars in her eyes.

"Is this how it works now?" I asked. "I mean, look at me. I'm forty. I don't know how to date anymore. Have all the rules changed?"

"Not really," Penny answered simply. "You could go online and see hundreds of hot women."

"I'd rather not."

"Why? Why are you such an online dating snob?"

I wasn't comfortable advertising myself like a product on eBay.

"I don't know," I said. "You put your picture up. What if a psycho sees it?"

"There's a risk with everything."

* * *

That Saturday, Maddie limped up the driveway in her pea-green Chevy Nova, which was on its last legs. She honked the horn, and Penny dashed out, with me reluctantly following. This would be our sixth trip to Bradley International Airport in the last two months.

"I really appreciate y'all doin' this for me," Penny said as she scooted into the backseat.

"You say that every time." Maddie pulled out of the driveway.

It was a drizzling, gray day in April with a slight chill in the air. As we headed up I-91, I got distracted again by patterns of rain on the window.

"How have you been?" Maddie asked.

"Hanging in there," I replied. "Penny's been great."

"Aw," Penny said. "It's been nice havin' you as a roommate."

"Until your dream girl shows up." Maddie's remark was directed at me; she was offended that I didn't bunk in with her. I would never, ever tell her about my dog thing. Instead, whenever I visited, I'd listen patiently to her struggles with their kidney transplants and incontinence. I'd dutifully pet them in front of her before going to the bathroom to wash the skin off my hands. She didn't understand the depths of my OCD, and I didn't have the heart to tell her.

"That's not true," Penny argued. "I wouldn't kick her out if anyone moved in. She'd always have a place. And I'm gettin' the basement finished."

"You've been getting it finished since you got the place," Maddie snapped.

"I'm not like her so-called friend Debra," Penny insisted.

"I know that," I said.

Maddie smirked and glanced at me. "Have you heard from her since?"

I shook my head. I didn't want to talk about it. But I really thought our friendship was doomed by her choice of the boyfriend over me.

"Sure, you can't have some friend staying indefinitely," I said. "But if one of you were in a crisis, I wouldn't tell you that you had to move out. I never saw that side of her."

"You're so naïve." Maddie struggled with the sticking windshield wipers. "Some of these straight girls would sell their mothers if it meant they could get a man."

"That's so not true," I exclaimed. "My sister would never do that. If anything, she takes in everyone, even people she shouldn't." Joanne had a little trouble saying no. She was the one who let our Uncle Bill with a gambling problem stay for two years before she had to pretend that one of the kids had a serious, contagious disease to kick him out. And she was a telemarketer's dream. She once signed up for the "Meat of the Month" club. They had to buy an extra freezer for their garage, which started to resemble a slaughterhouse. She quit only when there was no place left to store any more there either. She just couldn't hang up on anyone. She had a heart as big as a side of beef.

"Well, that's been my experience." Maddie grew silent, something rare for her.

"You're always in a bad mood," Penny commented. "You need a girlfriend."

I laughed.

"I already had the best," Maddie said softly. "Anything else would just be a disappointment."

Ever since Holly, Maddie didn't want to date. She seemed content to give all her love and affection to her dogs.

"Holly was the best?" Penny asked in disbelief.

"You don't know." Maddie turned toward Windsor Locks and tried to change the subject. "So what does this one look like?"

"Dark hair, dark eyes."

"You need to get another type!" Maddie exclaimed.

"She can't help who she likes," I said.

"Well, obviously, this type isn't working for her." Maddie turned up the ramp toward the airport.

We pulled up to the curb, where Penny started to climb out in the pouring rain.

"I see her!" she cried, making a dash for the doors.

Maddie and I watched the scene unfold like a movie. There was a tall, dark-haired woman with cocoa skin and a face that could be on the cover of a magazine. Penny came up to her. Smiles were exchanged, some talking. Then Penny turned around and returned to the car alone.

In the backseat she sat with her head down; all you could see was the glistening top of her wet blond hair.

"What happened?" I finally asked as we pulled out.

Penny had spent many disastrous weekends with strangers she'd met online, most all of them ending in heartbreak. But we'd never seen one end before the woman even got in the car.

"She didn't think we had any chemistry," Penny said sadly.

"In five seconds?" I shrieked.

"It's true," Maddie agreed. "You can tell if someone's getting in your pants in the first few seconds. It's a proven fact."

"What!" I was incredulous. "What about friends who grow to become more?"

"That's only in the movies," Maddie replied. "You either feel the lightning bolt or you don't."

"I thought *that* was from the movies," I said, turning around. "What about all those great phone conversations you had?"

"She told me she didn't feel that thing with me and didn't want to waste my time." Penny tried to seem matter-of-fact about it, but she looked heartbroken.

"Wow," I sighed. "What a judgmental bitch. She'd be lucky to have you."

That made Penny smile a little. But I could tell she was still in shock.

"Sydney," Maddie began, "it's either there or it isn't."

"You'll never find anyone with your standards," I replied. "What do you do? Take a measuring tape on your dates?"

"I told you. I've chosen not to date. I live vicariously through you losers." Maddie laughed. She had an endearing quality that took some of the sting out of her comments. Like Barbra Streisand or Pink Floyd—people either got her or they didn't.

"You know what you two need?" Maddie continued. "A night out." She looked at me. "You need to get your mind off money for a minute." Then she looked in the rearview mirror at Penny. "And you need to get to know women the old-fashioned way—meet an alcoholic in a bar."

"I'm not ready," I said firmly.

"I don't know. It scares me." Penny was whimpering softly.

"Of course it scares you," Maddie said. "It requires meeting people face to face. You younger chicks are always texting and crap. You have no social skills."

"That's not fair," I said softly, trying not to let Maddie push Penny over the edge. "Penny is social. I just can't believe…" I drifted off.

"What can't you believe?" Maddie persisted.

"Well, I…" I had to be careful. I didn't want to hurt Penny any more. "I just can't believe that woman had so much money she could afford to blow a plane ticket and not even stay a while!"

Maddie was right; lately all I thought about was money because I didn't have any.

That night, Maddie rounded up the gang, myself and Penny included, and I'd be going to my first lesbian bar in twelve years. At forty, I didn't know how to ask anyone out or even to dance.

Women really aren't socialized to pick each other up. It's a wonder we get together at all.

In the car, Maddie drove, I complained about my hair in the passenger seat mirror, while Penny and Ariel sat in the backseat, reading a Gay Guide to Connecticut.

"It's called Throb," Penny said. "It's men and women."

"Most of 'em are," Maddie muttered. "Not as many lesbian bars anymore." She looked at me, and we said in unison, "Cookouts." We all laughed.

"Am I missing something?" Ariel asked, confused.

We laughed harder.

Ariel slumped in the backseat, as always dressed in black from head to toe, with stringy hair and tattoos in places we weren't allowed to see. She believed we're all sexual beings, capable of feeling anything for anyone at any time. She was very different compared to many people I'd known and felt a little dangerous to me. I'm not sure why. Maybe I worried her influence would take me out of my comfort zone. And I wasn't very spiritually inclined, so half the time I didn't understand what she was talking about.

Maddie ejected the CD that was playing and threw it in the backseat. "Can we get something a little happier? Some gay guy music, dance stuff? We need some goddamn happy in here!"

I fumbled with some CDs until I landed on Jimmy Somerville's Greatest Hits. It was just what we needed. Immediately the car came to life with his wailing falsetto over the best dance music I'd ever heard. I must have been a gay guy in another life. Suddenly anything felt possible—until we arrived at the front door of Throb.

We could hear pounding techno music from behind the walls. Then the four of us were greeted by a guy dressed in leather from head to toe, with a dog collar around his neck and sharp studs protruding from the sides of his leather pants. His head was completely shaved except for a shock of flaming red on top, which he should have shaved as well.

"I'm sorry, girls," he said in a flamboyant, patronizing tone. "This is Men's Leather Night."

"It said in the guide that it's men *and* women," Maddie argued.

"Go to the website, dear," he replied. "It has the calendar of events."

"Any idea where we can find a lesbian bar?" Ariel asked. Her voice was thick and smoky from all of the clove cigarettes she puffed.

"You might try Flo's," he answered, already bored with us. "In Danbury. They're lesbian on days with 'n's in them, and every other Friday of every other month."

We headed back down the sidewalk, and it felt as though the angry techno music was shooing us away.

"See?" Penny whined. "This is why I go online."

"We could try the city," Ariel offered.

"And then get stuck seeing a New Yorker?" Maddie kicked at the ground. "Then one of you has to move, and it sure as hell won't be her. You think she'll give it all up to live in Connecticut?"

"Some people," Ariel continued, "are sick of the city, believe it or not."

"Really?" Maddie considered the possibility.

"Wait. Forget the city," Ariel suddenly said. "I may have slept with all the bartenders down there."

CHAPTER FIVE

"The Seven Species of Lesbians"

Flo's was located in a dark alley with no sign from the street. It was the kind of place you only knew about because a friend of a friend told you.

The minute we came inside, I felt old. The music was too loud. Everyone was underdressed. And I had a sudden urge to either pee or go home.

"I'm too old for this!" I shouted to Maddie over drums that shook the walls.

"We all are," she said and shoved me toward the bar.

I felt like a pubescent boy, staring at the bartender's low-cut, ripped black T-shirt and ample cleavage. Catching myself, embarrassed, I looked away and ignored her when she yelled "What'll it be?" at me. She was pretty for sure and very young— at least twenty years younger than I.

"Sam Adams, regular," I replied.

I scanned the room and realized some things hadn't changed in twenty years. The lesbians were not on the floor. Most of the dancing was left to the gay men, who cluttered the dance floor, lip-synching to Beyoncé.

I could immediately identify the various species of lesbians in the room.

Lesbius Action-Figurious. These women can only be found in bars after just coming in from a miles-long hike or bike marathon. They dress in Spandex and sip bottled water. They look with disdain upon meatier women, because they think they're the only ones who take care of themselves. You glance at them and imagine their sex must be incredibly acrobatic with swings hanging from the ceiling and moves like a double lutz or a triple salchow. I couldn't picture it exactly, but I imagined it must feel really good.

Granolas Birkenstockius. An older species of lesbian, these women can be found in coffeehouses more than bars. When they are spotted, they're usually arguing over a cup of chai tea or something grown in the ground. Usually vegans, these women like berries, nuts and twigs and vegetables that don't look too phallic like zucchini, and if they eat meat, they are shunned by the pack. Their hair hangs like stringy, unwashed gluten-free noodles.

Lesbius Lipstickius. A newly discovered species, this one is harder to spot out in the wild concrete jungle because they wear more makeup, especially lipstick. They look like models and, who are we kidding, they probably *are* models. They walk into the bar like they're on a runway with nine-inch stilettos and skirts so short they can't sit down without showing as much as a stripper. They communicate through raised eyebrows and often look too bored to be wherever they are.

Lesbius Studious. These women often wear eyeglasses to identify themselves to others of their kind. Dressed in black, they are usually found sitting at corner tables, leaning in to each other, having intense conversations about the subversive plot in any movie or books by Gertrude Stein and poetry by Sylvia Plath. Some can be very dark, like the Sylvia Plath fans, and are always super-intellectual. An opening line to break the ice with one of these women must include a reference to an obscure author or film director. Otherwise, they'd rather go home to Gertrude.

Years ago I was in this category, taking myself way too seriously and always dressing in black. It's the easiest color to match to the rest of your outfit, and the less time I could take getting ready, the better. Today, I'm usually not found wearing anything that isn't in the Lands' End catalog. Jeans and fleecy shirts have been the key to my survival in the cold when I wasn't in a work suit. As I'd gotten older, simplicity became the priority. I have two pairs of glasses, black-rimmed and brown-rimmed, in case one pair gets scratched. And I mostly wear sneakers or those earth-tone shoes that you can just slip your foot into, no fussing with shoelaces or Velcro. Just slide your foot into soft gushy comfort. That's why I immediately recognized this group, because one day, they too would continue their quest for simplicity and trade their boots for comfy shoes. They'll even crave a stupid movie every now and then that doesn't make a comment on the human condition. Oh yes, ladies, you will…

Lesbius Varietious. Some cute, some not, these women dress like all-American girls. Their camouflage enables them to blend in to straight society, whether it be a shopping mall or other public place. When threatened, they avoid predators by telling them they just want to be friends. I'll admit I had been a part of this group as well.

Stubbornius Mulletious. These women are creatures of habit, stuck in their ways, never to change. They either haven't yet gotten word that the mullet is dead or just don't want to believe it. But believe it, ladies. *It's never coming back.*

Butchus Aromaticus. Last but not least are the chunky butches who smell like men's cologne and wear boxers. This type can be found abundantly in their most comfortable habitats—playing darts or pool—but usually not on the dance floor.

Of course most women were a mix of these or couldn't be put into any type of box. But I liked to invent categories for each in my head to hide the fact that I was nervous just being there at all.

CHAPTER SIX

"A Blog is Born"

The strobe lights spun, the first beer didn't give me a buzz and I checked my watch. Then, like a scene from a movie, she emerged from the fog, dancing with a group of women. Were they her friends? Was there a girlfriend in the group? Lesbians needed nametags or color-coded bracelets to indicate single, recently split up and on the rebound, coupled off, etc. It was all so confusing.

"She so looked at you." Penny bumped my arm.

Me? Really? There it was again—a quick glance and a shy smile in my direction. She was the incarnation of Vivien Leigh, with flowing black hair, deep brown flashing eyes and a brooding stare that gave her mystery and intrigue and all those special little somethings that had me wrapped around her finger before I even knew her name. It had been a long time since the butterflies danced in my stomach. It felt good just to know I wasn't dead.

All this excitement made me so nervous I had to pee.

So I stood in a long line with Maddie, waiting for the ladies' room.

"What's taking so long?" I shouted, crossing my legs.

"You're gonna have to start shavin' again," Penny informed me.

"What?"

"The younger women don't like ya unless you're shaved." Penny was so certain. "I read it on a lesbian blog."

"They're stupid," Maddie said. "More infections are caused from shaving. I can't tell you how many I see in the hospital for some bacterial thing just because their boyfriend or girlfriend wanted a silly Mohawk."

My head spun. Was this what it was going to be like? I almost missed the comfort of Val and me growing old together. I didn't want to be with some young chick who was going to guilt me into shaving parts of my body that didn't like razors. My legs could barely stand it.

The restroom door finally opened and two men came out. Maddie was outraged.

"Hey, use your own bathroom!" she hollered.

"It was full," one of the men spat.

"See that door?" Maddie pointed to the WOMEN sign. "Unless you've had the change, that's ours. Just because we're not in here as much as you doesn't give you the right to have a quick fuck!"

"Is she drunk?" a woman in line asked.

"No," I replied. "She's always like that."

One of the guys came toward her, and a bystander had to jump between them. "Break it up! Okay! Enough!"

"Are you the owner?" Maddie demanded.

"No," the bystander responded.

"Well, someone should do something," Maddie continued.

Other women who were in line murmured in agreement. But nobody wanted to make a scene. As the line moved up, we could hear the next woman say, "Eew! The seat's still up."

I liked how Maddie said what everyone was thinking but was too afraid to say. Sometimes it got her into trouble, but sometimes it was worth it.

I was especially grateful not to be the next one in the bathroom. That had happened to me once a long time ago. Some things hadn't changed.

When I was back at the bar with a fresh drink, I watched the gorgeous creature continue to dance.

"You should go over there," Maddie said.

"And say what?" I shouted. "I don't know how to pick someone up. I'm not a picker-upper."

"What are you, a paper towel? Just start dancing and smile. If she's interested, she'll pay attention. If not, you'll get the hint."

"Oh, that simple." I downed the rest of my fizzy courage. "From the woman who doesn't date."

But Maddie was right. I meandered over to the dance floor and pretended to be dancing with no one in particular. The woman smiled at me and danced a little closer. In the distance, Penny gave me an embarrassingly obvious thumbs-up.

"Wish they'd play some better music!" I shouted over some Miley-Katy-Britney song.

"I know! Right?" She had a great smile. Even closer, I decided her eyes were more of a steel gray.

Feeling more confident, I added, "Where's Cher? Or Annie Lennox?"

"Yeah!" she yelled back over the music. "My girlfriend has every Cher CD!"

"Right." I donned my most natural fake smile and danced my way off the floor, pretending the whole time to be having a good time. My painted-on smile was absurd, aimed at no one in particular, as I returned to my friends, all of whom had question marks on their faces.

I ran past them and outside, toward the parking lot, shivering in the chilly, unspringlike air. Maddie, Penny and Ariel could hardly keep up. I felt so stupid, so deeply out of touch with the new lesbian dating world.

"What kind of woman goes out clubbing without her girlfriend!" I shouted.

"The kind that's looking to cheat," Maddie replied.

"Or," Penny offered, "that was a nice way of saying she wasn't interested. I've heard that one before."

"Great," I snapped. "That's just great. But she was looking at me!"

"Maybe she wanted a threesome," Ariel said.

I stopped walking. "How does that work?" I asked. "I mean, really? I can only focus on one body at a time."

"You should try it," Ariel responded, her eyes shifty. "It will release all this tension you've got."

"And give her a disease!" Maddie added. "Come on." She put her arm around my shoulders. "It's your first time out since when? Since dinosaurs walked the earth? So you struck out. Big deal. Next time you won't."

"Oh, suddenly you're positive?" I shook my head, walking faster. "No." Then and there I decided never to date again. I'd be one of those old lesbians who lived alone and planted vegetables. Never mind that I hated gardening. I'd find a way to like it. Sometimes I could appreciate an attractive tomato.

"There needs to be some kind of handbook," Penny said. "A guide to lesbian dating. 'Cause let's face it. Some gay women are just plain weird."

A lightbulb went off in my head. *That was it.*

"You're right," I muttered.

Maddie was irritated with Penny. "Gay women are weird? You'd better be including yourself. You go to the airport so much you should get a job with the TSA. That way you could frisk all kinds of women, and they'd know right away if you had chemistry."

"That's so wrong!" Penny cried, half laughing.

"Penny!" I exclaimed. "You're brilliant!"

Maddie said quietly, "That's not something you hear every day."

"*That's it!*" I kept repeating it over and over. I knew what I was going to do. I had a new purpose, a new calling. It was like the skies had parted and a ray of sun descended upon me. Never mind that it was nighttime.

When I got back to the apartment, I started a new blog: *The Comfortable Shoe Diaries.* There I would pour my heart out, kind of like therapy but with fewer tissues, talking about everything strange and horrifying in this new, mysterious world of dating when you're suddenly partnerless in a partnered-off world.

CHAPTER SEVEN

"Cat on a Hot Laptop"

I began writing. And writing. I went out to the bars, bookstores and coffeehouses. I wrote about every experience I had.

On one of these nights, I met Carrie, a pretty girl-next-door-type at the bar. She had brown hair with streaks of blond and almond-shaped, intelligent eyes. She seemed distracted or restless. I couldn't tell if she was looking for someone more interesting to talk to.

"Are you from Connecticut?" I asked.

"Yeah, Glastonbury. There's no place to go there, so I come here." Her eyes darted around as she chugged a beer.

"I'm from Florida," I volunteered. She wasn't interested.

"You're cute," she said. Okay, maybe she was interested.

"Thanks." I looked down at my shoes.

"Wanna get out of here?"

She wasn't much for talking. I'd never known anyone who moved so quickly. But I thought of my blog and decided to get out of my comfort zone.

We came through her apartment door, kissing. And even though it had been ages since it mattered what kind of underwear I was wearing, something didn't feel right.

"This isn't right," I said in between kisses.

"It feels right to me." Her eyes were now heavy-lidded and glazed. Was she drunk?

"No," I protested. "We should go for long walks in the park…get to know each other better." I pulled back. "We should have done that before our first kiss."

She looked at me and laughed. She thought I was joking.

"I'm serious," I said. "All I know is your name is Carrie, and you can't find gay bars in Glastonbury."

"You are so damn cute." She lunged at me again, and I'm not sure what she was trying to do to my bottom lip. I think she thought it was a piece of gum.

"I'm not into biting." I pulled away and headed for the door. "If you really want to get to know me, you've got my number." Then I left.

Of course I never heard from Carrie again.

Then there was Alissa, who, after one dinner date, had planned for us to buy a vacation home together in the south of France. Over dinner, she'd given me a résumé of herself.

"I'm a successful psychiatrist," she began. "I drive a Porsche, and I have houses all over. The right girl could travel the world with me."

She had long blond hair and intense green eyes. A little too intense. At first I thought it was just intensity. Then I realized it was psychosis. After dinner, she wanted me to go back to her place, but I declined, remembering the last time I'd done that with Carrie. By the time I'd returned to the apartment I still shared with Penny, I had six voice mail messages on my cell phone and two on our answering machine.

"Who is she?" Penny asked, looking up from her computer.

"A nutball," I answered simply and took my anxiety pills. "Why are women either aloof or stalkers?" I splashed my face with cold water. "There's no in-between."

"You got a stalker?" Penny raised an eyebrow.

"She seemed normal over the appetizers. Then it kind of went downhill."

"Dang," she sighed. "I wish I had a stalker."

"You did once. Remember?"

"It's better than bein' ignored."

I fired up my laptop and blogged my heart out. I blogged about the insanity of being gay, how it feels like you're going the opposite direction in rush hour traffic. I blogged about how hard it is to be a woman socialized to let a man call her but how you need to be more assertive if you ever hope to meet another woman. I blogged about how to tell if another woman is or isn't. Then I asked readers to explain to me the difference between a hard butch and soft butch. Of course, this made me think of hard-boiled eggs, and I was suddenly hungry for an omelet.

Little did I know, I had an audience. People were reading my observations on this varied topic—and not only lesbians. I was getting emails from straight women who said they found it fascinating and funny. Imagine that. I was proud again. It was the first time since I'd lost my job when I felt like I was contributing something useful to society. Was I finally writing that *thing?* I didn't know.

Night after night, I tossed and turned and dreamed of the woman I could never find. On the one hand, I was craving carnal pleasures. But when faced with a carnal situation up close, it never seemed right. I was used to the wooing and getting-to-know-you-over-dinner phase. I had to face it. I wasn't a one-night stand kind of woman. I had to know more than Carrie's name. Sure she was pretty. Sure she had the best body I'd ever seen in real life. Sure her body was even better than Val's. The more I thought about it, I felt like an idiot. Why did I turn her down?

"Who are you being loyal to?" Maddie asked.

We sat in the hospital cafeteria on her lunch break.

"No one," I answered.

"You're a vibrant forty-year-old woman," Maddie reminded me. "You have every right to hit the sheets if you want to. You don't have to answer to anyone."

"Hitting the sheets sounds so dirty."

"That Catholic girl inside just won't let you be happy, will she?"

On Saturday we strolled through the mall and complained about the rising hemline on girls' shorts, noting that boys' shorts were getting longer. Every article of clothing in the women's department looked like it had been made from really ugly curtains. As we walked, my eyes floated over every attractive woman. Tight jeans. Perfectly round posteriors. Or a curvy chest straining beneath a clingy sweater. So close I could almost touch it. And eventually I did...touch something. A topless mannequin.

Maddie shook her head, stifling a full-throttle laugh. "You really need to get laid."

CHAPTER EIGHT

"Penny from Heaven"

Driving back from another bad date, windshield wipers swiping at the pouring rain, I saw nothing but black ahead of me. Darkness for miles. I wondered when I'd see the end of the tunnel.

My phone rang.

"Why are you out driving in the rain?" Mom demanded on the other end.

"How do you know it's raining?"

"I hear it."

I turned around to make sure she wasn't in the backseat.

"I'm watching you on the Weather Channel," she cried. "There's a big red blob coming straight toward you!"

"I believe it," I sighed.

"Rain, wind, hail, flash flooding…"

Mom's favorite channel was the Weather Channel. Even if there was snow in Nebraska, where she knew no one, she'd be fascinated, staring at the map for hours. It used to drive Dad crazy. He'd yell, "Who the hell do we know in Nebraska?"

"Why don't you come back to Florida?" She blurted it out, like something she'd been thinking about for a long time.

"Don't," I pleaded.

Parts of the Merritt Parkway flashed in between blinding rain in the darkness.

"Come back home. What have you got up there? No home. No job. No one to take care of you."

"I can take care of myself!" My protest was volcanic, filled with molten hot rage and possibly completely untrue. Suddenly I remembered I needed to refill my anxiety medication.

"Are you sure it's really over with Val?" she asked timidly.

"Not again!"

"She had a good job, dear. She was a lawyer. You could have gotten that house with a second bathroom."

"I can't believe you!" I was wailing like a wounded squirrel.

"You're in a one-bath apartment with a friend you said you're not attracted to. So see? *That's* not going anywhere."

"I can't do this right now, Mom." I pulled into the driveway.

"Do what? Face reality? You never liked hearing the truth."

I had to end the call before her words sank in. But it was too late.

Mom's words echoed, as I threw my jacket on the couch that wasn't mine, turned on the lamp that wasn't mine and glanced at the one bathroom at the end of the hall. With my Irritable Bowel Syndrome, I was like that woman in the commercial who's always looking for a bathroom. She can't live her life because she's stuck in a bathroom. My mom also had IBS, and she used to count bathrooms wherever we went when I was a child. I was becoming Mom.

I went into the kitchen and looked over Penny's shoulder at the site she was visiting. It was called Venus Meet. Penny had a code name, but her photograph was prominently displayed.

"Don't you worry that some psycho is lusting over your photo?" I asked.

"I sure hope so."

She'd typed a list of things she was looking for in a woman. I read the criteria: "single, belief in God, employed…"

"That one leaves me out," I joked.

"You should do a profile," she suggested.

"No way." I laughed all the way to the living room. Then I turned on my laptop to write my blog. Tonight's entry was all about the meat market of online dating. Even though I hadn't tried it, I used my platform to condemn the practice as a cheap, embarrassing way to get a date.

When Penny came out to get ready for bed, she spied over my shoulder. "You know you're getting really popular."

"You mean my pseudonym is."

"Whatever. I tell my co-workers 'I know her,' and now I'm kind of a celebrity." She was beaming. Then she got a peek at what I was writing.

"That is so unfair!" she erupted.

"Everyone's entitled to their opinion!"

"Yeah, but…" Her eyebrows crinkled together. "You're makin' it sound like everyone who does it is desperate or something. I'm not desperate."

"I didn't say you were."

She pointed to my screen. "Take it back."

"Okay," I conceded. "I'll say it's just not for me."

"You know what you should do? You should try it. Then you'd have something worth sayin'."

It was a good idea. I hated that.

"I could share my experience," I thought aloud. "But why do I have to go through meeting all the psychos to talk about it? I already know I'll meet psychos."

"You should try it," she repeated like a wise, Southern Yoda. "Readers would rather hear your own story than you just goin' off about how dumb it is."

After she went to bed and everything was quiet, I decided to set up a profile. The whole time I felt stupid, describing my interests, likes and dislikes. It reminded me of grade school when a potential suitor passes you a survey to fill out. "Do you like me? What's your favorite color?" Everyone always said blue. I said it too, even though I secretly preferred red. On Venus Meet, they wanted to know stuff like that, as well as your favorite flower. I didn't know much about flowers. A rose would sound too common. I wasn't sure that daisies weren't weeds. My mind raced. Aha! I liked those tall flowers with the small red buds. I thought they were carnations, so that's what I typed.

Even though it felt silly and totally against everything I believed in, I did the entire profile on Venus Meet. The hardest part was choosing a photograph. It couldn't look too recent; I'd gained some weight, rationalizing that cookies were a natural part of the depression process. It couldn't be too old a photo with big eighties hair, because then everyone would assume I looked like Jabba the Hutt now. I chose a photo a friend took at a New Year's party a couple of years ago. It still looked like me, and I wasn't too drunk at the time. I clicked the "post" button and swallowed hard.

The next morning, I had five rainbows next to my name.

"What does this mean?" I asked.

Penny came over to look at my screen. She was impressed.

"Five already? You just started!" Maybe she was a little jealous.

"What does a rainbow mean?" I repeated.

"Someone's interested in you. They'll send you a miniature rainbow. Isn't it cute?"

"Yeah," I said, still feeling stupid.

"You just click on the rainbow, and it takes you to the profile page of the person who likes you."

So I did. I went to each profile page. There was only one rainbow who was attractive in her photos. I felt guilty for deleting the other rainbows. It seemed so mean. It was all about judging people based on how they looked on a screen. What if they took a bad picture? What if I'd gotten to know one of the deleted rainbows and realized I was eventually attracted to her and even found her to be my soul mate?

"It seems so superficial," I commented.

"Quit that right now," Penny snapped, sliding the remainder of her eggs onto my plate. "Isn't that whatcha do every time you go to a bar? You don't know how anybody likes their grits. All that catches your eye is how they look."

She had this sort of rare, down-home wisdom, like Dolly Parton.

"Okay, I'll give it two weeks. Then I'm getting off." That should be long enough to have something to share on my blog.

"Two weeks?" she retorted. "That's not enough time."

"What's enough time?"

"Two years."

I nearly choked on my eggs. "No way. I'm not selling myself online for two years. That just looks desperate."

The moment the offending words left my mouth, I wished I could take them back.

"I didn't mean you," I corrected. But the silence stretched out for an uncomfortably long time.

There's nothing worse than hurting a friend, one who's been so nice to you, taking you in when you had no place to go. I hung my head in shame.

"I'm not desperate," she finally said softly. "I just believe something will work out. I have faith."

Later that day, I sat out on the deck, soaking up the summer sun, scanning job boards and listening to birds chirp. I envied them for not having to get jobs. As I scrolled through the same old positions from places that hadn't gotten back to me or had just sent me form notices that they'd "keep me on file," I thought about Penny. She had faith. What was so bad about that?

Once upon a time, I used to have faith too. I had faith I would become a successful writer. I believed I'd find my soul mate, and we'd be planning our home renovations and adding a Jacuzzi to our backyard deck someday. I had dreams of traveling to Paris and exotic countries I'd only read about. But now, at forty, my faith was flickering off and on like when you start to lose power in a storm. Maybe I was at that age when if you didn't make it, you weren't going to. And if you had no one to cuddle with at night, you'd probably never find her.

I scrolled through jobs that I knew I wouldn't be considered for. I was in that clichéd "rock and a hard place" place, with too much experience to get even a crappy job and not enough experience to completely change my career and get something in an industry that needed people. It was like being in a room with two doors that were each bolted shut. Either way, I was resigned to getting a job I hated just to limp along. I envisioned myself doing something that required me to say, "You want fries with that?" And as more time passed, I thought I'd be lucky to land a job like that.

I stared at my little unsexy car in the driveway. I prayed it would stay in one piece as long as possible. I couldn't afford to have one thing go wrong in the engine. I couldn't afford to have Cookie get sick. I couldn't afford to fill a cavity at the dentist. I couldn't even afford a visit to the dentist.

After hours of searching, I looked up at the afternoon light streaming through the trees. It might not have been my home state, but Connecticut was pretty. It was like a Thomas Kinkaid painting—except for the parts of town that had run-down factories with the windows crumbling and boarded up. Except for those.

Then I had a vision. In the movie *The Perfect Storm*, the men in their little boat look up and see a towering black wave rising above them, ready to pound down on them with no mercy. When they push through it, they feel like they've beaten it. They're celebrating, all except for the captain, whose face is strangely somber as the sky above seems to clear, casting a yellowish light on them. Then he says something like, "She's not going to let us out." It's because he realizes they're in the eye, the calmest part of the storm, but they still have the other edge of it to get through. And those waves are going to be twice as bad as the first ones. Then comes the final giant wave that tips the boat over.

In keeping with my family's tradition of melodrama, I saw myself as facing that final black wave, the one that wasn't going to let me out. I saw no easy way through or around the storm.

Sure my blog was doing well. But I couldn't live on it. I was going to keep my subscription to Venus Meet for just two weeks. That was all I could afford. But maybe it was going to be just long enough. I had to keep my faith in something.

CHAPTER NINE

"Lesbians Aren't from Venus"

The following week, I landed my first interview. It was at a small, boutique ad agency that would require me to move closer to the traffic-infested area where all the industry was in Connecticut—Norwalk and Stamford.

Apparently, I'd done well. The interviewer, Constance McElroy, laughed several times, which I thought was a good sign in an interview. She was fiftyish with short and stylish gray hair and bold, dangling earrings like a high school French teacher.

"I'll be honest with you," she said and sat back in her important-looking office chair.

Here it comes. I have too much experience.

"You have a lot of experience," she continued. "And that's what we're looking for."

I smiled and nodded, a little surprised. Could this finally be a crack of light in my endless tunnel toward hell?

"But…" she sighed heavily. "We don't do much direct mail anymore. We need more of a web focus."

"I've done a lot of web marketing," I interrupted. I couldn't let this one get away. I just couldn't. My heart raced. The desperation oozed from my forehead. I hoped my bangs would cover up the beads of sweat.

"Yes, I see that." She picked up my résumé. "But to be honest, it's between you and another candidate who's done a little more with web and social media platforms."

Heat spread up my spine. The air grew thinner. My chest tightened. I needed the perfect response, and I needed it now.

"I understand," I replied. "But before you make your decision, please take a look at the samples I'm leaving. See the results I got from these." I heard myself sound like a desperate child, fighting for the last cookie on a plate.

She smiled warmly, but it was a hard-to-read smile. It could have meant "I like you" or "you pushy pain in the ass." I wasn't sure.

Did I sound argumentative? My stomach churned. Everything else was a blur until I shook her hand and dove for the elevator.

A few days later, I received a beautiful letter on beautiful company letterhead with Constance's lovely cursive signature below—a letter politely thanking me for wasting my time because they went with the other candidate.

I'd been knocked down once. Now I'd been kicked in the gut.

I called Debra Lansing. Even though I'd vowed to stay away from numbers for the rest of my life, she had a lot of professional friends. Surely all of them couldn't be in the financial industry. I was an idiot to burn a bridge at this time. I was in full sucking-up mode. I had no other choice.

"I'm sorry I was so dramatic when I left," I said.

"No, you were right. I should've told Kurt to deal with it."

"Forget it." I really wouldn't forget it for another ten years or so. "Are we friends again?"

"Yeah." She seemed distracted. She was at her office, probably doing something with a calculator. I didn't want to know.

"Maybe we can have lunch sometime?" I ventured. After all, I couldn't be too obvious. She'd think I was only making nice to get a job, which of course I was.

"Sure, that would be great. I'll give you a call. Same phone?"

"Yeah, my cell."

"How's it working out with Penny?" she asked.

"It's great. She's great."

"You guys aren't…" She stumbled awkwardly.

I couldn't tell what she was getting at.

"Aren't what?" I asked.

"You know."

"What? Penny? Me and Penny? Oh no. We're friends. Good friends."

"Oh, I just thought since you're gay and she's gay…" Debra was serious.

"Like Arnie is straight and you're straight?" I asked. She'd described her office mate, Arnie Duggart, as a slovenly mess of a man, who always had crumbs on his desk and who smelled like Fritos.

"I get your point. I just thought Penny was sort of cute."

"She is, but I think of her like a sister," I said. With Debra, I always felt like I had to explain things. Maybe it was because she believed every stereotype she'd heard. I could only imagine what she and her straight friends must have said behind my back. She was one of those people I wanted to trust but didn't. I wasn't sure why. Maybe it was her way of blowing in whatever direction the wind was going at the time.

That night, I turned on my computer to read the top headlines. One jumped out at me: "Anxiety Can Shorten Lifespan." Oh, great. I ran to the bathroom to take my anxiety medication. I hadn't noticed until I returned that Penny was at the kitchen table, holding her head and staring at her computer with glistening eyes.

"What is it, Pen?" I asked.

She shook her head. "No, you'll just make fun. You think this is all stupid anyway."

"No, tell me. I promise I won't make fun. Hey, I joined that Venus Meet for you, remember?"

She looked at me suspiciously, then softened a little. "Okay," she began. "I met someone I really, really like. But she's all about her farm in Kentucky. She breeds horses and has all this land. She'd need me to move to Kentucky."

Penny sat back and slowly raised her eyes to me. The world as she knew it was over.

"Penny," I said. "Are you that serious with her? I mean, so serious you're already talking about where you'd move?"

"That's what happens!" She burst into tears. "We've talked about everything! We get along so well. So naturally, it's gonna come up. You can't keep talkin' if you know it's goin' nowhere."

"I hate it when the other person expects you to move for her," I commented. "Like you don't have a life where you are, you know?" But then I remembered Penny was from Tennessee. "Would it be out of the question?"

She was surprised; she stopped dabbing her eyes for a moment.

"Whaddaya mean?" she thundered. "Give up my work? I'm the top sales associate. I have a reputation here! I'd have to go back to square one. I can't. No, I won't. What do I know about Kentucky anyway?"

"There's a derby," I quietly offered. That was pretty much all I knew.

"Yeah, I'm from the South, but that doesn't mean I like horses or cattle. We didn't live on a farm. We lived in a neighborhood. The closest I got to wildlife was the Nashville Zoo."

I smiled.

"What's so funny?" she demanded.

"I love that." I couldn't explain it. "I think it's cool you don't like horses. I never met anyone who didn't."

She smiled weakly in between tears. I could tell from the pink blobs all over her face that she'd been crying a long time. And I'd been too self-absorbed to notice.

"So did you break up?" I asked.

She nodded. "I don't have a choice. She said she won't come to Connecticut."

"Then she's not the one," I answered simply. "It's not meant to be."

Penny liked to believe in fate. I used to believe in it, until nothing turned out as I'd planned. I was leaning now toward the theory that everything is random and you'll pay for every stupid decision you make. But I wasn't going to tell her that. What I'd said appeared to give her comfort.

So Penny went to bed early, and I was left with my computer quietly humming on the couch. After the job rejection, I really wasn't in the mood to see if my one rainbow I'd saved had written me back. I couldn't take more than one rejection a day. But my fingers betrayed me, and before I knew it, I was back on Venus Meet.

Sure enough, the rainbow at least had the decency to tell me she'd hooked up with another rainbow. That was better than just ignoring me, I figured.

Then I noticed in the right column that Venus Meet suggested potential matches based on my interests. They flashed a few photos and profile teasers about people I might want to send a rainbow to.

Each one had dark hair, dark eyes and looked mysterious. I was attracted to every one of them. But they were also a little too young looking. Some of their expressions were vacant behind their perfect features. Then came a photo that stopped me. She had long blond hair with blue eyes like mine and a genuinely happy smile. She was in her late forties, with super-cute, well-defined features, giving her that depth of beauty only mature women can have. She was the opposite of my usual dark and brooding type, which never seemed to make me happy anyway. So I took a risk. I sent her a rainbow.

I shut off the computer and tried to fall asleep. But the darkness was where my worries hung out, waiting to pounce on me the moment I shut off the light. My car was going to die after six years. It would probably gasp its last breath in the middle of a busy intersection. How was I going to get a car loan with my credit rating? The good girl who thought she'd done everything right, whose face turned red if she didn't know the answer in school, now had a bankruptcy and foreclosure on her record. It might as well have said I was a serial killer too. I was going to be treated like one. I was going to be avoided like someone in medieval England with the plague. What was going to give me the strength to keep getting up and getting dressed each day?

Every morning, I'd turn on the local news and see commercials about depression. The commercials had begun to depress me even more—watching people who can't get out of bed, who can't smile at a birthday party or the woman who just stares at her dog while he holds a tennis ball in his mouth. Sad.

That weekend I would not think about my unanswered rainbow, just floating out there in the dark cyberspace all alone… I would go out to a loud club where I couldn't hear anyone and have fun, dammit.

So Saturday night, I met Maddie and Penny at Flo's. We sat at a high-top table and vented about the week's misfortunes.

"I'm thinking of changing careers," Maddie announced.

"You? Why?" I sipped my beer from the bottle, the lesbian way.

"Eh, I'm so sick of everyone whining."

Penny cleared her throat. "Uh, they're patients. They're sick. You're supposed to take care of 'em."

"Then *you* do it! You don't know what it's like. I'm burned out. I'm tired of hearing, 'Ow, the blood pressure cuff is too tight' when it's not. They're all such babies." She took a swig from her bottle, as Penny and I glanced at each other. "No," Maddie continued. "It's everything. The dumbasses I work with don't put things in the chart, like what the patient is allergic to. I think they want to get me fired."

"Are you this warm and fuzzy at work?" I teased.

"I'm wonderful to work with!" she fumed. "But I'm thinking of going back to teaching."

"No," I spat before having a chance to think. "Don't do it."

"Yeah," Penny agreed. "Remember how parents called and said their kids were crying?"

"And that was my fault?" Maddie sipped her beer.

It *was* her fault. She'd asked a class of fifth graders who had discovered America. One boy raised his hand and said, "Christopher Columbus?"

"No!" Maddie had shouted. "He came here accidentally. But he was really a greedy bastard who was looking for treasure. Only idiots think he discovered America!"

There was a reason for Maddie's bitterness. And it wasn't Holly, the ill-fated love affair. It was something else. But she never told any of us what it was.

"That girl winked at me!" Penny was excited. She hopped off her chair and made her way over to a very tall blonde at the bar.

"Wow, she has guts," I marveled.

"She could play a little hard to get. Geez." Then Maddie turned her attention to me. "So what's your deal?" she asked. "Still looking around?"

"Still like you," I joked, knowing she'd get huffy.

"You want to know what happened with Holly?" Maddie said. "You want to know the real reason I'm not getting out there again?"

I nodded slowly. This was like being given the map to the Holy Grail. I listened carefully.

"You already know she cheated," Maddie continued. "But you don't know how I found out. She sent me out for some things for our cookout. And when I came back, I found her in bed with the laundry chick I didn't know. And it wasn't just that they were having sex. I could see the other woman's bare back and Holly's hands gliding up and down it. But it wasn't that. It was the way she *looked* at that woman. I'll never forget that look, like she was in love with her. I knew I could never make it work with Holly, knowing she'd never look at me like that."

"What did you do?" I asked.

"The only thing I could," Maddie answered. "I was holding this cookout set in my hands, and I tried to beat her over the head with the spatula. If I had to do it all over again, I would have used the big fork."

I patted her back, touched that she shared this with me, this secret she'd kept stuffed inside. Maybe one day I'd learn her other secret too. She'd always alluded to something else but refused to talk about it.

"Holly was an idiot," I said.

"So was Văldemort."

"I told you it was mutual."

"It's never mutual." Maddie drank more of her beer, when Penny rushed back to the table, a little shaken.

"I didn't know," Penny kept repeating.

"What?" I leaned in and took her hand. "What happened?"

"I'm sure he's, I mean *she*, is really nice," Penny said.

"She's transgender?" I was surprised. You couldn't really tell from a distance. And she looked very cute.

Maddie squinted her eyes to study the woman. "You didn't notice her giant Adam's apple?"

I leaned across the table to get a closer look. "She doesn't have a giant—"

Penny's eyes filled with tears. "Am I a horrible person?"

"Yes," Maddie replied. "I'm joking! No, of course not."

"It may have hurt her feelings," I said.

They both looked at me like I was crazy.

"It's a matter of taste," Maddie argued. "She doesn't have to date anyone she doesn't want to."

"True," I said. "But running away like that can hurt a person's feelings. Someone did that to me on the dance floor."

"It was your dancing," Maddie joked.

I shoved her. "Bite me."

When I returned home that night, I found a reply to my rainbow. Her name was Ellie. What she wrote didn't sound like anyone I'd met before. I was immediately interested. Adding to the intrigue was her comment about signing up for only two weeks, just like me.

CHAPTER TEN

"When Sydney Met Ellie"

I had a girlfriend a long time ago, Justine. She always wanted to put on porn to get in the mood. Now I'm sorry, but whenever there was a scene with two women, say at the beach, oiling up each other's bodies, sometimes topless, rubbing oil over their curves, the whole thing would get ruined when a man came over to join in. Inevitably, they welcomed his presence. I'd get so mad I couldn't watch it anymore.

Justine would argue, "It's just a stupid movie! You gotta admit it's hot!"

And I would reply, "It reinforces the stereotype that all lesbians would like a guy to join in. After all, how can we possibly do anything without a penis?"

"You're too political!" she'd yell, like it was a bad thing.

"So? At least I think about the world I'm living in!"

"You're always pissed about something!" She'd slam the door and nobody would be having sex that night, except the actors in a very bad, grainy porn film called *Busty Babes at the Beach* or something equally dumb.

After we broke up, I'd often wonder if I *was* too political, too angry, too whatever. Aside from Ellen DeGeneres, lesbians had kind of a reputation for being pissed off, as reflected in angry acoustic music about getting screwed over by straight women. But I knew, at least among my friends, that we had the best sense of humor of anyone. We had to. We were living in a world that didn't exactly cater to us much at all.

Just watching an Old Spice commercial with a shirtless man telling ladies how to get their man to be like him—it's funny, but I couldn't help but notice how many commercials are *not* aimed at me. I'm not a demographic any company cares about, except maybe Subaru. Have you ever seen a woman holding a box of Tide and hear an announcer say something like, "Use Tide detergent, so you and your girlfriend can snuggle together in a soft, clean blanket?" Mmm. Sounds good, but it's never going to happen. Or in an ad when your legs get a nice silky shave, there has to be a man touching your legs at the end of the commercial to show you how wonderful your straight life will be with this product. I'd like to see another woman touching her legs. Now that would be worth seeing.

I wonder how much more interesting the world would have been for me growing up if I'd seen more images that reflected how I felt.

That was the first conversation Ellie and I had. The "conversation" was through email, but it seemed loud and intense, like we were discussing the media representation of lesbians at length at the corner table of a noisy coffeehouse or restaurant. She felt the same way. And she didn't think I was too political. Imagine that. I'd always tried to tone it down for people who needed to wear earplugs around my intensity. But not Ellie Hundersson. She liked what I had to say, and she had just as much to say. There wouldn't be enough time to talk about everything we had to say. Could this be my ideal woman?

At the same time, I didn't want to be a spokesperson for the lesbian community, which I worried my blog was becoming. I was many things, a person with hopes and worries, not only a woman who is attracted to certain other women. So I was a mixture of conflicting feelings—political but not wanting to be a mouthpiece. The two, however, didn't seem to go together. I could share these worries with Ellie too.

Most of all, I didn't want to get carried away like Penny. I saw the heartbreak a few emails could cause. I saw her get dumped at the airport just because the other woman saw her in person. Chemistry can't be predicted until you meet face-to-face. I learned that. I had to remember it. So I was cautious but wildly excited. I was almost excited enough to forget about the bills I had to pay.

Cookie would curl up next to me on the couch when I did my nightly ritual of responding to one of Ellie's letters. They were emails, but they read like letters. I also loved how she didn't try to say any of the same things all the other women said—how they loved hiking and camping, poetry and art museums, long walks at sunset. She said the opposite and didn't seem to worry how it sounded. I guess, like me, she figured if she was herself and that was okay, then she was talking to the right person.

In one of her first emails, she'd said: "I'm a little overweight, and I'd tell you I'm working on it. But I've been too busy at work to exercise. I'm not that active. I love food, all kinds. I make a wonderfully tangy and crunchy tomato-basil bruschetta. And I love strawberry cheesecake ice cream with the graham cracker bits left in. I hate the cheap kind that skimps on the graham crackers."

I smiled and laughed out loud—literally—when I read that. I imagined her body would be curvaceous, like an Italian painting. I could picture my fingers tracing her ivory curves under a cool, silky sheet. I had to slap myself out of my daydreams.

She continued, "I don't take a lot of long walks at sunset because of the bugs...or long walks at all unless I'm going somewhere in particular. I know so many women on here sound like they're always running and jumping and biking and always out at the ballet or an art museum. The last place I went was the hardware store to find the right bathroom fixtures to match my brushed nickel faucet. I wanted everything to match like they do on HGTV, my favorite channel, by the way."

Could this be a match made in heaven? I not only liked HGTV, but I hated fixing things, and it sounded like she'd put in her own fixtures. What a woman!

Before my membership expired, I gave her my email address, so we could stay in touch. Luckily, I did it just in time because her membership was expiring too. So we came within a feather of time, almost never meeting at all.

Tonight I got comfy on the couch, curled up with Cookie softly rumbling beside me, and got ready to savor Ellie's next entry. Reading a new email from Ellie had become the highlight of my day, or as she would say, the perfect dessert to complete the meal. I couldn't wait. And she never disappointed.

There it was. A new letter from Ellie. It was strangely much shorter than her usual emails. She wrote:

"Yes, I agree *The Bachelor and Bachelorette* TV series should do a gay version. Their ratings would spike, probably from straight but curious viewers more than gay people! I have to admit, I'm newer to this life than you. I haven't been out as long. Would you like to talk on the phone tonight? When you get this email, if you want to, call me at…"

My heart pounded as I read the numbers. I hadn't been this nervous since the time in high school when I bumped into Angie Helgenberger, my biggest crush, by my locker. I'd never spoken a word to her before that. And in that second, Angie said, "I'm sorry." I just stood there and stared at her with my mouth half open. Only she didn't know I was desperately trying to think of something to say. She probably thought I was a weirdo who didn't like people touching me or someone who was planning to blow up the school. Either way, it was a memory that stuck in my mind.

Why is it we always remember the most embarrassing, most heartbreaking, of all of our memories? Sure, the good times are scattered across your mind, fleeting thoughts. But the ones at the top of the pile that you tend to relive over and over are always the times when instead of coming across like a movie star, you most likely looked like a clumsy cartoon character whose head is screwed on backward.

Ellie wanted to *talk*. Why was that suddenly so terrifying? Why did that rank up there with giving a speech in front of the student body and throwing up the morning before? I knew why. Talking to her would make her *real*.

Right now Ellie Hundersson was the only light in my tunnel. Whether I'd meant to or not, I'd started to cling to the hope of something special with her, something corny that involved sunsets or at least flickering candlelight. She was a fantasy—still at a safe enough distance to not know any of her flaws, those annoying things that remind you someone is human and can hurt or disappoint you.

Even more importantly, she couldn't yet know about *my* flaws and quirks. I wasn't ready to lose my mystery by having a screaming fit at the sight of pistachio ice cream because I can't let it touch me. Things like that.

Pistachio was a big one that would surely prove my weirdness. What would Ellie think?

I stared at my phone and gulped. Then I cleared my throat. And cleared it again. No. I wouldn't do this. I couldn't bear to have Ellie learn the full depth of my weirdness.

My therapist told me I'd had a traumatic episode with pistachios as a child. But just because I'd gotten an explanation didn't make it any less weird. Then there was the chronic anxiety disorder. And the OCD. And the ADD. And the IBS. I had more acronyms than a dictionary.

In spite of my better judgment, I dialed her number.

"Hello?" Her voice was light and sexy, just like her photo.

My chest rippled with excitement.

"Is this Ellie?" I asked.

"Yes. Sydney?"

"Yes." I was beaming. If we'd been Skyping, which I still didn't know how to do, she would have seen me grinning like a giddy child.

Ellie sounded mature and sophisticated and calm and everything that made me swoon—all in that one voice.

"It's great to hear what you sound like!" I blurted. Already I'd lost my mystery.

"You too. Your voice is a little deeper."

"Is that a good thing?"

"Oh yeah." She laughed an easy, excited laugh.

I think the feelings were mutual. Of course I'd been so wrong about things before, but she seemed as happy as I was.

"So how are things in Connecticut?" she asked.

"Pretty much the same. My friends and I went out dancing, which was kind of unfortunate since none of us can dance."

She laughed.

"I danced to one of those loud songs where it doesn't matter if you're with anyone or not."

"Maybe next time I can dance with you," she replied.

I swallowed hard. After so many endings, something was finally beginning.

CHAPTER ELEVEN

"Ice Cream and Lactose Intolerance"

Before the conversation was over, we'd arranged to meet in Mystic, a halfway point from where I was in Connecticut and her in Massachusetts. Mystic was the little seaside town where the movie *Mystic Pizza* was made. And the pizza really was as good as it said in the movie.

Before I left, Maddie warned me not to move in with her too soon. I assured her that wasn't possible. I was taking things slowly.

"If you move up to Massachusetts," Maddie said, "you'll be dead to me."

"Will you get a hold of yourself? No one's moving in with anyone." Despite my attempts to reassure her, she was convinced that I'd be the cliché lesbian who starts packing boxes right after our first dinner.

Ellie and I each booked a room at a nearby hotel so we wouldn't have a long drive back the same night. Separate rooms were a good sign of taking things slowly. I was relieved that we were on the same page. And I couldn't wait to tell Maddie, who had said something about how she probably just wanted to get in my pants.

The morning I was getting ready to go, I was anxious—no, panic-stricken.

"Have some ginger ale to settle your stomach," Penny suggested, pushing a glass in front of me.

"No," I snapped. "Sorry. I'm just scared out of my mind."

"Of course you are," Penny said almost cheerfully.

"You've been through this. What's it like?"

"Well..." She thought a moment. "They never look as good as their picture. And they may have the wrong idea about how you look 'cause of your picture. It doesn't matter if you've had great talks or anything. If she's not attracted to you in person, it's doomed. She'll make an excuse to dump you, maybe lose you right there at the Mystic Aquarium."

I glared at her. Was this supposed to be a pep talk?

"Oh, but that probably won't happen to you." She tried hard to take it all back, but the fear and uncertainty had already been flung in my face.

I hit the highway, and as I drove down familiar hills, I pondered the green summer trees lining the road. They'd be barren and dead when winter came, with their beautiful days behind them and nothing more to give. I wondered if I'd still know Ellie when the trees looked like that. That train of thought led me back to myself, of course. I'd once been like these lush trees with summer light piercing through. Like it or not, I was getting older. What if my hottie days were all behind me? My best face and body had gone to Valdemort, who didn't really appreciate them anyway. And now Ellie would get the scraps of the woman I used to be.

I had to jump off this merry-go-round of mental misery. I had to get positive. Fast. Whatever I had left, I had to give Ellie the best me I could.

* * *

"You look beautiful," she said as we met in the parking lot. I dove into her bear hug and didn't want to let go.

She was beautiful too, more in person than in any photo. She wore a simple black top with a maroon corduroy jacket and jeans, very like my red corduroy jacket and jeans. We almost looked like twins. Up close I could see the features of her face, with the contours in the light and shadows…bursts of heat crackled up my spine. All at once I knew she had that *thing*. The thing that Angie from high school had. The thing that made me forget how to speak. The thing that could hurt me.

I fidgeted restlessly beneath the weight of her stare. Her topaz eyes danced in the gray light, and her long, blond hair blew gently off her shoulders in the breeze. She presented me with a single red carnation, remembering my profile.

"Want to go for a walk?" I asked, my smile giving away all my secrets.

"You can put that in the car." She gestured to the carnation. "I don't want you to feel like you have to walk around with it or anything." She looked around nervously.

"Sure." I placed the carnation carefully in the backseat, vowing to water it immediately, unlike all the other flowers I'd killed.

It was a foggy, misty afternoon, the kind that you imagine a day in New England is supposed to look like. You could feel moisture in the air, as clouds gathered overhead, promising a storm. We strolled by the boats that were docked and talked about how parts of the movie were filmed there.

I couldn't get over Ellie's stunningly gorgeous features, her shiny hair and her intelligent eyes looking back at me. I was nervous and sick. But that was a good thing.

"Want some ice cream?" she asked as we made our way up the bridge.

"Sure," I said without thinking. And before I knew it, I was standing in line trying to read a chalk-scribbled menu of flavors. What could I possibly order that wouldn't aggravate my IBS? What was the least likely flavor to kill me? Strawberry cheesecake? No. Chocolate? Hell no—a natural laxative. If I ordered that, I might as well shove a stick of dynamite up my ass. Panic seized me as I prayed to the ice cream gods to spare me just this one night...

Ellie made her decision first. *Not the pistachio. Don't get pistachio.*

"Chocolate chip," she told the cashier. *Whew.*

One crisis averted. My head was spinning. Butter pecan or death...cookies 'n cream...my insides were churning more than the ice cream had been. When the cashier looked at me expectantly, I panicked and blurted out, "I'm lactose intolerant! I have Irritable Bowel Syndrome!" The words dropped into one of those silences that mysteriously fall over public places whenever I say something stupid. Startled heads lifted and turned toward me, and I wanted to kill myself. I rushed out of there as Ellie gathered some napkins. "Forget that," I told her when she came out. "Rewind!"

She laughed as I tried to erase the moment, smacking myself in the head.

"I didn't know," she said apologetically.

"It's okay. It wasn't something I intended to tell you—and half of Connecticut—on our first date, but it's okay." I shrugged, and she put a reassuring arm around me as we made our way back to the dock.

We sat on a bench by the water in downtown Mystic that night. It didn't rain, but it was cool by the water, even on a summer night. I jammed my hands in my jacket pockets to give them something to do. I watched as lights from boats flickered across Ellie's windswept profile, outlining her nose and her cheeks, while she swirled her tongue along a lucky scoop of chocolate chip.

"Is it good?" I asked, so grateful it wasn't pistachio.

"Yeah, but not that good. I don't want you to feel bad for not being able to have it."

"You're so *gorgeous*," I gasped. What was the matter with me? I had violated all the rules I'd set for myself in the car on the way over. Rule number one—don't say anything embarrassing. That ship had truly sailed.

I saw her blush just a little. Then she slid her hand into my jacket pocket and grasped my hand. The wind battered our faces, freezing our awkward, shy smiles in place. It's funny. Everyone thinks that being by the water at night is romantic. Instead it's usually so windy you can't see and you have to blink a lot. So the first time we held hands was pretty much a blur for me, except for the memory of Ellie's hand in mine.

As we walked over the drawbridge, we passed a family with two worn-out parents trying to keep three toddlers from running into traffic. One little girl had ice cream running down her pink sundress. Her mother looked horrified and exhausted.

"Ashley!" The mother shouted. "I can't buy you nice clothes if you're going to make a mess like that!" Then she knelt down and tried to wipe the sticky mess.

"Kids," I sighed, shaking my head.

"What about them?" Ellie asked.

"Just look. You have no life once you have kids." I'd said I didn't want kids in my profile, so I was sure it came as no surprise. Then it dawned on me. "I'm sorry. I wasn't trying to say anything bad about your career."

"I didn't take it that way," she answered. "Actually, I don't mind the kids. It's the parents that can be annoying. If a child is falling behind in their work, the parents always blame the teacher. It never has anything to do with their home life," she remarked sarcastically.

"That has to be a pain."

"Yeah, parent-teacher conferences are my least favorite part of the job." She thought a moment. "'Yes, Timmy is an excellent student, except when he naps and snores in the middle of class and drools all over his desk. No, actually, your son is disgusting.'" She flashed a smile at me. "That's a conversation I'd never have, but could have."

We laughed on the way back to the car—me and the dignified teacher who had a deliciously silly streak just under the surface. That night I learned that she could imitate any accent after hearing it for a few seconds. She started parroting a lady from Wisconsin just as the lady came up behind us in a store. Ellie stopped abruptly, and we ran out, holding our laughter until we reached the street.

"I have to stop doing that," Ellie said between laughing spasms. "Someday I'm going to get in big trouble."

"Yeah, she seemed kind of pissed." We laughed harder.

Almost to the car…she squeezed my hand in my pocket tightly. The night was black except for the occasional store windows and lights from boats at the dock. As rows of car headlights darted toward us, slicing through the darkness, I wondered who was watching us in the dark cars behind the lights—skinheads, killers, members of the Christian Coalition who protested gay rights. My anxious thoughts, as usual, took center stage, when I really wanted to think about the way Ellie's hand felt like a silk glove, her skin giving me tingles all over. I didn't even notice how windy it was by the dock.

"You want to have breakfast tomorrow?" I asked shyly, pretty confident of her answer.

"No, I think I should get back," she replied. "I have a long drive."

"Oh." My heart leapt into my throat. It was as Penny had said, only Ellie was too polite to ditch me sooner.

Suddenly I was as humiliated as I was in department store dressing rooms, standing in front of the full-length mirror of shame. But this was even worse.

Ellie, seeing my worried face, leaned in to kiss me, a featherlight touch of her lips to mine. "I really like you," she said softly.

"Really?"

"Yeah, really. I really do have a long drive."

"But you got a room. You don't have to drive."

"Turns out I, uh, have somewhere I have to be tomorrow."

I wanted to believe her, but she sounded very secretive.

I spent that night in my motel room wide awake and wondering what I did wrong. She did give me a kiss, I reassured myself. She didn't have to do that. I alternated between "she hates me" and "she hates me not" until the first sign of dawn appeared through the drapes.

CHAPTER TWELVE

"Et tu, Debra?"

When I got back the next morning, Maddie, Penny and Ariel were all waiting for me in Penny's living room.

"How did it go!" Penny screamed.

"Really well," I said. "I think."

"You think?" I knew Maddie wouldn't let that go.

"Yeah, I think it did. I don't want to get too caught up." I glanced at Penny, whom we both knew, always got too caught up.

"Well, you did spend the night together," Penny said.

"Not exactly," I said. "She had to go home."

There was a collective "aww" until I glared at everybody.

"Did she give you anything?" Ariel probed. "A gift? Something that belongs to her?"

"A carnation." I reached into my bag, and it was already squished. "I need to get it some water."

"Not yet." Ariel grabbed it and rolled it between her hands.

"No," I said. "Don't do that thing where you try to sense her aura or something."

"Sure, be dismissive. But I can tell things." She handed it back to me with an all-knowing expression.

"Well?" I couldn't stand it. "What did you get?"

"I thought you didn't want to know." Ariel smirked, her eyes twinkling behind long, shaggy bangs. She reeked of cloves and patchouli.

"Come on!" I suddenly had to know.

"I'm getting…" Ariel was careful, thoughtful. "Some chaos, but it's good. She's a good person."

"You mean honest?" Penny asked. "Or not an ax murderer?"

"She has a good heart, a good soul." Ariel was looking to the heavens. Or at a crack in Penny's leaky ceiling.

Suddenly I felt like a high school girl who wanted to start scribbling our initials in all of my notebooks. I had a lightness in my steps as I went to the kitchen to pour some water.

"So you're moving to Massachusetts," Maddie concluded sadly.

"Let's not get ahead of ourselves." I washed my hands and picked up Cookie.

"How did she look in person?" Penny asked eagerly.

"Better than her photos. She's…stunning." I searched for words, but Ellie was like magic; you couldn't explain her. She had that special something, that wonderful whatever, that made me want to wrap her around me like a never-ending blanket. She also had a whole life that had happened before me, and I couldn't wait to uncover every detail, as long as she wanted to keep seeing me.

I caught Maddie's eyes, and suddenly I felt like I should stop talking. My whole face probably beamed with a joy that made her sad.

Friends should be happy for you. And Penny seemed truly excited for me. Ariel seemed stoned. But Maddie was seething beneath the surface. She'd once quoted Gore Vidal: "Every time a friend of mine succeeds, a little piece of me dies."

I felt the conflict radiating from her. My instincts were right.

"So, are you looking into teaching gigs?" I asked her, changing the subject.

"Ah, no," she answered. "That was the beer talking. I'm not giving up my retirement."

That was the theme for a lot of my friends. Now in our forties, it was as if they were superglued to their careers, even if they dreamed of doing more, flying higher, scaring themselves a little. They ignored those dreams in favor of the only security they knew in this world. I couldn't blame them. Nothing was certain anymore.

It was easy for me to talk about following long-held dreams because I had nothing to lose. But the truth was, I once had the "secure" job with benefits—that thing that's supposed to make you feel like you're going to be all right. But after years and years, moving into new homes that required a down payment and dealing with unexpected expenses, all of it was gone—the retirement, the 401k—and I hadn't even lived extravagantly. I'd never been out of the country. I'd never bought a new car unless mine was officially dead.

So the security I was supposedly working for was lost anyway. It never really existed. What I saw people clinging to weren't guarantees, but promises, too often unfulfilled.

Would Ellie understand this? I'd listed my occupation as a writer, which wasn't exactly a lie. But I wasn't writing for a company anymore. In Mystic, she asked what kinds of things I wrote, and I only told her the impressive stuff—billboards, brochures, things from my past. But I had lied to her, or rather, I had omitted the whole layoff part. Would she be angry? I was already starting off on a bad foot, lying to her. She'd never trust me now. And trust was important to me—right up there with good hygiene and good taste in music. I was violating my own standards. I'd have to tell her. My conscience was screaming in my ear. Anxiety spread its tentacles across my back and torso. She seemed to be an understanding person, I told myself. And downsizing was happening everywhere. Surely she'd understand.

I'd decided to write to her that night and tell her. I'd have to deal with whatever her reaction was.

That night, my hands shook as I typed. Cookie looked quizzically like she knew something was wrong. She had such awareness in her green cat eyes. Maybe it wasn't awareness, just the way they were slanted. Maybe the only thought in her head was when I was going to give her another treat.

I wrote:

> I'm sorry, Ellie. But I wasn't entirely honest about my work. Yes, I'm a writer. But I recently got laid off. I'm still in the embarrassment phase, so it wasn't something I wanted to volunteer. I hope you don't look at me differently. I swear I'm not a deadbeat who sits around eating Twinkies, watching daytime talk shows. I hate daytime talk shows. They're all about getting discounts on the latest shoes. I don't even like shoes. I'm probably the only woman who has like three pairs in her closet. And even then I usually alternate between two pairs. Okay, I'm rambling. I'm rambling because I'm scared. I'm sorry if I seemed dishonest. Please don't think I'm a pathological liar whom you can never trust again. In my spare time, I'm writing novels and screenplays and things I've always wanted to. I'm very ambitious, just not making any money at it yet. Well, I had a wonderful time in Mystic. I hope you did, too.—Sydney

It was a sad, meandering email and I wanted to delete the whole thing. I almost did, but Cookie kept climbing on the laptop. I was afraid she'd create a bunch of typos and make it worse. So I hit Send and took a deep breath.

Then I went to the kitchen to get Cookie a tuna treat. They smelled disgusting, but they made her so happy she swirled in circles like a dog just to get one. I figured anything that could make a cat do that, she deserved it.

By the time I got back, there was already a response from Ellie. I braced myself. My heart pounded. Now was the time when she was going to cut me loose. Now I'd learn the real reason why she wanted to leave so soon.

I opened it. It read:

Thanks for telling me. I completely understand. It's hard enough having to deal with the emotional stress of a layoff, let alone share it with someone you've just met. Honestly, I think novels and screenplays are way more interesting than billboards. I have things to share with you too. But there's plenty of time for that. I had a great time in Mystic too. —Ellie

What? That was it? Maybe she really was the one for me. But of course, I couldn't let myself be happy for more than thirty seconds, so my mind immediately drifted to "What things did *she* have to share? Did she have some deep, dark secret?" Of course she did, I decided. This was all too good to be true. She had to be missing a foot or at least a toe, something I wouldn't have seen. She was walking around with a prosthetic foot in a shoe. Not that I would care. I'd get used to it. Or did she really teach fifth grade? Maybe it was third grade. Wait. What was the big reason to lie about that? Even my inner voice was calling me an idiot. What if she was really a man? A very good drag queen? Suddenly I was sad. That would explain her not wanting to share a room with me—if there was something between her legs that she didn't want me to know about.

It was like getting a deal on a car. You find exactly what you want, but the price seems unbelievable. And there's a reason for it. There's always a catch. I had to figure out what the catch was. She was beautiful, nice, didn't rush me. Before her, I'd only known two kinds of lesbians—the cold, uninterested ones who can't remember your name and the kind that want to move in with you after you say hello. I had no point of reference for Ellie.

Penny came out of the bedroom for her nightly glass of milk.

"Hey," she called.

"Hey." I sounded worried.

"What is it?"

"I'm wondering if Ellie is really a man."

"Are you kidding me?" Penny laughed.

"She mentioned having more things to tell me."

"That could mean anything." Penny patted my shoulder.

She was right. A few moments left alone and my thoughts were runaway horses, galloping into all kinds of strange places. I already had her as a third-grade-teaching drag queen who was missing a foot.

"True," I agreed. "Maybe she just smoked pot."

"Eew. I hope not."

"Lots of people have, you know."

"Have you?" she asked.

"Well, no. But I've always been very square." I hung my head.

"Get some rest," she urged. "You seem like you need it."

"I guess…" I fumbled for words. "I guess when something goes well, I just wait to see how it's going to get screwed up."

"It doesn't always have to." She gave me a wise smile and went to bed.

My sister Joanne was right. She and I didn't know how to handle happiness. We were more comfortable when something bad happened. Maybe because it made more sense. Maybe it was more familiar. If I won the lottery, I'd probably stay indoors for fear of getting hit by a bus or falling space debris. I think my fear of success sprung from an article I'd read about Margaret Mitchell. First she writes this bestselling novel, *Gone with the Wind*, then she gets run over by a car. That was the reason I had trouble finishing anything I wrote—the fear that getting published was a sure way to get run over by something.

If I were Ellie, I certainly wouldn't want to get involved with me. I was nuts.

On Monday morning, I got a call from Debra. She said that one of her friends had a good job opportunity for me. I needed to meet her and a couple of women she hung out with for lunch at Le Jardin. It was an ultra-fancy restaurant. The entrées cost more than my rent. But Debra said it was her treat. So I donned my nicest business attire, a simple blue suit and crisp white shirt underneath, and headed for the little French bistro I'd always passed by with no intention of ever setting foot inside.

I met Debra there. She waved me over, dressed in her lime-green business suit with expensive pearls I'd never seen before.

With white linen tablecloths, the restaurant was the kind of place where you're afraid to sit down for fear of wrinkling something.

"Hi, you look great," Debra gushed, taking both of my hands in hers.

"So do you," I said, sitting down.

She sat back and studied me with her hand tucked under her chin.

"How are things with Kurt?" I asked.

"Oh, fine. We're fine. We're thinking about getting engaged."

"Thinking about?" I repeated. How did they decide to think about it, and what was that conversation like?

"Yeah," she replied defensively, rearranging the breadsticks in the basket. "You know they give you as many as you want."

"Great." I bit into one, not realizing how hard they were. The crumbs flew all over the flawless white linen. "So when are your friends coming?"

"Any minute." She checked her watch. "Look, you know the one I told you who might have a job for you?"

"Yeah?"

"It's Kirsten Foster. She's really glam, and she works for an in-house marketing department at Anne Hirsch Cosmetics."

"Anne Hirsch? Well la dee dah!" I was impressed. You couldn't open a magazine without seeing one of their advertisements.

"Yeah, and there's something you should know." Debra's eyes darted around; she looked nervous.

"She's a CIA operative? What?" I laughed.

"Kirsten and Susan, my other friend, Susan Kent, they know you're a friend of mine."

"Well, that's good." I shrugged my shoulders, completely clueless.

"But they don't know you're, you know." Debra looked toward the door.

"What? I'm what?"

"You know," Debra repeated, her voice almost a whisper. "Don't make me say it."

"Am I a criminal or something and just don't know it? You're acting really weird, Deb."

"They don't know you're a lesbian," she said softly.

"A what?"

"A lesbian!" Debra announced it to an older couple who was just leaving. The lady glanced at Debra curiously, probably surprised to see one up close.

"Wow." I sat back and stared blankly at her. We'd been friends for six years. I met her when she did some consulting for the company where I worked. A bunch of us had lunch one day, and Debra and I bonded over a love of Barbra Streisand, which the others at the table mocked. Once we started quoting *Yentl*, I knew we'd be friends for life. "I'm surprised you're making it such a big deal. If it's never come up before, it's never come up. I didn't expect you to introduce me as Sydney, your lesbian friend."

Debra smiled, looking a little relieved. "Well, I didn't know how out you wanted to be, especially with a potential job interview. I don't know all the protocol!" She took a sip of ice water with shaky hands.

"Calm down," I said. "It's okay."

"Look," she continued. "You have to understand. The Anne Hirsch company is kind of conservative. I didn't think you'd go for it, so I never mentioned it. But since it's been so hard for you...out there..."

"You mean there's been an opening for a while?"

"Well, yeah, but I know how you are."

"Debra, listen. I don't want to be some political poster child for lesbians. I'm not trying to make statements everywhere I go. I just want to live my life, okay?"

She nodded, more relieved.

"How conservative are we talking?" I asked. "Are there crucifixes hanging everywhere? Only white employees? What?"

"I don't think so," she answered.

I had been joking.

"I'll bet money their fashion department is full of gay men," I said. "And they're based in New York. Hello?"

"Just don't say anything like that to my friends, okay?" Debra looked solemn; she suddenly seemed embarrassed by me.

I didn't get a chance to say anything because her friends showed up right at that moment.

"Hey!"

"Hey!"

Kirsten and Susan could have been twins, with white-blonde peroxide accidents on their heads, similarly tailored suits and legs for miles. I stood up to shake their hands and felt like the odd sister who was kept in the attic.

"This is my friend, Sydney Gray," Debra said. "The one I was telling you about."

"Yes." Kirsten took me in with one expert glance and sat beside me. "You have great bone structure."

"Yeah, she does," Susan chimed in. "Look at those cheekbones."

"Thanks," I responded. "I pride myself on my cheekbones."

They both nodded intensely, not yet realizing that sarcasm was my first language.

"Oh, you're being funny!" Kirsten exclaimed. Then she laughed a high-pitched, squealing laugh. "She's funny too! Isn't that cute?"

"Yeah, she's a hoot." Debra glared at me from across the table.

"So how do you all know each other?" I asked.

"Oh, we go back a long way," Susan began. "About eight or nine months ago. Debra's in our quilting club."

"You quilt?" I looked at the alien across the table who had replaced my actual friend.

"Yeah," Kirsten added, "we get together and try to make blankets or those tea cozies..."

I mouthed "tea cozies" to Debra, who was not amused.

"The best part," Kirsten continued, "is how we get to rag on our husbands, or her boyfriend, all night long. It's great. You want to join?"

I smiled broadly. This was pretty amusing. "I'm an expert quilter," I lied. "I wouldn't want to make you look bad."

The two women seemed fascinated.

"I'm also Mormon. I make quilts all day with my sister wives."

"She's kidding!" Debra interrupted. "She has a warped sense of humor. Very warped." If the fire inside Debra could escape, the whole place would have burned down.

Kirsten and Susan stared at me with gaping mouths.

The waiter came and mercifully changed the subject. All of them ordered salads with balsamic vinegar. I had the double-decker pita with turkey and cheese and ranch dressing and fried fat thrown in for good measure.

They kept staring at me after I ordered. I could almost see their brains trying to compute who or what I was.

"So I hear you're looking for a job?" Kirsten touched my arm sympathetically.

"Yes, I've been an ad copywriter for nearly twenty years, but my company was downsizing, and you know marketing is always first to go."

"Right." Kirsten looked at me, sipping her water. "Did Debra tell you I work at Anne Hirsch? Not the queer fashion side, but the cosmetic side."

I almost choked on my breadstick. Did I hear her correctly? Or was she using "queer" in another way, as if peculiar? I hoped so. But Debra's face was now crimson, so I didn't think so.

"What's with the fashion side?" I asked.

Debra sank a little in her chair.

"Well," Kirsten explained. "We're the cosmetics division, so we write ad copy and design for all print and television ads relating to mascara, lipstick and her newest base powder, which is to die for."

"The kind that blends in no matter what's wrong with your skin?" Susan gushed.

"Yes," Kirsten confirmed.

"Oh!" Susan sighed. "I'd kill for some of that."

Kirsten turned back to me. "We get free samples of everything."

I was supposed to be salivating by now. But I got most of my cosmetics at drugstores, not high-end department stores. The skin care regime seemed like it would take forever if you really followed it, especially at bedtime. Cleanser, exfoliator, wrinkle minimizer, moisturizer—I'd be so exhausted I'd fall asleep in the bathroom sink.

"It sounds great," I replied.

"But we're in our own building on Park Avenue," Kirsten continued. "The fashion division is in another building, thank God."

"Oh, I know." Susan shook her head.

"It's all these flaming queens and models who won't speak to you." Kirsten sipped more water. "They do photo shoots and stuff over there. I couldn't stand to work near that, listening to those fags yakking about their boyfriends all day long. The way they talk, they're more feminine than most women!"

Susan laughed hysterically.

"Fags?" I repeated.

By now, Debra's face was covered by her napkin.

"I really don't care for that word," I said as politely as one could, I suppose.

"Really," Kirsten commented. "What does it matter to you? It's not like you're a dyke. You actually have hair!" She laughed uproariously along with Susan.

Obviously, my feminine suit, makeup, jewelry and the fact that I didn't have a buzz cut had them fooled. Clearly I was not one of *those* people. And suddenly, this small-town Florida girl who didn't really want to be an activist felt this fire shoot straight up her ass and up her spine until flames flew out of my mouth.

"Actually, I am," I replied. "We're sometimes able to blend in by changing our outer wear. It's how we survive in the wild."

Both women looked puzzled. They didn't get the joke.

"I'm a big, raging dyke. And I hate that word too, by the way." I stood up. "If working at that company means working with the likes of you, I'll pass." I started to leave, but I paused, gazing at Debra for a moment.

She was horrified, not because of what her friends had said, but because of me, for making a scene. I saw it all in one glance. She looked apologetically at them and followed me out the door. When we got outside, I turned to face her.

"How could you? Hanging around with these bigots? I'll bet they've said this before, and you don't call them on it, do you?"

"Is that my responsibility?" she asked. "I need to fight for the gay cause just because one of my friends is? No thank you. This may come as a shock to you, but I don't get the whole gay lifestyle. I'm not really for it, okay? I can be your friend, but I don't have to agree with your lifestyle."

I went numb all over. "No, Debra. You can't be my friend if you don't think I deserve the same rights as you."

"You mean gay marriage?" She had her hands on her hips, in full confrontation mode. If this had been an episode of *Wild Kingdom*, I'd have been the threatened elk right now.

"No, you have a right to your opinion," I said. "But I can't stay friends with someone who thinks she's better than me because I'm some kind of pervert who loves the wrong gender."

"I'm sorry if it hurts you, but I'm being honest when—"

"You know what, Debra? Go fuck yourself."

All the way back to the apartment I was blinded by tears—that and the regret I had for not choosing something more scathing, yet poetic, to say in the end. I had to resort to expletives? Why did all the perfect words always come to mind when I was miles away from the scene? I never wanted to see or hear from her again. I had enough straight friends. I didn't need her in my life anyway. But how could she be harboring these feelings toward me for six years, pretending to stand by me when all this time... I couldn't believe it. She was never really my friend at all. People always shocked me. With my age certainly hadn't come wisdom, I thought, pulling into a drugstore to get the cheapest brand of eye shadow possible.

And when I got to the counter, all I could think about was how ironic it was. Why was my only job possibility an opening with a homophobic company in one of the most liberal cities on Earth? What were the odds?

CHAPTER THIRTEEN

"A Tale of Two Lesbians"

Ellie was the bright spot in my day. No matter how bad things got, I could count on her emails to give me comfort. It was now fall, the perfect time for a getaway to Vermont. We'd planned to stay at a bed-and-breakfast for the weekend. Of course I was nervous. I'd never stayed at a bed-and-breakfast before.

"Did you make sure it was for lesbians?" Maddie asked over glasses of wine at Penny's place.

"No, I think it's just a regular—"

Maddie and Penny exchanged grim faces.

"What?" I always felt like the last one to know. "Is this some other rule in the lesbian handbook I don't know?"

"It's just not good," Penny sighed.

"Shit, Syd." Maddie threw her face in her hands. "A straight bed-and-breakfast? That's where you're going with your new girlfriend? You'll be stuck having breakfast with a straight couple from Minnesota yammering about their kids and having to act like you're just best friends or spinster sisters."

"It was her idea!" I exclaimed. "She thought it would be a romantic spot out in the country."

"Vermont is romantic this time of year," Penny mused. "You'll have lots of color up there."

Maddie smacked Penny. "Does this chick know the difference between straight and gay bed-and-breakfasts? Wait, you say she hasn't been out long?"

I nodded.

"That explains it," Maddie continued. "Just tell her you need to pick a different spot."

"I can't. She made reservations." I started packing and tried to ignore their admonitions.

* * *

I drove up to Massachusetts; I was going to meet Ellie at her house. Then we'd take her car up to Vermont. I worried over the winding roads. I took my anxiety pill. I tried the breathing exercises my therapist recommended. They never worked in any situation, but I kept trying them, hoping to have a different outcome.

Massachusetts was dotted with reds and golds, as autumn had just begun. Old Victorian houses lined the roads, as well as handmade signs for apple orchards with arrows pointing to dirt roads. I kept checking her directions. Every back road seemed to lead to nowhere, until I saw a gas station or old inn that she told me would be there. My car sputtered as I crawled up a small hill. Behind a clump of trees a sprawling lake glittered with the reflections of color. It was the perfect place. A writer's retreat, I fantasized. As I made it all the way up the hill, I found Ellie's little ranch house in a small enclave on a dead-end street. It was a little tucked away place that made me want to stay a while.

But Ellie came out to the driveway with a suitcase in each hand, clearly intent on leaving immediately. She greeted me with a warm smile. "The place is a mess," she said apologetically.

"That's okay."

"My brother's fixing the oil tank. It's not safe, uh, to breathe the fumes."

"Oh." I didn't see another car in the driveway. "You sure he'll be all right? Should we leave him?"

"Yeah, sure." She unlocked her car. She couldn't wait to put our suitcases in, it seemed. As I handed her mine, she winked at me. "You made it."

"Great directions." I waved the paper with her directions written on it. Amidst the smiles, I had an unsettled feeling. Why didn't she want me to come inside? Was she a hoarder? Did she have so many knickknacks we'd hardly be able to open the front door?

She backed the car out.

What if she collected primitives? Like cloth roosters?

We started down the winding road to Vermont. I told myself to stop being negative and just enjoy the damn scenery.

Ellie programmed her GPS, hit it a few times, then tried to fasten it to the inside of the windshield. It kept falling down, and I tried not to laugh because she was getting increasingly irritated.

"You want me to hold the wheel?" I asked.

"No, it's fine. It always does this." Another smack on the GPS.

A road trip was a good way to really learn about someone. I saw her impatient side—yea, a sort-of flaw. It made me feel better.

I took in the Vermont landscape, a patchwork of cows and hills and red barns that had probably been around since the first settlers. I glanced at Ellie and smiled. Her flannel shirt looked so soft. We brushed hands, and I got those warm flutters inside.

This was a lightning bug moment.

Although I was the kind of person who waited for—and expected—the bad news in any situation, I knew I'd never forget this day. The light in her hair, the general stores with crudely drawn cow pictures on wood signs and the weightless feeling I had—this was what it meant to be alive.

We arrived at the bed-and-breakfast, The Rooster Inn, which was an intimidating, stately Victorian mansion.

"This isn't exactly my style," Ellie told me apologetically.

"It looks pretty," I said, reassuring her.

She squeezed my hand. Her hand felt like the safest place in the world. With her slender fingers woven through mine, there was a strength between us, like we could conquer anything together.

We checked in at a dark, cherrywood desk, complete with an old woman who was wearing a dress that must have been made from the same fabric as the busy, flowery drapes in the lobby.

"One room?" she repeated.

I thought Vermont was liberal. Wait. Vermont was, but Maddie was right—a straight bed-and-breakfast might not be.

"Yes," I answered firmly. I sensed that Ellie was uncomfortable.

"They all have one bed per room," the old lady informed us.

"That's fine," I said sharply.

Ellie looked around at the line of husband and wife couples forming behind us in the lobby.

"But you're two women!" the old lady protested.

A rush of heat flashed up my spine as I got ready to climb over the front desk.

"Hey, this is Vermont!" A man behind us yelled at the desk clerk.

Ellie lowered her head; she wanted to disappear. I could tell.

"Yeah, gay marriage is legal here," another woman added. "So deal with it!"

I turned and gave a quiet "thank you" to the crowd of supporters with New York accents, while the old lady reluctantly checked us in, punching the keys of her computer harder than was necessary, I was sure.

We entered the ornate, overly Victorian room that looked so formal I didn't want to touch anything. Ellie collapsed on the bed.

"I'm so sorry!" she cried. "I didn't know…"

"That you had to make sure it was gay-friendly?"

She breathed a heavy sigh.

"It's okay," I said. "I know you haven't been out long." I tried to sound like the wise lesbian even though I had had no clue, either. "How long have you been out?" I asked.

"Not long."

I wasn't learning much here. And I was hoping to get to know her a lot better.

"When did you know you were?" I continued.

"All my life," she answered. "You want to grab some dinner?"

"Where?" I took a brochure off the nightstand. "The Dead Moose Inn. That's, uh, forty miles away."

Silence.

"I think they want you to eat *here*," I said.

"No." Ellie peeked out the window. There was nothing for miles but bales of hay, grass and an occasional barn.

"I doubt she has the energy to come up here and kill us in our sleep." It was a bad joke, from the look on Ellie's face.

She seemed so upset. "I'm not used to this."

"Me neither," I replied. "I never had anyone act like that in a regular hotel."

"This was a bad idea."

"It doesn't have to be." I took her hands and pulled her close.

But neither of us wanted to go to the dining room that night, being in a fishbowl with a spotlight on us, subjected to staring straight people, even the nice ones. I especially didn't want that for Ellie. Since she hadn't been out long, I wanted her to see how good it could be. But another thought nagged at me; it was the annoying inner activist waving signs on my shoulder.

"If we don't go to dinner," I said, "the haters win, and we starve. Or drive to the Dead Moose. God, I hope that's not on the menu."

She laughed so easily in the midst of her fear. I loved that most about her, an infectious laugh that spilled out even in times of stress.

Over a candlelit dinner in the middle of the dining room with the stone fireplace, we ignored the crowd, which seemed mostly supportive, except for a handful of older couples who were trying hard to figure out if we were sisters.

"Have you ever been to Provincetown?" I asked.

"No."

"I've heard it's a place where people like us can go and hold hands in public. My friends always talk about it."

Ariel had called it the Key West of the North. Years ago, I'd been to Key West with my family. We stayed on Duval Street where I remembered seeing mostly gay men walking hand in hand, and nobody seemed to care. That left the biggest impression on me. Well, that and the hot stickiness of sauna-like air that hit you every time you went outside. Our clothes stuck to our skin as we watched the orange sunset touch the horizon, at the southernmost tip of the US, in Mallory Square, to the applause of other tourists on the pier.

My ADD was taking over. I'd forgotten I was in Vermont and instead was remembering trained cats jumping through hoops of fire in Mallory Square. How could anybody train a cat? I couldn't even get Cookie up from her nap.

"I was thinking of visiting there sometime," I continued.

"Then we should."

I gazed into her full, blue eyes, with candlelight swirling in them. This made her self-conscious; she turned her head and looked everywhere but my eyes.

I smiled to myself.

"So tell me," I said, "when did you know?"

"First grade," she answered without a second thought.

"No, I mean when did you decide to come out? What was the catalyst?"

She hesitated. "It wasn't long ago. I'd taken a night class in painting, and I got a crush on my teacher, who happened to be a woman."

"Ooh, that's exciting." I was like a little kid, wanting to hear all the juicy details.

The waiter, who himself seemed gay, was very kind to us as he presented our plates of linguini garnished with some herbs grown in the owners' garden.

"Thank you," Ellie said, not looking at him.

"It's okay." I took her hand, and she jumped a little. She was obviously uncomfortable, so I took my hand away, tortured, trying to think of ways to put her at ease. Luckily, there was wine.

We toasted to new beginnings. After another glass of wine, she stopped looking around the dining room.

"You think it's exciting I fell in love with my teacher?" she whispered.

"Oh, yeah. That's hot."

She tucked her hand beneath her chin. "It's not so exciting when she turned out to be straight."

"Those straight women, always messing with your head." I winked at her, and in the firelight, there was a glow all around her. Maybe it was just the way she looked to me that night. Her smile, her features, everything about her had a glow. There was no one else in the dining room, and all I could feel was my heart pounding as I wondered where this night would lead. The flames cast intermittent light across her face, making her eyes dance in a way that seemed to suggest she wasn't quite so innocent after all.

We returned to the Victorian bedroom. I pulled back the gushy, down comforter, grateful it was there to combat the draft coming from the cold windows. Places that had character always seemed to come with cold, drafty air.

I took off my earrings, as I sat on the bed, suddenly aware of Ellie's fearful expression. I reached out my hand to her.

"You have slept with a woman before, right?" I asked. It never crossed my mind that I might be the one to initiate her into the lesbian club. That would be way too much pressure.

"Yeah," she answered, hesitating. "But it didn't go so well. I guess I didn't do it right."

I tried to imagine that. There was no right or wrong if you're with someone you want to be with. It's not like the Olympics, where you can get a perfect ten on your dive and earn a gold medal in lovemaking. Maybe the woman she was with was too mechanical.

"You can't do it wrong," I said softly, starting to kiss her, trying to relax her. I was pretending my hands weren't shaking or my heart wasn't thundering out of my chest.

I'd heard or read somewhere that you're never more dishonest than when you're in bed with someone. Ironically, it's probably true. You want everything to go so well. You want her to remember you the next morning with a smile she can't erase for days afterward. But it's never like the movies. It's sometimes clumsy and awkward, with you kneeling on her hair or her accidentally bending your arm in a direction it doesn't naturally go.

But once I figured out how to dim the Victorian lamp, there was a mood, a feeling, that reminded me of a movie. And all of my senses were overcome. I inhaled her soft, velvet skin, so warm, wrapped around me. When I looked up at her, brushing her long hair back from her face, I was struck by her beauty, with bare shoulders peeking over the sheet, like a painting or artistic photograph. I wanted to remember the way she looked at me, her eyes heavy-lidded and full of desire, a look I couldn't get enough of. I wanted to make her look at me like that always.

With the sheet tangled around our waists, she held me like she'd never let me go, kissing me all over. Her touch was gentle yet urgent, as if she couldn't wait to explore all she'd imagined, just like me. This woman of my daydreams was sharing a bed with me. The thought crossed my mind, reminding me to savor every second.

Reality is a funny thing. It's always different than what you imagine. But this was the first time my reality was better than my dreams. That had never happened before.

She smiled at me as I traced her lips, my fingertips inching down over her chin. "You're so beautiful," I sighed.

She closed her eyes a long time.

"What?" I asked, raising up on my elbow.

"You have no idea how long it's been since someone said that."

"You're kidding." I saw the hurt in her eyes. I couldn't believe a woman like her wouldn't have heard those words every day of her life. "Obviously, you've been with the wrong people."

"I guess so," she said softly and looked away so I wouldn't see.

I turned her face to look at me. "I meant it," I said. For some reason, I had a feeling she needed to know it was the truth. This was a woman who had been betrayed before or underappreciated. I had to show her I was different. Each caress was a silent promise that I would never hurt her, at least not intentionally.

My lips melted into her soft, silky skin. I was discovering every curve for the first time, with endless wonder. I traced the lines around her mouth, as she smiled in the dim light. Her body like poetry, her skin steamy hot to the touch—she was perfection. I only hoped I was deserving of this newfound treasure.

Moonlight streamed in and outlined her exquisite breasts, as she arched her back, moaning with pleasure. I couldn't get close enough, and I dove beneath the covers, discovering her with my lips, my tongue. She thrashed against the pillow, her body shaking into a frenzy, then quiet. Peace.

We breathed deeply, holding each other with the soft cotton sheet still wrapped around us.

I woke up after a few minutes and felt her arms around me. She whispered in my ear, "I want to go take a shower."

"Okay." I closed my eyes and breathed a luxurious breath. It had been so long since my body felt like a rippling liquid of total relaxation, something so foreign to me.

As the shower ran in the bathroom, there was a strange buzzing noise. I noticed it was her phone. I glanced at it, and on the screen it read: Shirley. It was a text. The curiosity ate away at me. The shower water poured forever. I couldn't stand it. I picked up the phone and saw an unfathomable text message: "Call your husband."

My heart sank like a heavy boulder. I sat upright in bed, hurriedly put on my clothes, feeling used and humiliated.

Ellie came out of the bathroom in a fluffy, terrycloth robe, her hair a shade darker from the water. She looked so good it hurt even worse.

"You got a text," I managed. "Someone named Shirley."

"She's the school principal," Ellie explained, picking up the phone. Then she saw what I'd just read.

"You forgot to mention him in your profile?" My eyes filled with tears.

"It isn't that."

"Then what is it?" I was too paralyzed by my own shock to hear anything. After what we'd just shared, how was I supposed to think of us now? How could I trust her? I wanted to take a long, hot shower to feel clean again.

"On that Venus Meet, no one would've contacted me if I said I had—"

"Oh, so you just lied," I interrupted. "And I was your girl-on-girl experiment."

"I wish you'd let me explain," Ellie said.

"There's nothing to explain. As long as you have a husband, there's nothing to explain." I hadn't felt this stupid since high school, when my eyeglasses-and-braces-wearing situation overlapped for a year.

She went back to Massachusetts alone, and I hitched a ride with a sweet older couple, ironically from Minnesota, who rattled on about their grandchildren all the way back to my car. When we pulled up to Ellie's driveway, she wasn't back yet. I imagined she must have made a stop somewhere to pick up some other unsuspecting lesbian. I was bitter—not your usual bitter, but the shriveled up, never-going-to-trust-the-human-race-again bitter. I went straight to my car and sped away as fast as I could. I wouldn't be returning to Massachusetts.

CHAPTER FOURTEEN

"Going with the Flo"

I returned to Connecticut and insisted my friends not ask me any questions about Vermont.

"I never want to talk about it ever," I declared.

Maddie kept filling my glass with wine, hoping I'd spill every detail.

"Did she do something freaky in bed?" Maddie asked.

"No. I'm the freak, the freak who agreed to go anywhere with her!" I left the room, knowing they were dying of curiosity. I sat out on the small deck off the kitchen. I sat under the full moonlight, mad at myself for wondering if she was looking at the same moon through the beautiful, tall pines that surrounded her house. I was mad for fantasizing about sharing that house with her someday. I know, I know. I did that thing where I got ahead of myself just like Penny.

I went out to clubs with my friends, night after night. I became a regular at Flo's. I got so discouraged with the job hunt—the interviews and everything that always went with them.

Before long, it had been a month since I'd seen Ellie. No more calls. No more emails. I'd pass houses, rows and rows of pumpkins on porches, wishing I could go back to September, when I still had hope of something special with her.

One day Joanne called and woke me from my fog.

"Where does she live? I'll come up there and kick her ass!" Joanne was barking every time I heard from her. I almost thought she wanted any ass to kick. Maybe she wanted someone to pay for something she herself was unhappy about. I wasn't sure.

"There's no point," I answered. "It doesn't change anything."

"No one messes with my little sister."

"I appreciate your support. I really do. But you can't swoop in and fix everything like you…used to." We both knew I was referring to an ill-advised relationship with a young woman with whom I moved to Ohio because her job had transferred her. We'd hardly known each other very well, but I couldn't wait to set up house. So there I was, carefully placing juice glasses into a cabinet, staring at the Ohio winter through the windows. Joanne came for a visit and helped me come to my senses. It was no one's fault. I was emotionally immature.

That's the part in the lesbian handbook they never tell you about. You spend your days in high school dating the wrong gender. By the time you've reached your twenties and know it's women you prefer, you don't have the social skills to date them and understand who fits best with you. I'd always thought of dating like trying on shoes—you try on several pairs until one feels really right. But when you're already in your late twenties and all of your straight friends are getting married, you feel it's time for you to settle down, too. So the first woman you're attracted to ends up being "the one" in your mind. You move in together and attempt to start a whole new life with someone who should have been a few dates in one chapter of the book of your life.

Even though you went through puberty in high school, you spent more time suppressing your feelings than learning how to act—or not act—on them the way your straight friends did. That was my personal theory as to why so many lesbian relationships didn't last until the women were at least in their forties.

But here I was, forty and frightened. I wondered if it was possible for there to be no Ms. Right at all. Everything is a fantasy, even the fairytales we learned as little girls and even if they involved princes to come and rescue us. Where was our *princess?* How did she fit into the picture?

"I want you to come down for a visit," Joanne insisted. "Please? I need to see you, and you definitely need to see me. So come on. What do you say?"

"What's going on with you?"

"Nothing major, but it has been a year."

"I know. I just have to find a job."

"Job shmob! I'll pay your way." She loved to say that. It was the solution for everything. Only Joanne never had to be the recipient of the charity. She didn't know what it did to my sense of pride. She didn't know how humiliated I already felt. She couldn't understand, because money was not her biggest worry as it was for me.

"I can't." It killed me to hurt her or even disappoint her. But I had no choice.

The next day I had an interview at a local newspaper in Danbury. I met with the editor in a busy newsroom. I'd dressed in my most professional attire and practiced in front of the mirror all morning long. What was my biggest weakness? Working way too hard, sometimes staying late and having no social life—I'd repeated the lie so many times I'd begun to believe myself.

"You've been writing ad copy?" He grunted, chewing on his pen. He was totally underwhelmed, with a faded yellow shirt, dangerously receding hairline and touches of gray around his ears.

"Yes, but I worked on the newspaper in college. It won awards." I was chirping like an eager bird.

"Why advertising? Why didn't you go into journalism?" It was a fair question. His eyes squinted at me in judgment. I had to have an answer. And it had to be good.

"I had some personal issues," I began carefully. "I was offered a good deal of money. But that's not usually my motivator! It just was…at that particular time. Then, you know how life takes over and you start moving up the ladder…" I drifted off, certain I'd lost the job already.

"I understand." He sat back and smiled slightly, even warmly. "Don't apologize for taking a good offer. Money's moved me before, and anyone who says it doesn't is a liar." He scanned my résumé too quickly; I can't imagine what he actually read. "Opinion pages? Well, you won't start there. We need more basic reporting. If the grade school has a track and field day, we need you there. I know it's crap. But it's a start. And if you show us a good work ethic, there's lots of room to move up, like say, to obituaries."

"That's great," I lied. But it was still a writing job. Could this be the beginning of some good luck?

"Just one thing," he added. "We're a small-town paper, a small family paper. We cover local neighborhoods. We don't go in for a lot of wacky stuff, if you know what I mean."

"Not exactly."

"We don't cover stories like that girl who wanted to take her girlfriend to the prom. Keep it family-oriented. Kids, school, PTA meetings, that kind of stuff."

I was frozen. This was the ultimate test—to be broke or give up all of my principles and have money.

"You know why?" he asked, leaning forward.

I shook my head.

"Because newspapers are dinosaurs!" he thundered. "We're a dying breed. Everyone gets everything on the Internet. Now our core customer base are the old folks, eighty-year-olds. You put some shocking story in there, you'll give 'em a heart attack." He seemed troubled. "They don't care what you or I think about current events. Only reason I bring this up is because we had a gal in here two days ago for this job. We hired her. Then she wanted to do something about lesbians and pride parades. I don't have a problem with it. But our readers might, you see? I don't even think I need to tell you about this. You don't seem like it would be an issue."

"Why's that?"

"You look like there's a boyfriend somewhere in the picture." He tried to smile, even chuckle, while noticing no rings on my fingers.

"I'll have to get back to you," I said like a true coward. "It sounds great, but I'm going to have to talk it over with family." I scooted out my chair.

"Well, listen, we hope to see you here Monday morning early." He shook my hand. I had the job. It was in my hands. I just had to accept it. And I needed the money. It was probably a no-brainer for any sane person.

That night, everything on the news was like my conscience screaming at me. A gay Congresswoman: "Every time the LGBT community is omitted from the media or classroom discussions, it's as if we don't exist. It keeps us invisible."

But this was a small-town newspaper. It wasn't setting out to change the world. It was a simple reporter job, writing copy about lemonade stands and other crap. I scrolled through my emails. There were no other interviews. Hundreds of résumés had gone out, contacts had been contacted and there were no other prospects. And there was the car insurance bill, the car payment—I couldn't let go of those in my bankruptcy unless I wanted to lose my car. They'd have to be paid somehow. And I told myself I'd already stood up for my rights by turning down what could have been the most lucrative job ever with Anne Hirsch Cosmetics. My principles sure weren't paying the bills. Me and my principles were getting lonelier and more stressed out with each passing day.

Life isn't like the movies. Staying true to your convictions doesn't always win in the end. Sometimes it gets you nowhere or poor and homeless with no teeth. No, I said to myself. Principles be damned. Just because the editor made a stupid comment didn't mean I couldn't take a reporter job for as short a time as possible until something better came along. After all, I wasn't going to be the poster child for fighting homophobia. That wasn't my role in life. I kept telling myself that.

I lay in the couch bed and the silence screamed at me that I was a traitor to my people, a coward! How could I take that job?

But I would. I would so I wouldn't have to spend another night sleeping on someone's couch bed.

I told my friends I got the reporter job and didn't mention the little bit about swallowing my spine to get it. I couldn't bear the judgment I'd get from Maddie or the sad look on Penny's face. Maddie didn't have those concerns in a hospital. There were too many people for the whole place to have a shared viewpoint. And Penny was in sales, surrounded by gay men who, I can only imagine, made each day fun to go to work. Neither of them knew the life of a struggling writer.

Okay, the pity party was getting old. I turned to my blog, where I publicly flogged myself. It would only be a matter of time before Maddie and Penny let me have it.

Maddie came over for breakfast on Saturday, and Penny made a buffet of egg-white scrambled eggs that didn't taste like eggs and fake bacon strips that mushed in your mouth, very unlike bacon.

"I guess you read the blog," I began, bracing for the backlash.

"Yeah," Penny said, handing me a fruit plate. "Do you realize you got hundreds of followers now? It's pretty huge."

"No, I didn't. I never look in the corner there, where the stats thing is." I took a sip of coffee and studied Maddie's face, while she chewed the bacon over and over again.

"What the hell is this?" she finally asked, pointing to the fake bacon strips.

"It's made of soy but tastes like bacon," Penny answered cheerfully.

"The hell it does." Maddie shook her head and washed down the aftertaste with strong, black coffee.

"So, Maddie," I began. "Go ahead. Say it. I know you read my blog."

"Uh-huh," she grunted.

I knew they read it. They knew my pen name. There was no hiding.

"Say it, whatever you're thinking, that I sold my soul? I have to make ends meet!" I protested.

Maddie held up her hand. "Hold on. No one's judging you. We're your friends."

"Come on. You always judge me."

"Not this time." She continued chewing her fake eggs. "Hell, I slept with someone to get that rotation at Johns Hopkins. That wasn't an easy place to get in, you know."

"No, you didn't," I barked. "You're just saying that."

"Dr. John Samter might disagree with you." She sipped her coffee, her eyes shifting to Penny.

I couldn't believe this. Where was the lecture? I expected more from them, from myself. If I was going to be a coward, surely they weren't going to condone it.

"Are you really Maddie Kimball?" I demanded.

She pointed her fork at me. "You're a hell of a writer. Go do it."

There was silence. Nobody seemed to care. But deep down, I'm sure they did. They just felt sorry for me, being on the edge of poverty.

"Okay," Maddie finally said. "I didn't sleep with anyone to get Johns Hopkins. But sometimes you have to suck it up just to support yourself. Anyone who says different is an idealistic idiot."

Like I used to be.

CHAPTER FIFTEEN

"The Book of Revelations"

My first assignment was a girls' soccer game at Hancock Field—much further to the east of Danbury. The school they were playing was from south-central Massachusetts, just over the state line. It was the Hancock Ravens versus the Walten Warriors of Walten Middle School.

I arrived with my notepad and photographer, Joe Ellis, a no-nonsense guy who bathed in Marlboros. But since we got to use his truck instead of my car, I didn't care. We made the small hike up to the chain-link fence. I'd come a long way since the Clio Awards, now writing about something taking place among the cow pies in a field where only a handful of bundled-up parents were watching. It was a pretty sad scene, to be sure. The small crowd watching sat in those fold-out chairs with cup holders in the armrests. Some people were huddled over their thermoses filled with hot chocolate. We arrived on the field just as the game was getting underway. I approached the woman who looked like the head coach and one of the mothers.

"Who is the star player on the Hancock team?" I asked.

"They're all stars in our eyes," she answered with a forced enthusiastic smile.

"Of course. I'm with the *Danbury Gazette*, and we want to do a piece about today's game."

You'd have thought I said I had Cher waiting in a limousine behind me.

She got so excited to hear we were the press, she gave me the name of every girl on the Hancock team.

"How well have they been doing? Is there a championship game?" I asked.

"They don't really have the same number of games the boys do. We encourage them to play just for the sake of playing." The other mothers smiled and watched excitedly as I took notes.

"Really? No championship? How many wins have they had?" I persisted.

"So far they're unbeaten." A husky, older woman waddled up to me and announced this very important fact.

"That's terrific! Now we've got a story." I wrote frantically, while Joe took some action photos of the game.

I noticed that not all of their shirts matched.

"How can you tell who's on whose team?" I asked. "Don't they have uniforms?"

"We don't have enough money to buy matching uniforms," the head coach replied. "We tell them all to wear red, but some forget." Then she screamed, "Lisa! Get in there! Be aggressive!" She shook her head. "Poor girl, just doesn't have that killer instinct. I think she really wants to be a violinist."

Now I felt like there was a reason I'd taken this job. I could encourage all interested parents and teachers to help donate money for the girls' soccer team. Encouraging young girls would surely be well received in the newsroom.

As the sun started to set, Joe and I headed back toward his truck.

"Sucks, doesn't it?" he muttered.

"Yeah, they're unbeaten and no one talks about them. They can't even get freaking uniforms!"

"No," he replied. "This school kids beat. It's boring as hell, isn't it?"

"Well, I guess the challenge is finding the story where there doesn't seem to be one."

He shook his head. "Trouble is, nobody's gonna care about whether these girls have uniforms. It's a waste of print."

"The boys have them," I argued.

"More people go to their games. So they get more money. That's how it goes." He climbed into the truck. He reminded me of the blue-collar friends my dad used to drink beer with. They liked to get together, play card games and not rock the boat. They liked to complain about the boat, but they sure didn't want to build a new one. All were clinging to their jobs like they were life rafts, and they needed everything to stay as familiar as it was.

I looked at Joe disdainfully. He had that same attitude, now spreading like a disease, as millions of people say that things just are the way they are. I guess that's why change happens so slowly.

"I forgot the coach's card," I told him and ran back onto the field. She'd mentioned having a card, but as we talked, I never got it.

I rushed back onto the field toward the setting sun, which was turning the October trees a flaming crimson. I noticed the parents of the opposing team, especially one in particular. A woman in the crowd who had her arm around two of the girls looked a lot like…but it couldn't have been.

"I'm sorry," I said to the coach. "I never got your card."

"Sure." She handed it to me. "If you ever, ever have any questions or want to do a follow-up story, you call me, okay?"

I nodded.

"Our next game is in Tolland."

I glanced over at the Walten Warrior bus. It was Ellie. She looked in my direction and stopped walking. She said something to one of the girls and came back toward the field.

So there I was, making chitchat with an overly exuberant coach when Ellie came over to us.

"Hi," she said.

"Hi," I answered.

"Well, we've got to get truckin'." The coach smiled and waved.

"Thanks!" I called to her.

Around us kids and parents were folding up their chairs, gathering their thermoses and not noticing the drama in the middle of the field.

"You never let me explain," Ellie said, just as she'd said a month before.

"What did you need to explain?" I asked, trying to hide the pain still in my eyes.

"Marc is my soon-to-be ex-husband," she said. "Do you have any idea how hard and expensive it is to get a divorce?"

I stared blankly at her.

"I wanted you to know," she continued. "I planned to tell you. But I wanted to get to know you better. I wanted to make sure it would be okay. You weren't some experiment to me."

"What was I then?"

"Someone I was falling in love with," Ellie said. It was so simple, so dramatic. And yet I couldn't enjoy the moment because I was too busy feeling confused and awkward.

"I don't know what to…"

She turned and headed back to the bus.

"Wait!" I called. "You're just going to leave it like that?"

She turned around. "There's one other thing, but I don't think you can handle it."

"Give me a chance!"

"Why?" She waited a moment, but I couldn't speak, like those dreams you have where your legs are stuck and you can't move. She turned around and kept walking.

I couldn't believe she was walking away without another word. Then I heard Joe calling me, and I turned toward the truck. One quick final glance back at Ellie nearly stopped my heart. She again had her arm around the girl she'd spoken to earlier, and there was a young boy dragging behind them, holding her other hand. Ellie wasn't riding on the bus. She got into her car with the two kids. Unless she was a foster parent or a really involved soccer coach, there was something even bigger than a husband that she neglected to mention. Two kids. And all I knew about them was that at least one of them played soccer.

That night I started what would be a flurry of emails: "You didn't lie to me," I wrote. "You just forgot to mention an entire family?"

"I heard your opinion of kids," she shot back. "In Mystic. That you'd have no life. I was falling for you, and I wondered if you could change your mind if you got to know me. That's why I invited you for the weekend in Vermont."

"You messed with my head, telling me you loved me."

"Tell me this…if you'd known I had kids, would you have written me back?"

I stared a long time at the blinking cursor. I guess that gave her the answer.

She wrote, "I didn't think so."

"You didn't give me a chance," I wrote. But it was a lie. I wouldn't have gotten involved with anyone who had kids. I knew it. She knew it. My cat knew it. "So see what you did?"

Somehow I had to make this her fault.

She was now offline.

I was irrational, a crazed bee flitting about the apartment, wishing I could sting something.

I called Joanne and told her Ellie's big secrets. Joanne laughed a long time.

"All right," I snapped. "What's so damn funny?"

"You and a woman with kids! You'd forget you had a cat if you didn't occasionally trip over her."

"What's your point?"

There was an agonizing pause. "This could be kind of interesting karma. You, who swore you'd never have kids, meeting this…mom."

"She lied to me," I reminded her.

"She was right. She was smart. You wouldn't have given her the time of day."

It was true.

"So now what do I do?" I whined.

"There's an expression," she said. "Something like, 'Life is what happens to you when you plan something else.' So it doesn't match your plans. So what?"

"But I'm not even a good aunt!" I protested. "I forget my own nephews' birthdays. I suck with kids."

"No, you don't. You helped Cabbot put together that Lego thing."

"The castle? It came with an instruction book."

"Don't be so hard on yourself."

"I'm easily overwhelmed," I reminded her. "I need my anxiety meds to go into a Super Walmart."

"You're better at it than you think." Joanne was suddenly calm, reflective. "I remember when Cabbie was three or four, and we were in that store. I took forever trying on outfits, and he was getting restless. You started popping wheelies with his stroller, getting him to giggle at himself in the mirror."

"Yeah." I remembered. "That got old really quick."

"My point is, you had good instincts."

But she was the only one who thought that I could be a parent. And maybe she was just saying it because she was my sister. There's a rule in the sister handbook that you should always say the other one is good at something, no matter how far you have to reach to find it.

For the next few days, I moped. I went to work, then went back to the apartment to mope. I think Penny was getting frustrated. And I was tired of her sunny attitude. Just once I would have given anything to see Penny punch a wall or something.

"What do you think of me with…kids?" I asked.

She literally spit out her beer in the kitchen sink. "You're gonna do artificial insem…uh," she stammered.

"No. That ship has sailed. Ellie's a mom."

Penny studied me for a long time, searching for some answer in my eyes.

"Do you love her?" she finally asked.

"I think so. We were just getting to know each other. But this is so messed up."

"It doesn't have to be." She assumed the Yoda pose again. "Not if you just let life happen."

CHAPTER SIXTEEN

"The Discomfort Zone"

I was working again, and it didn't matter if I was reporting on the local bake-off, the retirement center ballroom night or the Palmertown Piglets jump rope competition. I was saving up for the day I could take my life out of boxes and have a place of my own.

There was just one problem. I couldn't get Ellie's face out of my mind. I'd see her among the dancing couples at Flo's. I'd see her in the coffee shop where I went to work on my blog. But worst of all, I'd see her every time I closed my eyes at night.

It wasn't long before the Macy's Parade was on TV, and the aromas of Thanksgiving filled Penny's apartment. In the kitchen Penny and I were debating about the perfect stuffing, arguing over whose family recipe was the greatest.

"You know, you got tons of followers," she repeated.

I shrugged, sampling her stuffing. "I like the raisins."

"I'm serious," she continued. "It's really taking off. Maybe a publisher will want to put your blog into a book."

I wouldn't say I'd never considered that. But I kept any enthusiasm under wraps. I preferred to wear my sadness like a favorite shirt. It was comfortable, familiar, even if I was acting like a real Debbie Downer to my friends.

"Aren't you excited about that?" Penny asked. "What if it happens?"

"That would be great."

"Oh, don't sound so thrilled." She shook her head as she mixed real cranberries into the sauce.

"You do have a can version too?" I asked. "I mean, cranberry sauce out of a can *is* the true meaning of Thanksgiving."

She nodded and smiled, opening the cabinet. Ah, yes. Thanksgiving was saved.

I started to set the dining room table and wondered what Ellie was doing. What if Joanne was right? What if I allowed life to just happen instead of trying to stick to a plan?

No, even though I missed her, I still didn't want kids. I knew it in my gut. I wasn't one of those people who drove by the park and, when seeing parents pushing their toddlers in swings, felt a sudden surge of baby jealousy. I didn't want that life. Of course it looked like Ellie's kids were a bit older than toddlers. I couldn't tell ages very well, though. Age nine looked the same as ten or eleven to me.

The biggest truth of all was that when someone mentioned my turning forty and wondered how I felt about my biological clock, it never occurred to me. If I'd wanted something so badly, wouldn't I have at least stopped to notice my age in terms of child-bearingness? But I didn't. It never even crossed my mind. A lot of weird thoughts had crossed my mind over the years. Interestingly, that was never one of them.

Penny came in and saw me staring at a bowl of mashed potatoes. I quickly wiped my eyes and donned my party face.

"Almost forgot those cute little napkin rings," I said. "What are they? Pilgrims or pumpkins?" I rushed toward the kitchen.

She stopped me.

"Call her," she said. There was that wisdom again. "I've been writin' to women on the Internet for what, two years now? Do you really want me to remind you about the airport?"

"No."

"What I've learned," she said, "is that life is short. If you find her, don't let her go."

"But she has…"

"Two of God's greatest creations."

Was she serious? They probably fought like wild dogs, whined when they didn't get their way, made Ellie's life a living hell. I thought of God's greatest creations; among them had to be the Grand Canyon, not these two monsters I didn't even know.

"I don't want to hear about the kids," Penny argued. "Be open-minded. You were once a kid." She patted my shoulder the way she always did when she really meant something.

That afternoon everyone finally arrived. First came Ariel, who refrained from talking about our chakras for a change. She looked like she was wearing a burlap sack dress and brought us a bowl of organic hummus. She took my hands in hers.

"I'm feeling you're conflicted," she spoke in a hushed tone.

"Yeah," I laughed. "Trying to decide which beer I want to start with."

"I meant what I said when I read the flower. She's a good person," Ariel repeated.

I looked down, unable to talk about it. This was what depression felt like, and it lasted longer than I'd expected. But I couldn't fold it up neatly and put it away like the laundry. So I strained to smile through my mask of gloom.

Next came Ruth Lassiter, the school crossing guard, who liked to wear an orange safety vest and say things like "secure the perimeter." I think she was a frustrated cop who never went to the police academy. She was incredibly tall and always tucked her shirts into athletic swishy pants. She wore a whistle and spoke gruffly even when she was in a good mood. We'd all taken bets on whether or not she was gay, but she insisted she had a boyfriend in Italy, Antonio, who was never able to visit because of visa problems. No one would argue with her. I think we were all afraid to.

"Congratulations on living together," Ruth said, shoving a six-pack at us.

"Oh, Penny and I aren't—" I stumbled over my words.

"Oh, okay. Well, it's been a while since we caught up. I didn't know what you meant by 'living together.'" She did air quotes.

"No, we're good friends," Penny confirmed. "Very good."

"Maybe you should be more," Ruth mused, chomping on tortilla chips. "You're both cute."

"We're just friends," I said again.

"Hard to tell with you gay chicks," she joked.

Then two of my dearest friends finally showed up in their SUV. Morgan and Fran, who had been together so long they were thought of as more of a unit like Morgafran or Franamorg, still looked the same and were still bickering as they'd always done. They lived up in Vermont in a barn that had been converted to a house. They were the kind of lesbians who lived off the land and were so loyal, so caring, the day we met, when I was newly out, I knew we'd be friends for life. They never spoke a bad word about my ex, no matter what they actually thought. But they were shoulders to cry on when I needed them most.

How they argued with each other was something legendary. From outside I could hear them.

"Don't start with me again!" Fran shouted.

"Nobody's starting with anybody! I just said we could bring something from the goddamn farm, not the same old fizzy piss!"

"Morgan, they like beer! I'm not listening to you anymore! This is why I didn't take your name!"

"Who asked you to take it?"

"I could have, but I didn't!" Fran hollered.

Then the doorbell rang.

"How you holdin' up?" Morgan asked. She was a plump, sometimes temperamental butch with a jolly face and fuzzy brown hair. She hugged me hard like my grandma used to, squeezing the life out of me and pushing my face into her puffy, down vest. Of course it was navy. She always wore navy.

"I'm good," I said, taking the case of beer from her.

Next came Fran, smiling. She had platinum hair spiked and sprayed so much it would hurt you if you touched it. She had the heart of an activist and came across like a gentle dove.

"Hey," I said. "I like your coat."

It was a long, black wool coat, the kind my sister wore when she came up to visit. I'd rarely seen Fran in anything other than a hoodie.

I, on the other hand, had gone with my simple black turtleneck, the color of the Grim Reaper.

She hugged me and stepped back to appraise me.

"Wow," she responded. "It's been almost a year."

"I know."

"You've got to come up sometime soon," Fran said.

"Actually, I was there not too long ago. The Rooster Inn." I lowered my eyes.

"That stodgy place?" Morgan bellowed. "What, were your grandparents visiting?"

"They're dead," I replied.

"Oh, sorry." Morgan's eyes darted at Fran, who was giving her the death stare.

"It was a mistake, the whole trip," I explained. "I didn't know what kind of place it was."

"Real stuffy," Morgan said. "Old people love it."

"I'm sorry I didn't give a call while I was there. I had a lot going on." They followed me into the kitchen. "There's been so much with the new job and all."

"That's good, right? You like the work?" Morgan's hands were planted on her hips.

"It's all right." I didn't sound very convincing. I started pulling various beers out of the cooler.

"Sometimes I still can't believe you and Val are over," Fran said.

"Don't," Morgan warned.

"It's okay," I said. "I know what you mean. I'll have dreams that we're still together, and I wake up and we're not. But honestly, when I wake up I'm relieved."

"I still remember meeting you guys at that lesbian poetry slam."

"Yeah," I laughed. "None of us even liked poetry."

Fran's gaze was distant, her smile twisted, as she reflected on that night. "She was all over you like white rice."

It had been so long since I'd seen them that I'd almost forgotten how much Fran loved to use popular expressions. Just one problem—she never said them correctly. Everyone knew what she meant, but Morgan couldn't let it go. Morgan had an annoying need to get everything perfect. Exact. Precise. Together, they were a human atom bomb.

This also explained their incessant fighting for the past nine years.

Morgan rolled her eyes. "It's white *on* rice."

"What does *that* mean?" Fran retorted.

"Nobody says like white rice, unless it's unusually sticky or something." Morgan begged me for help. "Can you explain this?"

I'd always thought that deep down inside, Morgan was a frustrated English teacher.

"You're on your own," I laughed and left the kitchen. Their bickering reminded me how much I missed them.

As the night trudged on, I found myself looking up at the brilliant full moon from the deck, blowing smoke in the chilly air and wanting to share scenery like this with Ellie. My heart hurt.

Maddie cornered me on the deck. "What's up? You can tell me."

"Nothing is up. Really. Let's talk about you. What's going on with you?"

"Oh, the old turn-the-tables thing." She sounded a little drunk. "There is someone kind of cute. She's an anesthesiologist. We ran into each other in the hall. I was getting ready to put in an IV." She stared off dreamily.

"There's nothing like a romance that starts with an IV," I mused. "Miss never-gonna-date again."

"I didn't say we're dating. I don't even know if she's gay. She's probably married or something." Maddie glanced at Penny through the open sliding door. "You need help?"

"Nah, I'm good." She was rinsing dishes.

Maddie shivered. "What the hell are we doing out here?"

That was my cue to lead us back inside. I closed the slider.

"You should bring Ariel to the hospital," I suggested. "She has great gaydar."

Ariel raised her beer in agreement.

"Gaydar is bullshit," Maddie announced. "Now what's with the mom you won't date 'cause she's a mom?"

"That's not it," I said, realizing that the living room noise was suddenly quiet and several pairs of eyes were on me. I didn't want to seem shallow. "Okay, it kind of is. But isn't it good to know who you are and what your limits are, so you don't ruin another person's life?" Funny, it sounded like such a good argument when I'd kept it inside my head.

But everyone descended on me like a pack of wild dogs.

"If she makes you happy..." Penny yelped.

"You emailed us a while back," Morgan joined in. "You said you were falling in love. You've never said that, not even about, you know." She exchanged knowing glances with Fran.

"Love has to mean something," Fran said quietly.

"What about the kids?" I protested. "It's a huge lifestyle change you have to admit! You can't just say, 'Oh, I love her, so I'm willing to live a life I don't want.' I'd end up resenting her, and the whole thing would end in disaster."

"No offense," Ariel began. "But you like to poo-poo any good thing that ever happens to you. It's like you don't want to be happy." She blinked innocently after dropping that bomb and excused herself to go "tinkle."

I stood there, dumbfounded, shocked at my friends' reactions. Morgan and Fran never wanted kids, either. What if one of them had kids? Would they be happy?

The party had begun to clear out.

"It's her decision," Fran argued.

"Damn right," Ruth agreed.

"Shut up, Fran." Morgan shook her head.

"I don't think it's everybody's business," Fran insisted.

"We're her friends," Ruth told them. "She knows we care." Ruth patted Fran on the back, said something about it being nice to meet them, and she left.

A few candles had burned down to the wick. Penny had fallen asleep in a chair in a turkey coma, and Morgan and Fran were lingering in the living room. I think they were afraid to leave me alone, and Fran was getting drunker by the minute.

"I'll be driving." Morgan snapped up the keys. Then she looked at me. "You okay?"

"Yeah." I nodded too enthusiastically. "I will be."

"Morgan, tell her what you said to me? When we first met?" Fran bumped her arm repeatedly. "You know the thing…"

"I don't remember."

"Yeah, you do!" Fran sat up, then seemed to forget what she was talking about. "Don't feel bad, Syd. It's not natural to meet women. Nobody just goes up to someone and says, 'I'll show you yours if you show me mine.'"

"It's 'You show me yours, and I'll show you…'" Morgan was exasperated. "Never mind."

"Whatever." Fran's face turned red, then she scrambled for her dignity.

I could still hear them fighting on the front porch when they left.

"Why do you always act like I'm an idiot?" Fran said.

"I don't act like you're…you know what? Never mind!"

Their voices faded as they got to their car.

I already missed them. They were the kind of friends I might not call for months, but when we did talk, nothing had changed. Now Vermont seemed so far away. I considered paying them a visit, until I remembered the rising cost of gas.

Cookie finally crawled out from behind the couch, checking to see if the coast was clear. She didn't like loud voices; that's why she hated me especially during football season. But seriously, I wasn't going to whisper "touchdown" just because the little fur ball was one giant nerve ending.

I refused to check my computer that night. Instead, I went to bed, clutching Cookie like she was a life preserver. I'd see my therapist soon. She always told me I had the answers within me already. What a great job—just tell everyone they already know why they came to you because you don't know. They finally make a decision, and thank you for having the wisdom to know that they knew what they thought they didn't know. Not a bad career, if you can stand to listen to people complaining all day.

* * *

Connecticut in November…it looks a lot like England with a white, sunless sky and the wind whipping dead, brown leaves around the yard. My assignment was to go to a local school and ask any kids I could find about their holiday food drive.

I found a young boy who had created a tower of cans of baked beans so big it could blow up my colon just looking at it. His mother, who looked ten years older than she really was, grabbed him by the collar.

"No, Braden!" Her voice was hoarse. "We don't play with the food." It was too late. He'd already turned long boxes of pasta into missiles that tore down the tower. I imagined what their house must look like.

His mother looked at me apologetically, noticing that her son had opened a juice box that had splattered on both of them. Most mothers I saw looked tired—not a normal tired, but a please-shoot-me kind of tired. So why would I ever want kids?

"Excuse me?" I called. "I'm with the *Danbury Gazette*."

"No comment," the mother snapped, yanking her son by his sticky hand and trying to wipe up the mess with a tissue.

"We'd like to feature your son in the paper," I added quickly. That always got parents' attention.

"Oh," she said.

I bent down to be at eye level with him. "What's your name?"

"Braden Lester." He got instantly shy, but he stopped throwing things, at least.

I took some notes. Joe, the photographer, snapped a toothless grin. But we weren't done yet.

Not being good with ages, I couldn't tell who would be best to talk to. I roamed the school gymnasium where most of the canned food was being collected. But what I saw were adults more excited about the holiday than the kids.

A teenager said, "Uh, I don't remember what we brought."

"Really?" I was sure the kid was at least fourteen or fifteen.

"My mom brought stuff we don't eat." Not a quote I could use. "I think it's pretty lame." The teen wandered off.

It took about two hours to piece together some kind of heartwarming food drive story. Joe looked so bored he wanted to cry or have a stiff drink.

So, older kids thought everything was stupid, and the really small kids screamed and put things in their mouth they really shouldn't. We annoyed the big kids and frightened the little ones. This day was further proof that I was not, nor ever would be, good with kids.

As we started back for the van, one little girl ran up to me. She'd been watching us a while and shyly said, "I brought corn because that's my favorite, even though Mom says you can't digest it." She looked so innocent and clueless, desperately wanting to share this information with me. Her tiny hand tugged at my shirt, as if to say, "notice me."

"That's great," I said awkwardly, getting her name and a photo.

"Mellanie with two l's," she announced proudly.

Her big brown eyes were so bright and her little body so animated, she reminded me of myself at her age—minus the princess dress and pink shoes.

I smiled at her. When I got back in the van, I wondered if I might not have another side to myself I hadn't yet explored. But even if I did, I decided, being an aunt was better because it wasn't full-time. After all, how could anybody spend a whole day with a child covered in sticky juice or a teen who doesn't want to talk to you? No thanks.

CHAPTER SEVENTEEN

"And a Partridge in a Pear Tree"

It was a cold December day. The windows were foggy, the ground covered in snow and more flakes fell in weird surges; the sky was constipated. I had the Sunday blues, imagining having to go to work the next day, because no doubt the bulldozers would plow the roads soon. Those overachieving bastards.

"I miss snow days in Tennessee," Penny said dreamily, staring out the kitchen window. "They didn't have plow trucks like y'all do up here. So we'd get an inch and be out of school."

I glanced at her, but my mind was spinning in a funnel cloud of crazy thoughts. All at once I knew what I had to do.

* * *

It was the most impulsive, strange, out-of-character thing I'd ever done. But there I was, passing the "Massachusetts Welcomes You" sign, then suddenly at some elementary school I'd Googled. I managed to get directions when I saw that there was a big event today.

In the school cafeteria, there was a stage where third, fourth and fifth graders were butchering "Jingle Bells." Since there were so many doors to the building, I had no idea which one was the front door. Of course I chose the door that led to the cafeteria stage. In front of a room full of parents snapping photos, I appeared in the background among the children. I lowered my body to appear shorter and moaned my way through part of the song. Some kids laughed at me. Some parents laughed. When I finally saw some steps on the side, it was my salvation. I ran into the audience, down the side aisle. Though it was dark, I searched for her face. I knew she'd be there.

And she was. With a big zoom lens on her camera that looked like she was with the press, Ellie was shooting the proud mom moment in a seat a few rows back from the stage—that is, until she saw me. She seemed shocked and confused, as I shuffled through the seats, disrupting other proud parents. I even had the audacity to ask another mother to switch with me so that I could sit beside Ellie.

I plopped down, breathless. "You have too many doors at this school," I said. "Which one's yours?"

"Third row, second one from the left."

Her son was belting out the song with great enthusiasm. He was cute, with light brown hair, freshly cut bangs and a dimple in his chin. He looked harmless enough, not the monster of my nightmares.

"What are you doing here?" Her eyes were intense. She was suddenly so close again.

"I missed you." I wished I'd rehearsed this. "You're the first woman I can laugh with, have deep conversations with, and… you're pretty. You're the total package."

"I'm your UPS."

I laughed out loud. Some annoyed parents thought I was laughing at their children.

We applauded the end of the song. I applauded because I was grateful that it was over. Shortly after, though, there was a band on stage, ruining "Frosty the Snowman." I didn't think trumpets belonged in "Frosty the Snowman."

Then I noticed another woman sitting on the other side of Ellie.

"Unless I'm too late." I swallowed hard.

"She's the science teacher," Ellie whispered.

"She has a lazy eye," I continued like an ass. "Not that there's anything wrong with a lazy eye, unless you're into freaks." I seemed to be more hostile whenever I was nervous.

"Am I supposed to be happy to see you?" Ellie asked.

"Are you?"

"You really hurt me. You ran away just like that. You didn't give me a chance to explain."

"I know. I was an ass. And the stuff I said about kids ruining your life, I'm sorry. I want to give it a try." It didn't come out nearly as eloquently as I'd hoped.

"What?" She leaned in. The music was getting louder, if that was possible.

"I was an ass!"

But everyone started clapping, and she still didn't hear me.

"I was an ass!" I shouted into the now quiet auditorium. The word "ass" seemed to echo all the way down to Connecticut. That was a moment I'd never forget. Ever. It was right up there with falling off the stage during my first school play.

Crowds poured into the halls as parents tried to find their kids.

"I think you should go," Ellie said.

I lowered my head. I deserved it. She was obviously the mature one, and I had some growing up to do, I suppose. "Good decision," I said, turning away.

"You're not going to run away again?" she asked.

A ray of hope.

I shook my head.

"Good," she said. "But you should still go. I'm not ready to introduce you yet."

I nodded like an excited puppy. "Good motherly instincts there." I fumbled with my gloves. "They always make the fingers so hard to find," I said, tripping over my own feet. This major embarrassment of a day more than made up for my hasty departure in Vermont, I'd decided. It was worth every mile on the highway.

CHAPTER EIGHTEEN

"Mini-Putt Poo-Poo"

Understandably, Ellie was in no rush to introduce me to her kids. I think she wanted to make sure I wasn't going to flake out first. And I too was putting it off as long as possible, getting used to thinking of her kids as vague concepts rather than actual people with thoughts and feelings. It was better that way.

We'd meet occasionally on weekends, always in neutral places. Weekdays were the hardest. I'd sit in meetings to decide which stories should make the front page—a disgusting hot dog eating contest or a mysterious animal in some granny's backyard. When I came home to Penny's place, I'd find Cookie scratching the couch. I'd get so angry and clap my hands loudly. More and more, that black and white ball of fuzz represented something that I wanted to forget. I'd see those nails ripping the couch, the curtains, even my leather briefcase to shreds, and I'd remember how Văldemort didn't want her declawed. At the time I understood. But now I resented every clump of hair in the corners of the small apartment or the light sounds of licking, which meant barf sounds were soon to follow, along with a hairball for me to clean up. I felt guilty at how every little thing about her had begun to irritate me. Then my OCD took over, and I couldn't let her sleep with me anymore. I'd worry that she'd scratch my face off in my sleep or leave fur balls in the sheets. We still had our moments, when she'd climb into my lap and I'd be too tired to push her off. So we'd sit together and watch TV, Cookie softly purring as she shredded my pants.

When the drama at home wasn't going on, my thoughts drifted up to Massachusetts. Summer came, and the day I'd been putting off finally arrived. Ellie and I decided to go to the Cape, to the more kid-friendly area of Yarmouth. There was mini-putt golf off the main road that Ellie thought her kids might like. We pulled up to Pirate's Landing at the same time. I got out of my car, and she got out of hers. Then she prodded her kids to come out.

First came Megan, who was fifteen, hiding behind her long, blond hair and portable video game. She thought everything was lame, Ellie had informed me, so I'd have to win her over by hiding my lameness. The ten-year-old, Matthew, was more interested in what we were doing and, more specifically, in meeting me.

"This is Sydney Gray," Ellie said proudly. "The woman I was telling you about."

"Hey," Megan said, squinting and putting on her sunglasses. She was a smart-looking, attractive girl, but you couldn't really tell behind the long hair that was falling over one eye.

"I'm Matthew," the youngest said shyly and extended his hand to me. He was so cute, with Ellie's blue eyes, two plump cheeks and freckles over a wide smile. He belonged in a hamburger commercial. I shook his hand and caught Ellie watching us.

Ellie's eyes were twinkling in the sunlight, relishing the moment. Yet something inside of me didn't want her to get too excited. It was a Gray family trait—don't ever get too excited during happy moments or someone will get hit by a bus.

We went to an information area shaped like a pirate ship to get our clubs and balls. Ellie picked up each club and made a face.

"They're not the right height!" she shouted. "This one is crooked! How am I supposed to hit a ball in a hole with a crooked club!"

Megan went to her mother. "Chill out," she whispered. "You're embarrassing me."

"I'm your mother. I'm supposed to embarrass you." Ellie examined each club carefully.

I had seen hints of Ellie's temper before and today it was off the rails.

"Okay," Megan said. "Is this all because you're worried we won't like her?"

I tried not to listen, but the pirate ship wasn't that big.

Ellie's face softened; her daughter obviously was more perceptive than she realized.

"Maybe," Ellie said.

"Well, chill. She's fine," Megan assured her.

Matthew began telling me all the subjects he'd be taking next year in school, so it looked like things were going well with him too.

* * *

The next Sunday, I went up to Ellie's house for the day. Luckily, she lived just over the Massachusetts–Connecticut state line, so I didn't mind the drive.

At long last she gave me a tour of her house—the quaint cottage on a hill near a lake. I was relieved to see that she was not a hoarder. Her furniture was an eclectic mix of rustic and Pottery Barn, which I loved. Wood floors, cappuccino leather couch, walls painted in earth tones instead of neon colors from the seventies—her house was as warm and inviting as she was in her soft, flannel shirt. Today's flannel had more of a blue pattern than the last one I'd seen. I figured she must have had several of those shirts. As she was showing me the kids' rooms, we sort of bumped into each other in the hall, and warm flutters engulfed my whole body. Everything was going a little too well. It made me nervous. After seeing that there wasn't even any mildew in the bathroom, I got even more nervous. Everyone had to have just a little mold, after all. In the kitchen, I saw photos of Megan and Matthew at different ages stuck all over the refrigerator. School pictures. Then family outings with a man I didn't know. It must have been her ex. Seeing me staring closely at those photos, she said, "Their father. I didn't want to erase him from the house."

"Oh, yeah. I get it." *Yikes.*

We talked for a while in the kitchen, while the kids stayed locked away in their rooms. When dinner was ready, Ellie shouted, "Come help me set the table!"

"I can help," I offered.

"No, it's their job," she insisted, getting more annoyed by the minute.

It wasn't long before she stomped back to the hallway, a door creaked open, and the muffled sounds of yelling ensued.

"Well, if you didn't wear that freaking headset all the time, you might've heard me!" Ellie sounded like a very experienced mother.

I looked around the house, trying to keep an open mind about kids, families…but the more I heard, the more I wanted to run in the opposite direction.

"Don't use that tone with me!" Ellie hollered. "You know the silverware is your job."

So reluctantly, the kids wandered out of their caves and set the table. Matthew was a bit more eager to acknowledge my presence.

At the dinner table, both of them sat with solemn faces.

"What did I do?" I whispered to Ellie.

"It's not you. They're just upset because their show isn't on tonight," Ellie explained. "They get forty cartoon channels that run all day long, but their particular show isn't on."

"Forty channels!" I exclaimed. "We only had three growing up. And cartoons only came on Saturday mornings."

"Yeah," Ellie agreed. "And they ended at noon."

"Yeah," I continued. "Followed by *Soul Train* or something even worse, like golf."

I shuddered, as Ellie and I laughed. Then I looked up at the two faces staring at us. Megan and Matthew were looking at us like we were from the Stone Age.

"Here you go with the old-timey talk," Megan muttered.

"What did you *do?*" Matthew asked, as though he felt sorry for us.

"We went outside and played!" Ellie fired back. "Something you might try someday."

"What if it was raining?" he persisted, deeply disturbed by this new information.

"We read," I said. "You know, books."

Ellie and I laughed and eventually noticed the kids weren't laughing. To them, books were like medicine, to be taken in only when necessary.

Later on, describing our first video game, two lines and a dot hitting each one, drew much the same reaction, except with an extra jolt of horror and pity.

During dishwashing time, Ellie's mouth tightened as she watched the kids put the dishes in.

"You're not doing it right," she groaned. "Why don't you go do something else?"

The kids dutifully left, and soon the voice of SpongeBob echoed from the family room.

"What?" Ellie said.

I wanted to say something, but my mouth could get me in trouble, so I thought carefully. The look on my face said it all, though.

"You think I should let them do it," Ellie said.

"It's your house."

"No, tell me."

"Well, how else are they going to learn?"

"I know." She took a deep breath. "I've been called a control freak. But they don't do it right."

Control freak. Red flags waved in front of my eyes. No, no, no. My mind was flooded with visions of Valerie as she hovered over me while I folded towels the *wrong* way.

"They may do things differently, but that doesn't mean it's wrong," I said, sounding like I was talking to someone else.

"But they don't fit!" she protested.

I was brought back to Earth and the dishwasher. "You can teach them."

"You're right. I lose patience sometimes." She ran her hand through her tangled hair, took a long breath, then called the kids back in and showed them what she wanted.

When Ellie was satisfied that things were running smoothly, she left the room.

"So you got Mom to stop freaking out?" Megan asked me.

I smiled triumphantly. "Uh-huh."

"Great," she snapped. "Now we have to do dishes every night." Her voice dripped with attitude. I'd known from the start she'd be harder to win over.

That first time at Ellie's house wasn't exactly persuading me to take on the role of a parent. But I started considering it more and more as time went on.

I spent several weekends at Ellie's. I was getting to know more about video games that looked like gladiator movies and especially more about SpongeBob, though I never discovered the answer to why he wore pants at all, being a sponge. Matthew told me I was overthinking it.

I learned about the difference between Playstation and Wii. I also learned how to play tennis without a racquet or tennis ball, just a TV and a "nimchuck," a new word I learned that sounded like something obscene.

Megan spent most of her time in her room doing something called "face time" with her friends. These kids didn't use phones. They texted or talked over their phones, face to face. It was like *Star Trek*. The whole house was a mess of cords and wires, and suddenly I thought of how my grandfather must have felt when I showed him my electronic microphone at Christmas. He was probably used to wooden toys, and then everything had become a science fiction movie.

The Comfortable Shoe Diaries began to buzz with new entries about the possibility of being a step-parent. It's the only role in the family that no one asks for. It's like being the last one invited to a party. So if you are eventually trusted, even loved, by the family, then it means even more because you earned it.

Back in Connecticut, the day came for cutbacks at the newspaper, which was already dropping in circulation. I wasn't sad about it. The editor had come over with an especially long face. He couldn't even look at me. I knew what was coming. I found myself consoling *him*. Honestly, I felt relieved while cleaning out my desk, and I had a strange faith something better would come along.

CHAPTER NINETEEN

"Weapons of Mass Destruction"

Ah, the sweet breath of autumn in New England—the gentle kisses of colors in the trees, a hint of chilly air heralding a new season—and it was hell. Ellie had to go to a teachers' seminar for the weekend, and I stupidly volunteered to stay at her house and watch her kids. I thought of it as a test run. If I could handle this, maybe it wouldn't be such a drastic lifestyle change, like on *House Hunters International* when they move from California to Bangladesh.

Penny didn't mind watching Cookie, which relieved some of my guilt about the cat. So I packed a small bag and off I went.

I arrived Saturday morning, and Ellie showed me where everything was in the refrigerator. Then she showed me the phone numbers for the police and fire departments taped to the door.

"Fire? What are you expecting to happen?"

Ellie darted nervously from room to room. "You never know. Hey, Megan! Have you seen my phone?"

"Why would I have it?" The teen called from her sanctuary.

"You used my charger!" Ellie ripped apart her bedroom until she found her phone under the bed.

I walked her outside.

"Thanks for doing this," she said over and over.

"It's no problem. Have fun." I shut her car door.

"Yeah," she said sarcastically. "Trapped in meetings with teachers. Fun. I didn't want to go, but I was told I had no choice."

"It'll be okay," I assured her.

"No. They'll make us do team-building things like carrying eggs on spoons. Ugh."

I kissed her through the driver side window. And she pulled out, leaving me alone with the Children of the Corn.

Actually, it wasn't that bad. At first.

Matthew couldn't have had more energy if he'd been on steroids. He told me all about his class and everyone in it, including Amanda, this girl who was obviously accident prone. Her latest claim to fame was stapling her fingers together when she volunteered to put up construction paper ghosts on the bulletin board.

"Ooh," I responded, riveted by his enthusiasm.

Matthew was impressed with the ambulance and the way they took her swiftly away to the hospital. I think he was especially impressed that she'd gotten excused from all of her assignments that day. I hoped he wasn't getting any ideas.

"Wow, that's…uh…" I didn't know what to say.

Then he began to play a concert on his tuba for me. The sound, probably similar to a hippo's mating call, filled the living room.

"Stop that shit!" Megan hollered from the doorway of her room. Obviously, the sound was messing up her "face time."

"Don't swear," I said. "Maybe we can work out another time for your brother to practice."

"Just not now!" she raged and slammed the door.

I was appalled by her attitude, but I didn't want to get the "you're not my mother" reaction, so I played my cards carefully. I knocked on her door.

When she answered, I said, "Hey, I know you're frustrated. But your mom wouldn't want you to slam anything, okay?"

"Yeah. Sorry." She shut the door.

I was surprised. I'd managed a situation like a *Facts of Life* moment—a show, which, by the way, these kids wouldn't even have known.

But for Matthew, if he couldn't make noise on the tuba, there would still be noise. Out came the nimchucks, and soon sounds of explosions and machine guns overtook the small house.

Megan came out of her bedroom, a storm trooper in sweatpants. I had to say things carefully, like, "Would you want him hitting *you* like that? Or sticking *your* iPod down *his* pants?" Or in the worst-case scenario, "If I have to call your mother, you know she'll take a game away. Is this really worth it?"

By the time Ellie came home on Sunday night, there was a rotten, burned cheese smell from an ill-advised grilled cheese sandwich in the toaster, underwear strewn about both kids' bedrooms and nimchucks running amuck, and I was drained of every ounce of energy in my body.

"I'm sorry," I said. "The kids were very good, but I've got to get home."

"Now? It's late. You sure you don't want to spend the night?" She smiled slyly.

"I couldn't move even if I did." I left before dinner. I couldn't imagine how she could work, see her kids and make dinner all in the same day. I had a new respect for my sister and for every mother who ever lived throughout history.

Seeing the "Connecticut Welcomes You" sign brought a mixture of emotions, but mostly relief. What did that mean? It had to mean I was doing the right thing, running as far away from that lifestyle as I possibly could.

I came back, rain-soaked and tired, seeing Penny, as usual, on her computer.

"Give it up," I joked, as Cookie ran to me.

"Hey," she called. "I didn't expect to see you back tonight."

"Neither did I. Thanks for watching my fuzz ball here."

"Oh, no trouble."

Yes, I thought. A cat isn't much trouble. They don't make you listen to tubas or explosions for hours. The worst they can do is cough up a hairball. That's it.

That night, Ellie and I had a difficult phone conversation.

"I know you're careful about who your kids meet. And I've been honored to get to know them," I said.

"You *have been?*" she repeated.

"I just can't do it. I can't live the life you do. It's too much for me. I felt like a bowl of Jell-O when you got home."

"So? There are nights like that." She paused. "Heck, there are days when I can't stand my own kids!"

"Really?"

"Of course. But you never hear June Cleaver say that, because she'd sound like a bad mother."

"I don't think I can do it." I was scared. If I went too far down that path, it would affect not only Ellie, but two other lives as well. Better to admit it now.

Finally, she accepted it. "I wish so much you'd change your mind."

"I know," I answered. "But I can't." I had to hang up quickly, so I wouldn't hear the sound of Ellie's tears and she wouldn't hear mine.

CHAPTER TWENTY

"Anger Management"

"I hate my kids all the time!" Joanne blasted me on the phone.

"You don't understand," I interrupted.

"Oh, no, I think I do. It got a little hard and you freaked out. But I have to break up two Sumo wrestlers every day. I've had to pull broken glass out of Cabbot's hand, and the little one likes to roll around in the grass with the dog. The grass in Florida! You know the kind filled with red ants and pesticides! I might as well just take the gate off the pool, for God's sake!"

Then I knew why I was running away. I didn't want to become like Joanne. She used to be so fun and creative and actually enjoyed life, well, when she wasn't worrying about death. Then she got married, had kids and transformed into this Momzilla who was always roaring at everyone: "Get that out of your mouth! We don't eat Elmo! What did you do to your father's computer?"

I didn't want that. And something else I realized. Once I knew I was gay and I was different, I embraced the opportunity to follow the road not taken. But let's get real—it wasn't for poetic, artsy reasons. It was because I thought maybe it would make me immortal. If I didn't have a traditional marriage, I wouldn't have that slightly faded forty-year-old wedding picture hanging on my wall reminding me of the passage of time when I was old and wrinkly. I wouldn't get old and wrinkly if I didn't get married. It made perfect sense in my warped mind.

And kids? Forget it. They're the cause of aging, I'd confirmed. Gray hair, deep frown lines, all things caused by your new baby chewing on jagged glass or a toddler eating plants then running out into traffic—all the things Joanne was dealing with. Or just the really gross things that my OCD didn't want to fathom— little Cabbot picking his nose at dinner and spreading boogers on the drapes. That was my earliest memory of him at age three.

Kids make you age. And that wasn't going to be a worry of mine. Until it was.

* * *

"My sister told me I was an idiot." That's what I blurted out on the phone to Ellie. "Well, not exactly like that, but it's basically what she meant."

"What?"

I had to back up. "I'm sorry. I had to talk to Joanne, get a little perspective..." I'd entered a new realm of extreme fidgeting. "What I'm trying to say is, please forgive me! I want to make it work with you." There. Nothing like diving head first into shark-infested waters.

But there was a long silence. She wasn't going to let me off the hook easily.

"Are you sure?" she asked. "Because I haven't even asked you to move in, and you were already breaking it off."

"I realize that."

The hum of more silence.

"I need to know this is really going somewhere. Because I'm a mom, it can't be a casual, on-again, off-again thing. I've got more than just me to think about." Her voice cracked.

"I know."

"I want to be more than an entry in your blog," she said.

Whoa. I couldn't feel my legs. "You read my blog?"

"Yeah. I hope it's okay. It's really entertaining, by the way."

After a conversation that seemed to last all night long, we started seeing each other again.

Then, after soul-searching conversations with Joanne and Penny, I eventually decided to move in with Ellie and her kids. That was it. I was taking the plunge!

Moving day was bittersweet. As the last of the boxes were being taped, Maddie stopped by.

"I meant what I said," she growled. "You're dead to me."

"I love you too." I was too excited to let her upset me.

"You're really going out to the boonies," she continued. "I tried to Google the town. I'm not sure you can get cable there."

"We're right over the state line," I assured her. "You can come and visit anytime."

"The highway goes both ways." Her arms were crossed. Her big blue eyes were extra shiny today. "This sucks, Syd! You can't do this!"

"I'd think you'd want me to be happy, just like I want you to be happy."

"No! I want you here so we can have lunch and shoot the shit."

Penny helped me carry the last box to my car. Cookie was already starting her pitiful cries from the cat carrier, which would get louder and more disturbing with every mile.

"I'll miss you so much." Penny hugged me tightly, then dabbed at her eyes. "I'm not doin' this. We'll still see each other."

"Of course we will," I said.

"No, we won't." Maddie marched toward her car.

"No hug?" I stood there with my arms outstretched.

"I told you," she said, "if you do this, you're not my friend anymore."

As her car door slammed, Penny took my hands. "Don't worry 'bout her," she said. "She'll come around. I think she didn't want any of us to find a partner before she did."

"She doesn't even look for one!"

"I know, I know. Preachin' to the choir." She closed my door after I was all set behind the wheel.

As I drove off, I saw her waving in the yard and felt good to be closing this tumultuous chapter of my life.

None of my plans to be immortal worked out. The very next morning after I moved in with Ellie and the kids, I saw crow's-feet in the mirror, followed by a double chin, ten more pounds on the scale and a giant butt. It could have been related to the fat-free Fudgsicles I kept eating; fat-free does not mean sugar-free. Even though sugar was the enemy, I preferred to blame it on the kids.

Living there was an adjustment, to say the least. Sometimes I'd have to babysit the kids when Ellie had a late meeting, and all would be fine until somebody pulled out a water gun. Now at ages eleven and sixteen, they were like two powder kegs just looking for a match. I heard myself talking like Ellie, Joanne and even my own mother: "Someone could lose an eye—or a hand. Don't call your brother an asshole. Please turn down the TV. You'll go deaf!"

So the kids basically ruined my plan to be immortal, and because of them, I was now going to die like everyone else.

If the kids didn't kill me, the job search would. Looking for work when you live beyond the boonies in Massachusetts is like that scene from *The Karate Kid* when they try to catch a fly in between chopsticks. Impossible. So here I was, trying to find a job, adapt to a new life, while realizing that Ellie sometimes had anger issues. One minute, she'd be warm and sweet, and we'd be having a great conversation. Then she'd fly off the handle as if a switch had been flipped. She was Ms. Jekyll and Ms. Hyde.

"I'd better not find another M&M in this couch!" she'd scream.

I never knew when one of these outbursts was coming. It was usually provoked by the kids, who would do their best to get in a fight with each other, especially on days when their mother was already in a bad mood. They had no instincts for bad timing. I'd warn them if I could, but it would be too late.

"If you'd thought of that last night, we wouldn't be late, looking for it now!" Ellie would scream across the house.

Cookie would run and hide under the nearest bed, and the kids would scramble to find whatever that thing was that they absolutely needed.

"What do you need your iPod for anyway?" Ellie would yell. "We're just going down the road." She'd turn to me. "I don't understand it. They can't have one waking second without that crap." Then she'd make an executive decision. "You know what? You kids are coming right now, and I don't give a crap who has their iPod or who doesn't! You can survive without it!"

Matthew would smile teasingly at Megan, because he had his.

"That's so not fair!" Megan would whine.

I'd be making the cut-throat symbol behind Ellie to warn Megan not to pursue the matter further. But she wouldn't take the hint.

"If he has his, why can't I have mine?"

"Because you can't find yours!" Ellie thundered. "Now get in the freaking car before I get in a bad mood!"

Everyone, including me, would scamper into the car. Sometimes the lost item would vary, but this was the typical scenario.

For Cookie, it was an adjustment as well. She sniffed around and rubbed against walls to claim her territory. She favored Megan's room because it smelled like lavender-scented candles. But Ellie, like me, wasn't a big animal person, and we both screamed whenever we saw Cookie rolling around in the freshly warm, washed clothes in the laundry basket. But the little fuzz ball made her way just as I did. As long as she knew where her litter and food were, she was good to go. It was probably a bit more of an adjustment for me.

I managed to find a job in advertising again. There was just one catch—it was an hour train ride to Boston. Every morning I'd watch this weird little culture of train riders. No one seemed happy to be there. Everyone faced straight ahead unless they sat opposite other seats. Then they'd look out the windows or at their iPhones. No one wanted to be that creepy, staring weirdo who made other people call security.

There was the businessman complete with coffee thermos and briefcase seated beside the fidgeting young woman, also with briefcase, who was fighting with her significant other via text. You could tell because she'd huff and puff after each new ding.

What hit me hardest was the realization that I wasn't the youngest one on the train anymore. So many of these bright-eyed professionals in matching suits seemed to be straight out of college—base powder on young women couldn't completely mask the traces of acne still clinging to their faces. I sometimes felt like Methuselah.

When I first started working at Push Industries, it seemed a far cry from the places I'd worked down South. I needed an ID badge just to get off the elevator at the floor where the company was located. And my first day I was escorted to the little cubicle, not much bigger than a rat's cage, that I'd be calling home every day. There it was—an L-shaped desk pushed against a bare partition under a fluorescent light with the wattage of a thousand suns.

I set down my purse. With some photos, some plants, a few personal decorations...I still couldn't make this place look any better.

As the days slumped along...I thought of a line from a Siouxsie & the Banshees song: "The day drags by, like a wounded animal..." How fitting. Every day at Push was a wounded animal, which turned into a dead carcass by five o'clock. For a supposedly creative company, it was quieter than a library. I certainly couldn't talk to myself as I sometimes did when writing. Even in meetings you felt like you had to whisper. In the breakroom, people didn't talk much, but kind of nodded. The loudest thing were the notes taped to food in the fridge, which featured exclamation points as they warned others not to steal their pastrami sandwiches or whatever. The first time I'd seen one of these Post-Its, I'd thought, "At last. Some emotion." Frankly, it was the weirdest, deadest place I ever worked. But they paid me.

One morning, during the long, tedious train ride, I thought about Siouxsie—the most iconic of rock women—whom I deeply admired for reasons I could never explain to a record store clerk. Siouxsie would never be caught sitting in a cubicle. She was the quintessential badass, doing as she pleased and finding a way to make a living at it. Somehow she found a way to live her life on her terms and fought tooth and nail to keep it that way, in spite of record companies and all the forces that wanted her to capitulate to their demands. Not Siouxsie. Maybe I was so drawn to her because I always seemed to be doing the opposite in my own life.

I compromised for everyone. I took the safe route because it paid the bills. I didn't even walk out of the newspaper room when the editor talked about not doing lesbian stories. Where was my spine? In your forties, you're supposed to have a stronger sense of who you are and what you'll put up with. What had happened? I guess the shock of a layoff and never-before foreclosing on a house rattled my sense of security to the core. It forced me to crawl even further back into a shell of safety. I suppose moving in with Ellie and the kids was the wildest, out-of-my-comfort zone thing I ever did.

That night, I shared these thoughts with Ellie.

Then we settled into bed to watch another episode of HGTV. There was a show on about renovations.

"We could really use a new toilet," she lamented. "Have you noticed it wobbles?"

"I've noticed Matthew pees on the seat."

I watched her in her soft, oversized Boston Bruins T-shirt, popping cookies from a ninety-calorie snack pack into her mouth. We had become an ordinary couple, I realized. And for the first time, even something as mundane as watching yet another house show didn't seem so mundane as long as I was with Ellie. Of course, that wouldn't make the greatest line in a poem, but the realization meant a lot to me.

"Matthew! That better not be a video game!" Ellie suddenly yelled.

"Mom! Come on!" he wailed pitifully in the next room.

"You didn't finish your paragraph!" she shouted.

"I did most of it!"

"Most doesn't count! It's one freaking paragraph! You can do it!"

I leaned in closely. "What's it about?"

"Something he's going to do over the holidays," Ellie replied softly. "He can think of something."

My eyes darted; the wheels were turning in my brain.

"Don't help him," she warned.

"How should I know what I'm going to be doing?" Matthew called from his room.

"We're going to bond as a family, dammit!" Ellie yelled and winked at me. "Our first Christmas together." She wrapped her arms around me and pulled me over to her on the bed. We both started giggling, something we hadn't done in a while.

"Thanks for putting up with me," she whispered.

"Hey, you put up with me." I touched her face the same way I'd done at the awful bed-and-breakfast. I realized I could be moody, a roller coaster of emotions and ideas—some realized, some fizzled. And she rode the bumps with me without blinking an eye. It took a special person to do that.

Yes, she sometimes had a volatile temper, but her shout wasn't as big as her heart. And that's why I stayed with her.

CHAPTER TWENTY-ONE

"Naughty and Nice"

Since Ellie knew so much about kids, I always listened to her advice.

"Don't rush the affection" was one of the first things she ever told me. "They'll come to you when they're ready."

Sometimes this was a tough rule to follow because Matthew would come out in his Buzz Lightyear pajamas and kiss Ellie goodnight, and I'd get a goodnight wave. She'd look at me, silently telling me not to worry about it. But I did. What if I waited too long until it just became too weird to ever hug me? She said that wouldn't happen, but she could be wrong. She'd gotten the cords wrong for turning on the DVD player. So she might be wrong about this too.

It was extra tough on me because I'm a hugger. It was all I could do to keep from squeezing Matthew's cute little Muppet-size body. But I always remembered Ellie's words. If I forced a hug, it would feel awkward for them since I was the newbie.

Megan, on the other hand, was at the age when her mother had to sneak a kiss because, to a teenager, it just wasn't cool.

Ellie would give her a goodbye hug before a long school field trip, and Megan wouldn't want any of her friends to see.

"I'm not cool," Ellie told me, starting the car.

It was a Saturday morning. And I remember pulling away from the school, feeling bad for her.

"Doesn't that bother you?" I asked.

"Nah, but sometimes I miss my cuddly bear. That's what I used to call her. You should have seen her before first grade." Ellie's face lit up, remembering. "She cried before I left her at school. She held on to me so tight."

For a split second, I wish I'd known Megan back then. I'd look through old photos and feel like I missed out on a huge part of their lives.

One morning, Megan came into the kitchen while I was making my coffee, and she said, "I'm never calling you 'Mom.'"

"I understand," I said.

"I mean, I only have one mom."

"So do I."

She smiled because I seemed to get it. "Okay, cool. Just so you know, it's not that I don't like you or anything."

"I want you to call me whatever you're comfortable with. You could just call me Sydney. That *is* my name."

We smiled at each other. I was all about not making things awkward, and I thought we had a good moment there.

Our first Christmas was tricky. Matthew and I put ornaments on the tree, while Ellie lamented not being able to find the right Christmas jazz CD to play. We were nearly done before she found it. The tree was a blend of ornaments—mine and hers. Some had belonged to Val, or I just remembered her picking out some of them. I hadn't unpacked any of my Christmas boxes while I was staying at Penny's because her apartment was too small and her decorations were plenty. So this was the first Christmas I was slapped in the face with symbols of my past life. But as I watched Matthew excitedly hanging an ornament he'd made in second grade, and Ellie teasing Cookie with bubblewrap, I knew my old life was getting smaller in the rearview mirror. I didn't just see a new beginning, I could feel it.

Then the jazz music stopped, obliterated by the loud phone ringer that none of us could figure out how to turn down. All I heard next was Ellie pacing in the kitchen.

"You call me the day before Christmas Eve? I don't care what you thought! Oh, you're so full of shit, Marc."

Marc Parks. The famous ex-husband I'd only seen in photos.

"Let's leave it up to the kids." Ellie came out with the phone.

Matthew first. "Hi. Uh-huh. Yeah. Sure." He shrugged and looked questioningly at his mom.

"Give it to Megan," she said.

When he was out of the living room, she said in a hushed tone, "Their father. He decides to breeze through town and wants to see them Christmas Day."

"Tell him no. He didn't give you any notice." It seemed so logical to me.

"True, but I don't want to rob the kids of the opportunity to see their father."

"You're more noble than I am."

"Not really. I wanted to say no."

Megan came back with the phone. "It's cool with me as long as it's cool with you." This was a calm and respectful Megan. I hadn't met her before.

"Okay." I could see the struggle on Ellie's face. But for me, that was another huge lesson in momdom. When you have an ex, you put the kids' feelings first, no matter how you feel about the ex.

So we spent Christmas Eve opening gifts, including ones from Santa. The living room was an explosion of Legos, video games, DVDs. And Ellie and I each dog-eared our favorite page from a Lands' End catalog and got each other the same red fleece pullover. We laughed so hard. In the dim Christmas lights, her eyes sparkled. And just as I thought we were going to become an unromantic, ordinary couple, she took my hand and we danced by the tree. I don't even think music was playing. In that moment, I could tell we still had that spark.

So we danced.

All of a sudden, Matthew cried, "Sandwich!" and slammed into us, putting his arms around both of us. Ellie was right. He came when he was ready.

I don't want to be corny and say it was one of those Hallmark movie moments when everything comes together at the end. But it seemed like it.

On Christmas Day, Marc rode up in his very loud red sports car. There was barely enough room for two kids in there. Ellie and I both had uber practical, four-door cars in slightly differing shades of tan. They didn't reflect our quirky, lovable personalities. Then again, good gas mileage is very lovable.

I didn't get a good look at Marc because I didn't want to stand so obviously in the front window and stare at him like some sort of creep. All I could see was Ellie standing with the kids in the driveway, no doubt telling him what time she wanted them back.

When she returned, her expression was heavy and she slumped alongside me on the couch.

"Do you realize," I said, "this is the first time we've been alone in the house in forever?" Relishing the quiet, I took both of her hands in mine.

She was distracted; she kept looking out the window.

"It's okay," I said.

But she still seemed disturbed, craning her neck as far to the window as possible, even after his engine could no longer be heard.

"Is it Marc?" I asked.

"No, the damn Ms. Claus!" She bolted up and went outside to fix her yard display—an animatronic Santa and Ms. Claus. Santa was moving just fine, but Ms. Claus was stuck. Apparently, as Santa moved back and forth, Ellie insisted there was a moment when it looked like Ms. Claus was giving him a blow job. I didn't see that at all.

In spite of what she'd said, I could tell she was distressed by Marc's emergence on this day of all days and that she wouldn't relax until the kids returned.

* * *

"Happy New Year to you too!" Penny's voice was light and joyful on the phone. "You're still popular with that blog, you know."

I laughed. "Aw, well, tell me when you figure out if anyone has ever made money from a blog."

"I just really don't know."

"Nobody knows," I said. It was like we'd had the same conversation before. "Can you put Maddie on?"

"She's uh…" Penny struggled. "I think she's in the bathroom."

"It's okay. I get it." Maddie hadn't talked to me or returned my calls since I moved to Massachusetts. "I hope she forgives me soon. Tell her happy New Year anyway and that I miss her."

"Will do," Penny said.

That was it. My family and Morgan and Fran had been called, and Ruth had left to join the National Guard. I was all caught up for the year.

"Hurry up!" Ellie called from the next room. "The ball's about to drop!"

"Coming!"

When I got to the family room, *New Year's Rockin' Eve* was on TV, and Cookie was nowhere to be seen. She must have heard loud noises on the TV and gone flying off the couch.

Ellie put a glass of champagne in my hand and wrapped her arm around me. "Happy New Year," she said softly in my ear.

"Same to you," I answered, gazing at her.

Megan covered her eyes, as if we were doing something X-rated. Matthew had long since fallen asleep in his room.

"You guys aren't gonna do it, are you?" Megan asked.

"Don't talk like that," Ellie snapped. "That's inappropriate."

"We're all adults here," Megan said.

"Some of us aren't." Ellie squeezed her cheeks.

"Whatever." Megan slumped off to her room and closed the door. That was where she lived most of the time.

Then we adjourned to our room. When we came in, Ellie picked up her book about coming out stories.

"What is lesbian 'dead bed'?" she asked.

"Bed death," I said. "It's a myth." A moment passed. "Okay, maybe it's not a myth. It's the idea that without a man to initiate sex all the time, women get comfortable in their routines and neither one initiates it, so the sex part kind of dies down."

"Did that happen to you?"

"There were other reasons for…that." I came closer to her, threw her book on the floor and began unbuttoning her pajama top. My breath quickened as more of her silky chest was revealed, more of her cleavage exposed.

She jumped up to lock the bedroom door.

Moments later, we were naked and writhing around, soft and sweaty skin sliding up and down each other. Our breasts pressed together, legs wrapped around the smooth skin of our hips. She felt so good. I wanted to devour every inch of her perfectly curvy body. Just when we were in the moment of hot, unbridled rapture, I started to let out a moan that was so loud Ellie had to cover my mouth. We started laughing.

Then there was a knock on the door.

"Mom?" It was Matthew. He was trying to open the door!

Quickly we scrambled for our clothes. My underwear was somewhere at the foot of the bed. When we were decent, Ellie pretended to try to open the door.

"Is it locked?" Matthew asked.

"No, honey," Ellie said calmly. "It sometimes gets stuck." She tried to be serious but was hanging on the edge of a laugh. She winked at me.

Then she opened it.

"Happy New Year," Matthew said. He'd just awakened and realized it was a new year. His hair tousled, his eyes sleepy, he squinted up at her.

"Happy New Year, sweetie." She put his arms around her neck and carried him back to bed.

"Happy New Year!" I called from the bed.

When Ellie returned, I stared at her in amazement. "You're brilliant," I whispered.

"It's every parent's little secret," she said, kissing me over and over. "We don't have to stop." She breathed in my ear, and my whole body tingled.

I didn't expect this. So many nights we'd end up watching some *Nightline* special like "Is the Fruit You Eat Killing You?" Then we'd fall asleep.

But tonight was different. And when we managed to steal some time together, everything made sense.

CHAPTER TWENTY-TWO

"Something Fishy on Cape Cod"

There's nothing like a New England summer. The ground is an electric green, the sky a deep blue—like the front of a Claritin box. This particular June morning, Ellie and I were getting ready for a trip to a beachfront cottage on Cape Cod. Our neighbor, Greta Swanson, who already had four kids, actually volunteered to have Ellie's kids stay with her. That's what Ellie told me. All I could think was that the woman had to be a saint. Megan was thrilled because Greta had Playstation in the basement, so she wouldn't be seen all weekend. Greta, who was also a cat person, agreed to look in on Cookie and even change her litter. I'd vowed to get her a nice present. Anyone who willingly scoops up your cat's poop and pee deserves some reward.

In the two years I'd been living with Ellie and the kids, this was our fourth visit to the Cape. It was our getaway from life. I'd found a certain groove in the family, where I could finally see where I fit in. But when everything was too stressful, it was nice to know the Cape would be waiting for us.

We used to leave the kids with Marge, a kind lady who lived across the street, until she died. She was too kind to tell us if they'd ever pushed her over the edge, so I wondered about that. But Ellie insisted that heart disease ran in Marge's family.

Anyway, it had been just long enough that I couldn't wait to return. I could just imagine listening to the lapping waves, seagulls squeaking to each other, and inhaling the salty air.

Only this time, it was a recipe for disaster. There were so many anxiety-provoking situations awaiting me that I saw my therapist twice the week before.

Don't get me wrong. I know it sounded like paradise, but we weren't staying at our regular hotel. We were meeting my sister, Joanne, my brother-in-law, Nathan, and my two nephews. Even though I loved them all, they gave me anxiety attacks. I'm not sure why. Maybe it was because they're a more fast-lane kind of family while I prefer a pace closer to an old lady driving on the shoulder.

You can tell a lot about people by the way they drive. My sister is the kind of person who likes to ride in the far left lane and wait until she's one inch in front of her exit to cross over four lanes of traffic. It made me nervous. But I couldn't tell her that, or she'd get offended and not talk to me for months. She took after my mom's side of the family. They were kind of like the Mafia—only instead of guns they'd just not speak to people for years and years. You had to pick your battles.

Since Joanne's husband, Nathan Hutchins, came from a wealthy family, it was his family's cottage we were using for a couple of days. We'd be meeting them there, because they had to fly up from their home in Florida.

Every time I tried to explain to them where we lived, they always seemed confused. Ellie and I lived in south central Massachusetts, the part no one ever talks about. It looks like Vermont, a landscape dotted with lush greenery, glassy lakes and old cemeteries dating back to the 1700s. It's a nice mix of scenery and death everywhere. It puts everything in perspective. Just as I'm enjoying the majesty of a sprawling oak, I'll see some old tombstones in the distance, reminding me how short life is and how I'd better get a good look at that tree, because it will be around longer than I am. *Happy, happy.*

Anyway, this morning Ellie was packing a giant cooler with enough slabs of meat and seafood to keep us fed should the world come to an end.

"It's only two days," I said.

"We need to be prepared," she insisted. "Food is expensive over there." Ellie was still attractive underneath her stress lines and desperate need to be in control. Given the papers and family mementos strewn about the kitchen table, it was obvious that having control was as elusive for Ellie as happiness was for me. But she tried hard to gather her things each morning, inevitably leaving her phone or wallet behind. Lately, every now and then, I could still catch her blue eyes beaming at me the way she did when we first met in Mystic. But bills and kids and stress had been chipping away at the brightness in her eyes. I hadn't seen it much in a while.

I didn't know what to call Ellie. She was my girlfriend, but that seemed like we just dated, so I guess she was my partner since we lived together. "Partner" sounded like we owned a paint business together, so I guess there was really no good word for what we were. Even though gay marriage is legal in Massachusetts, we hadn't considered anything like that yet. When it was mentioned on TV, she'd wave her hand dismissively and say, "You're not ready for that yet, I know." Maybe she wanted to be the one to say it first so I wouldn't hurt her when I did. But honestly, it never crossed my mind, being someone who had lived much of her life in states where it wasn't an option.

This past winter, she made a big announcement about her divorce going through, and I was glad to hear it. I'd felt funny about living with someone who was still technically attached.

"Isn't that great?" she asked.

"Yeah, sure." I was munching on chips in front of the TV. When I saw her face fall, I knew I'd failed some test. "I'm really happy about it. But I guess I've always thought of us as kind of married anyway."

"But we're not." It was more black-and-white for her because she lived in a state where we could marry. Before moving to Massachusetts, I'd learned to think of marriage as more of a state of mind. It was a difference in perception, I guess, but it didn't worry me since all that mattered to me was that we were living together.

Ellie had most of the trunk packed. When I added a suitcase, she moved it to a better location. I didn't know there were eggs perilously close to my suitcase. I didn't know there was glassware near every space I thought I could move it to. *Wait.* Why were we packing glassware?

"*You* do it," I sighed. "You know where everything is."

"No, it's okay. You can help. Really." Ellie's face was contorted into a painful expression that looked like she was about to have diarrhea. She'd been trying so hard to work on her control issues. I had to give her credit for that.

The night before, I blogged about being in your forties in *The Comfortable Shoe Diaries*. I talked about all of the weird changes you go through during this time. It's the decade of desire—to be something different from who you were before but fearful of any changes that will mess up your security. It's a time when you think you've accrued enough wisdom to teach others, only to realize you know as little as you did in your twenties. All that can really be said about your forties is that you should now know what you'll put up with and what you won't. Past relationships have left you scarred and limping along, still trying to be optimistic.

I remembered feeling that way when Ellie and I met. Though we hated to admit we met online, we had to tell people whenever they asked us.

We'd get the same reaction: "Oh, you know lots of people are meeting that way now." It was as if they thought they needed to make us feel better.

The truth, both of us were bruised from past relationships and lugging heavy chains of baggage around like Marley's ghost. Sitting on each side of a pizza in Mystic with our invisible chains from the past, we'd made small talk and tried to present the sides of us we'd always wanted to be.

"I like foreign films," I'd said, though I hadn't watched one since film school. I thought it made me sound artsy.

"I enjoy reading," Ellie had said, sipping her wine in that casual, sexy way she still does today. Later I'd learn that she has major Attention Deficit Disorder and can't focus on a greeting card, let alone a book.

That morning I carried the last heavy group of bags out to the car. My cell phone rang in my pocket, and when I reached in to try to answer it, I lost my balance. Everything was top heavy, and I fell over on the driveway.

"You okay?" Ellie rushed to my side.

"You packed too much!" I snapped, grabbing the phone.

It was Joanne.

"What? You haven't left yet?" I looked at Ellie with alarm. "Uh-huh. I get it. No, I understand."

Ellie and I got in the car but couldn't get out of the driveway. She kept slapping her GPS because it had her going to Connecticut, and she couldn't figure out why.

"What did your sister say?" she asked, smacking the device over and over.

"It's Nathan. They missed their flight."

She looked quizzically at me.

"He couldn't go right away," I explained, giving her a look. I'd told her about Nathan before. He had a kind of agoraphobia, so sometimes he didn't like to go anywhere that seemed overwhelming, like a mall or airport. He never went to crowded restaurants either. But Joanne had managed to convince him that a couple of days on the Cape would be good for him and that there wouldn't be too many people, which was a lie. It was June, after all.

We started down the road. Ellie wasn't good at doing more than one thing at a time. But she tried anyway. I grabbed the wheel when she grabbed her phone.

"Who are you calling?"

"My brother," she answered. "I need to check if he needs a ride."

"Which brother?"

"Bryan."

"You might've told me this." It was already getting crowded and we hadn't gotten there yet.

"You're seeing your sister. Why can't I see my brother?"

"You're right. Sorry." I didn't like being the last to know about things.

"No answer." She put down the phone and held my hand.

"Sure you don't want both hands on the wheel?"

She sighed in frustration. "You're so romantic."

"Is he coming?" I asked.

"He may show up later. I don't know."

"He's the only one I haven't met, right? What's he like?"

"We think he's gay, only he doesn't know it yet." She smiled.

Bryan was her only sibling who lived in the same state. He owned a candy store in Rockport, and apparently her whole family worried about his survival. What they didn't know was that his peanut butter dream drops were about to go national. We'd find that out later.

CHAPTER TWENTY-THREE

"P-town"

Ellie and I fell in love with Provincetown, not only because it was the only place where we could hold hands in public without worrying about hateful stares, but because it had that feeling of history and seaside ambience and that special something that makes you want to stay a while longer. I'd cry every time we'd leave. I'm sure she wasn't looking forward to that. I was miserable to be with in the car for seventy miles down the Mass Pike—seventy miles of sobbing, tissues, wiping my swollen, pink eyes. She'd ask if we needed to pull over, and I'd wave my hand forward, unable to talk. Ah, good times.

Joanne and Nathan had never been to the Cape. Even though his family owned the little cottage where we were going, he hadn't seen it. So we couldn't wait to show them what paradise looked like.

"So when will they get there?" Ellie asked.

"About four o'clock."

"Fuck you!" Ellie screamed at the woman in the GPS who kept telling us to turn around. Finally, she threw the box in the backseat. We already knew how to get there anyway.

Snapshots of highway flashed by my window until finally I saw the sign for Cape Cod. My eyes got misty. I could hear Patti Page singing. Then anxiety set in. Worries tumbled into my head like waves at high tide. One after another. I pictured Joanne and Nathan with stopwatches, setting out itineraries for us—snorkeling, bike riding, parasailing—all before seven in the morning.

"Did you take your medicine?" Ellie asked.

"Yeah," I answered defensively. "Why?"

"Just, you seem…I was just checking."

"I seem what? What do I seem?" I couldn't let it go. It was a skipping record in my brain. I had to have the answer.

"You seem kind of nervous."

"What?" I barked. "How can you tell? I didn't say anything."

"I sense it. I feel your energy."

"Oh, stop. You sound like Ariel."

"When am I meeting her?" Ellie asked.

"You won't be until you can stand the smell of twenty packs of clove cigarettes," I replied.

Ellie made a face.

The truth was, I didn't know how to relax. I'd bought six books on how to relax. Not one of them helped me to relax. When someone told me to relax it just made me angry.

"Just think," Ellie said. "You'll be seeing your sister soon."

I did miss Joanne since I'd left Florida. Unfortunately, every time we got together, she had schedules and blueprints for each day, which somehow made it even more impossible for me to relax.

Then there were the rogue worries that drifted in and out, teasing my mind. I was afraid no one would be paying attention to their younger son, Tayler, and he'd drown in the sea. I was afraid Nathan would freak out and they'd have to leave before they saw Provincetown. I was afraid their older son Cabbot would blurt something out at a gay couple walking down the street. I was afraid my IBS would kick in during the trolley tour.

Determined not to live my life in fear, I did a few breathing exercises as we looked for the cottage. Then I decided that breathing exercises were stupid and tried to shift to positive thoughts, like the shacks that lined the sides of the road. These weren't ordinary shacks. They were homes to lobsters, clams, oysters, crabs—temples of seafood worship—where you sat in boat parts underneath massive nets strung across the walls and waited for your overflowing plate of fried goodness.

I sighed a contented, orgasmic sigh.

"You all right?" Ellie looked sideways at me.

"Oh yeah."

I hadn't noticed the curvy brunette sunning in a bathing suit at a resort pool we'd just passed. I was still imagining a drop of butter clinging lightly to a sweet chunk of lobster meat. I licked my lips.

"Put your eyes back in your head, will you!" she barked at me. Did I mention Ellie's temper?

"Why? Can't a girl lust after a lobster?"

"I thought you were looking at the brunette," she said.

"What brunette?"

A huge smile spread across her face, and she squeezed my hand.

We sounded like an old couple who couldn't hear what the other was saying anymore.

We decided to stop and have some lunch, especially since Joanne and family would be late. We didn't have the keys to the place, so there was no sense in sitting in the driveway for two hours.

Sunlight flickered across the windshield when we pulled back onto the road. Suddenly we'd driven onto a movie set, and everything looked perfect—as if the ocean, the trees, even the electric blue sky, had been put there just for us. I was so content, remembering my plate of sweet fried clams.

I sighed and held Ellie's hand, which reminded me of our first date in Mystic, when she put her hand in my coat pocket. I snuck a smile in her direction, and it was as if she knew what I was remembering. She gave my hand another squeeze. It was nice to be alone, just the two of us.

Sometimes she had a shy smile like a little girl looking for approval. Then she could seem so regal, like when she was instructing everyone on how to put the spoons in the dishwasher.

There were many shades of Ellie, light and dark, like sun and shadows through the windows. I was so surprised at how I'd found her in this world of mazes that so often lead to nowhere. Somehow I found my way to her picture on a computer screen, and my life would never be the same.

We rolled down the windows, letting the salt air inside. I breathed in the sunny scene with high dunes all around and almost relaxed, feeling almost light, like the thin sea grass swaying in the breeze. I could have been in one of those feminine napkin commercials.

"Are we there yet?" I asked.

"You're worse than the kids," she laughed. "It's coming up."

CHAPTER TWENTY-FOUR

"The Third-Year Hump"

The cottage stood high on the dunes, overlooking the bay. It had gray, clapboard shingles and white trim with a deck in back. It was the perfect New England house.

Then I noticed Joanne's white SUV rental car parked in the gravel beside us.

"I'll beat you in!" It was Tayler, a blur of blond hair, running up behind us, darting toward the water.

"No! You'll wait for everyone else!" Nathan called helplessly in his Southern twang.

And there was Joanne, already looking tired and defeated, her tumbling red curled hair scattered across her shoulders. No one knew where her red hair came from, but there was a rumor that Mom had had an affair with a plumber years ago. *Go Mom.*

"You made it!" I threw my arms around her waif-like body.

"Yeah, we managed to get another flight."

"You look great," I exclaimed.

"Thanks." She seemed distracted, pulling out gigantic bags from the trunk. "I'm doing this new workout video. She makes you do all these awful crunches and positions that make you wish you were dead. It's great."

As we carried our bags to the front door, Joanne lowered her voice so Nathan wouldn't hear. "He freaked out in the airport, worse than ever. Made a huge scene. I pretended not to know him."

"Tayler!" Nathan scooped up the boy's little seven-year-old pale body, sprayed him in a cloud of sunscreen mist, then insisted he wait on the back porch until the adults were ready to go outside. For a child, this was torture.

Joanne exchanged hugs with Ellie.

"You look great," Joanne said.

"I have an extra chin, but thanks." Ellie never could take a compliment.

Joanne unlocked the cottage. First we were hit with a musty smell like an old basement. But the views of water from every room quickly distracted us.

"This is…wow," Ellie sighed. "Just…wow." It was an almost spiritual moment of peace, everything you come to the Cape for. That was until the back sliders opened and Tayler scream-cried, begging to go swimming.

"Not until we're with you," Joanne said firmly. She unwrapped the furniture and began digging for cups and dishes in the cabinets. "We have to have lunch first, for Christ's sake."

"Nooo!" Tayler wailed. His little face was scrunched up like a used tissue.

Then Cabbot emerged from underneath a giant suitcase. He grinned sheepishly like he was up to something when I lifted him high into the air. At age ten, he already started to look like a handsome little man. It was painful to see. It meant I'd be getting older and dying sooner.

"How's my guy?" I nuzzled my cheek against his.

"Fine." He had that shy, just-getting-to-know-you-again face. It happened with every visit. Then after about fifteen minutes, he'd be explaining his Lego battleship features and what homemade rocket ships he'd demolished.

"So you like building things?" I was always trying to figure out what he was going to do for a living.

"Yeah." He nodded proudly.

"Why?"

"'Cause I like tearing them down." He smiled like a Cheshire cat and ran outside to torment his little brother.

So I decided he'd either be an architect or a terrorist. I looked around the living room and tripped over all the bags.

Joanne had packed as much as Ellie. There were more bags than furniture in the room.

"I wasn't sure what the last renters left," Joanne sighed, glancing around in a circle.

Down the hall were two bedrooms with one tiny bathroom we all had to share. After sizing up the sluggishly flushing toilet, I decided that while on this trip I wouldn't eat any more fried foods, dairy, tomato sauce or anything with sugar. I began obsessing about my Irritable Bowel Syndrome and thought it might be best not to eat at all.

We took nearly an hour to unpack all of our crap. And crap it was. We weren't going to need most of what we'd brought. Or were we? Was there something I didn't know? Then there were the silky, linen napkins. Why were they necessary?

"They never have enough napkins at these places," Ellie complained, looking for something under the bed.

"Why all the stuff?"

"I like to be prepared." Ellie's mouth hardened into a thin, tight line. I knew she'd lost something valuable but was afraid to say so. She was always losing things, and she spent half her life looking for them. I'd given her an expensive watch for Christmas, which was a huge mistake, because she'd promptly sucked it up in the vacuum. Then there was the charm bracelet, which was either lost in the car she'd just sold or thrown into the garbage with the cat poop. I had then vowed never to buy her anything over five dollars.

"What did you lose?" I asked. "Your keys?"

"Never mind. I'll find it."

"Great, she doesn't want to tell me. Must be something bad."

"No, just a phone number." Her voice trailed off, and she began looking in weird places, like the closet neither of us had opened yet.

"What number?"

"Why do you have to be so nosy? Just a number. It's no big deal!" She stormed out of the room.

Nosy? She'd never called me that before. Maybe it was true what they said about the third year of a relationship. You start to get sick of each other and break up. I'd read in a lesbian magazine that if you can survive the third-year hump, you'd make it as a couple. We had been fighting a lot more lately. But the first Christmas when she got along so well with my family, who are all just older versions of me, I thought she had to be the one, because she came out unscathed. But now...here we were in this romantic place and she was already yelling at me. Not a good sign.

Tired before the day had even begun, I went out to the living room and saw Joanne watching her husband tiptoe along the water's edge. The ocean was liquid ice, which only made Tayler cry harder because he couldn't go in.

"I tried to warn you," I said. "It's not like a Florida ocean. It's more of a taking-photos-holding-hands-at-sunset kind of beach. You can't go in."

Joanne nodded. "Tell *him* that. He thinks he's in that polar bear club." She was watching Nathan and most likely frustrated that she was stuck unpacking everything.

Then I noticed Ellie had found a brochure or whatever it was that had the phone number and had scurried toward our bedroom. It was strange that she didn't want to tell me what it was. I looked at her like a kicked puppy. She met my eyes and a certain calm washed over her face.

"I'm trying to surprise you," she explained. "Sorry I yelled."

She hugged me and all was magically restored again. It was amazing how just one or two words from Ellie could change the entire landscape of the world. It was either coming to an end or just beginning. For me, that was what real love felt like.

When Ellie retreated to the bedroom, Joanne turned away from the window and looked at me in that way you do if you have earth-shattering news.

"Sydney," Joanne said with a dramatic pause, "my face is falling."

I flopped on the couch, trying not to laugh. "It is not."

"Oh, yes it is," she insisted. "My cheeks have been lowering for a while. I've measured them."

"I haven't seen you since Christmas. You'd think I'd notice."

"No offense, but you don't notice details." She sat beside me.

"Ouch!"

"Seriously, when I made that Easter wreath and emailed you a photo, you never said anything about the tiny chicks in the middle."

"Chicks? I thought it was just some yellow fuzz."

"You only notice things that are about you."

"That is so not true!" I screeched indignantly, even though it might be true.

"I'm considering a...lift. I'd like your approval. You're my sister. I need to know you think it's okay."

I gasped.

"Before you give me the misogynistic society speech," she continued, "I just really want to do it for *myself*."

"What if you come out looking like one of those Hollywood wax figure women?" I closed one eye then the other, trying to picture it.

"I don't know."

"Or get a really bad surgeon? Then your face won't look like you anymore, and as you get older, you'll look scary."

"I knew I shouldn't have told you. Never mind."

As she got up, I noticed her face in the light. A few more freckles from the Florida sun, and some crow's-feet creeping along near her eyes, but she still looked like herself, the girl with the knobby knees who I grew up with, the girl I rode down to Sanibel Island with every summer who fought with me over the last piece of grape gum in the backseat. I didn't want that to change.

CHAPTER TWENTY-FIVE

"If You're Happy and You Know It..."

The sun shone so brightly on the water that it hurt my eyes. I turned away from the white glare, reminding myself that I was having a good time. This was a vacation, after all, the thing people take pictures of to put in brochures that demonstrate happiness.

"Are you happy?" Joanne probed, digging her toes into the sand.

There was that word again. I'd decided that "happy" was an ideal everyone strived for but didn't quite know what it was.

"Yeah." *Like it said on our Christmas card.*

"So you are…happy," Joanne repeated.

"Yeah," I grunted. There was sand in my butt crack, little bugs zipping around my face, and bites itching on my legs from some sneaky mosquito. But I was on a beautiful beach, where it seems like something's wrong with you if you say you're not completely happy.

"I mean with your life." Joanne liked to get deep and dark to fill in the cracks of happiness that found their way into her own life from time to time. She couldn't let that happen.

Joanne had earned the nickname "The Angel of Death" in our family because of one particular Christmas. Years ago when Dad was alive and we were all singing carols around the piano—in between songs when everything was quiet for a moment—Joanne suddenly said, "Just think, one of us will die first."

You can imagine the rest of that evening and following morning. Mom was crying over her Christmas coffee cake and Dad was reading the obituaries to see if any more of his friends had died. Good times.

We didn't celebrate Joanne's birthday, at her request. I knew she'd have trouble aging ever since the first time she had to shop for her first bra. But I tried to send a card one year, and she blew up at me, so the boycott was official.

"What is it?" I asked.

"Well, how happy are you supposed to be? I've seen the vitamin commercials."

"What are you talking about?" I was completely confused.

"You know, those multivitamins for every stage of your life. They show you graduating from college, then married, with kids, then with grandkids and riding bikes with your equally gray-haired husband. Your whole life is planned out for you. And I'm one scene before the old people on the bikes!"

Was this what a nervous breakdown looked like?

"Don't…you can't…" I was choking on sea air. "Don't let Centrum dictate your life!"

"But it does! Don't you get it? Oh, you don't."

"What does *that* mean?"

"You didn't get married. You're not following the plan." Her words came down as a butcher knife. There was some resentment deep inside of her, though what other plans she had were still a mystery to me.

"I guess not, unless same-sex marriage is legal everywhere someday." I thought about it.

I wasn't exactly living the life I'd envisioned. But after three years with Ellie and Matthew accidentally calling me "Mom," I can't say I minded it. I don't know why. It even made me smile sometimes.

"Actually, I am living a similar life to you," I corrected. "Now."

Joanne nodded, realizing I could now relate to her in a way I never could before.

"I've changed," I continued. "The old me used to freak out about adopting a cat, remember?"

"Yeah. But you totally lost it when you found out about Ellie's kids."

"You want to hear something weird?" I said. "We're starting to feel like a real family."

Joanne smiled a different smile at me. It was a mixture of pride and awe, like she was proud of her baby sister. Maybe I wasn't such a mess now after all.

"Especially with her ex always out of town. He hardly sees the kids, so it feels like it's just us." I leaned back in a rare, contented posture.

"You're okay with that?"

"Well, yeah," I replied. "Sometimes I have to get over that 'oh God, she slept with a man at least twice' feeling. But it passes."

She was studying me carefully.

"What?" I was beginning to get nervous.

"I'm happy for you," she said simply.

There was a pause that followed, the kind of pause that wasn't going to go away. "What's wrong?" I finally asked. "You're not happy or you wouldn't have asked if I was."

"Nathan and I fight. I mean like crazy. We fight over which brand of hand soap to buy. After twelve years…you think that's normal?"

I wasn't sure.

"Is the hand soap worth divorcing over?" I asked.

She shook her head. "The soap is a symptom. It seems like we fight over everything, big and small. And he's always working. It's *his* business. He could come home and let the employees work late."

"You think it's an affair? I'll kill him right now." My butt was almost off the sand when she held me down.

"I don't know that! There's no one good looking there. They're all super religious nerds with acne even in their thirties."

"You still love him?"

"Y...eah." And there it was. She said it with two syllables, like she was thinking it over as she said it.

My heart sank. A cold rock settled in my stomach. Joanne and Nathan were something I could count on, like the sun rising or the Rolling Stones doing their millionth tour. Now what would I do?

I stared out at Nathan, taking Tayler by his little hand, skipping waves that crashed dangerously close to their feet, and I suddenly felt sorry for him, for what he didn't know.

"You only get one chance and life is short," she said. "How do you know if you're not missing out on something?"

"Some people go looking for what they think they're missing, then realize they had it all along and are now trapped in a new relationship with a drug dealer who somehow got custody of your kids."

"How did you get me married to a drug dealer? That's not what I'm saying."

"Isn't it? You always do the 'road not taken' thing, but maybe that road has a million potholes. Ever think of that?" I was on a roll.

"I'm sorry. This is really bad timing."

"Why?" I looked around. Everyone was busy doing something else. "What's wrong with the timing?"

"Well," she hesitated. "This weekend isn't exactly..."

"What?"

"It's not about me."

"Am I missing something? Not about you? What does that mean?" Something was strange, and she was a bad liar.

"I'm not good at keeping secrets." She tucked in her legs protectively and traced patterns in the coarse sand with her fingers.

Before I could ask anything else, Nathan was shaking off his wet hair over me like a dog.

"Is that a guy thing?" I snapped. "As much as I love getting soaked by you."

"Oh, sorry," he lied, toweling off and puffing out his chest like he could convert me.

"It's funny how straight guys always wonder what lesbians do without a penis," I told Joanne, pretending that's what we had been talking about. "I wonder what gay guys do without a vagina." I smiled to myself, enjoying Nathan's stunned silence and my ability to still shock him after all these years.

He let out a high-pitched, nervous laugh, and his flip-flops were a blur on the landscape as he scurried back up to the cottage. My work there was done.

* * *

That night, Ellie and I lay in bed with moonlight streaming in.

"I'm worried about my sister," I whispered. "She doesn't seem happy with Nathan anymore."

"Well, they're under a lot of stress. Tayler seems kind of hyper."

"I think it's more than that. She said something about keeping secrets."

Ellie stirred uncomfortably. "Don't make her problems your problems. Just focus on what you have control over."

"You sound like my therapist." She couldn't see, but I was smiling at her in the dark. "Do you think we'll ever get to Paris?"

"I'm happy just being here." She squeezed me tightly. "There's too much cheese there."

"Now I know you're not with me for my money," I whispered. Ellie turned. "Will you stop?"

"You do know this is my brother-in-law's cottage, not mine?"

"You'll get back on your feet soon. And maybe…you shouldn't go back."

"I already have. What do you mean?"

She sighed, her breath catching in her throat like she was holding something back. "You really seem to be hating it."

She was right. I'd lost the spark for advertising. I came home one night and said that I'd spent my whole life trying to sell things that people didn't need to people who didn't want them. "This job is the worst," I admitted, resting on my arm. I remembered a photo shoot, spreading Vaseline across a green pepper to make it shinier. Food ads were harder than I'd realized. "I don't know. I feel kind of lost."

"What about your dream of being a writer?"

"We'll never get to Paris if I go for that. You've heard the phrase 'starving artist'?"

"I believe in you. Screw Paris."

"All these galleries here…you think these photographers make enough to quit their day jobs?" I exhaled painfully. It was a reality I was always fighting with. And I knew I wasn't the only one. I hated reality. I hated the words "reality," "realistic," and "practical." There was definitely a theme there.

"Your stuff is good," Ellie insisted. She was that reassuring angel always sitting on my shoulder. When she wasn't yelling, of course.

"You only saw a seventh grade poem, a bad one."

"I saw your newspaper articles," she said. "You actually put some suspense in a story about a bake-off. Would it be the reigning champion, Gladys Lisbert, from Fairfield, or her arch-enemy, Louise Compton, from Waterbury?"

"The editor hated that."

She laughed. "What about some of that stuff in your blog? Did it all really happen? The drag queen who sang to you under a spotlight?"

"Unfortunately, yeah. In a crowd of hundreds, I got the spotlight song."

We laughed, and the more we tried to be quiet, the harder we laughed.

"I believe in you," she whispered again.

I rolled over and touched her cheek. "You say that to all your students."

"Only the ones who aren't in gangs."

We laughed some more. "At age ten?"

"You'd be surprised."

In the immortal words of Kenny Rogers, she believed in me. But there was a feeling gnawing at me. I wanted to make enough money to add on to the cute ranch house we shared. I wanted to make enough to whisk her away to Paris and have too much cheese. How would I ever be enough for her?

CHAPTER TWENTY-SIX

"The Woman I Love"

Provincetown is a dream. You don't believe it's real because you think it's a place that would have had to come from the imagination of some brilliant writer or artist. Maybe that's why so many writers and artists flocked here—to absorb some of its mojo and put it into their work.

Ellie and I and the rest of the gang made our way down the cracked sidewalks that reminded me of what winter must be like here. We scanned the shops on Commercial Street. I took Ellie's hand under bright sunlight, out in the open, where all eyes would see us and other couples who were like us would smile secretly proud smiles at us.

Shops nestled inside old Victorian houses with lovingly cared for balconies and neatly manicured flower gardens surrounded us as we felt the cool breeze off the water. A seascape from a postcard could be seen squeezed in narrow cracks between the houses we passed. There was one pink house that demanded to be noticed. Soon we were immersed in all of the sights and sounds of Provincetown. We passed two men pushing their adopted

Asian daughter in a stroller, two lesbians each yanking hard on their boxers' leashes, a drag queen on a unicycle advertising his nighttime comedy show. And there were the straight couples passing us without any bulging-eyed stares or double-takes. Most of them didn't seem to care at all.

We went down to the pier, and I spotted the little red boat in the bay. Always there year after year, the red boat was happily sitting on glassy water amidst all the white boats, many much larger—okay, some were yachts. But it was the red boat that *was* Provincetown. It was the one with color, unashamedly taking its place among the other more imposing boats and just as proud to be there as they were. It was different, but happily there anyway, reminding me that so was I, reminding me to hold Ellie's hand without looking over my shoulder, to hold my head as high as I did in ballet class when I had no clue that I was shorter than everyone else in second grade. My dance teacher told my mom that I carried myself like I was ten feet tall. As I watched the red boat rock a little, I realized I'd almost forgotten how I used to be. How I *could* be again.

I'd let the layoff and bankruptcy poison my self-esteem, and Ellie had become the only light in my life, warming me all over just when I felt like the world was cold and I was unlovable.

Back on Commercial Street, we poked around in different shops. Even in the crowd, Ellie caught my eye and her smile filled my chest with excited anticipation like Christmas Day, right before opening presents. Now as the late afternoon sun took hold of the street, spilling a hazy pink summer glow across everything, the shadows across her face and her serene smile gave me a peace greater than my anxiety pills.

In one store, I vaguely heard the chatter going on around me. Cabbot picked up a rustic sign and read, "'It's always five o'clock somewhere.' Mommy, what does that mean?"

"Don't worry about it," Joanne said casually. She was an experienced, unflappable mom.

I was lost in a daydream, smiling back at Ellie. I'd begun to follow her into another store. My sister grabbed my arm and pulled me in another direction.

"What about the cool music place?" Joanne urged.

"Yeah," I answered. "It's up a little further."

"Let's go there."

"But Ellie's going here."

I started to follow Ellie's golden-streaked hair, and when she turned, her bright blue eyes were anxious little sapphires, giving Joanne a secret look. Something was definitely going on.

"Let's give her some space," Joanne said. "You know the key to a good relationship is giving each other space."

"You're giving me relationship advice?" I tried to lower my voice. We were now standing in the middle of the sidewalk.

"You see her all the time, and you never see me." She was becoming an even worse liar.

"Something's going on. Will you just tell me because the not knowing is going to kill me!"

"I want to see it now!" she exclaimed. "We have to go before Nathan freaks out." She looked all around. "Then I won't get to see it."

"Oh." That made sense, but I knew it wasn't the whole truth. We raced up the hill to my favorite little used music shop.

Nathan looked bewildered but followed us anyway, with my nephews dragging along. They only cared about the pool later and were showing the patience of saints waiting for it.

A fan rattled overhead, and the musty smell of old vinyl albums filled the air. I could've stayed here all day. Because of me, Joanne knew some of the best gay singers and bands, and her knowledge even surprised the flamboyant guy behind the counter. With a receding hairline and skintight tank top, he came out from around the counter to get a closer look at her species.

"You like Erasure?" he marveled, still a bit suspicious.

"Oh yeah," Joanne exclaimed.

Because she was straight, Joanne got extra-credit points for being gay-friendly.

"She's in Florida," I told him.

"Yeah," she continued. "I caught them in Tampa, and they're still as good as they were in the eighties."

"I saw them in New York," he replied. It was now a contest to see who knew them better.

While they buzzed about that, I flipped through some CDs, always searching for a new Jimmy Somerville import I hadn't seen before. I couldn't help but wonder what Joanne meant about secrets yesterday. Something was happening. Ellie was in on it. Joanne was in on it. But I had no idea what Nathan knew. He seemed distracted by all of the people.

"I'm gonna take 'em next door," Nathan interrupted, scooting the boys toward the door. He didn't see enough Tim McGraw to be comfortable in this particular record store.

"I don't think it's a good idea, honey." Joanne gritted her teeth behind a smile.

When the counter guy took a phone call, she erupted at Nathan.

"There are naked people on the walls in there!" she exclaimed.

You could see X-rated advertising in the windows, and I pretended not to notice so Joanne wouldn't get ruffled. It didn't work.

"So?" Nathan shrugged. "They might as well see human anatomy."

"How can you be so matter-of-fact about this? What if it traumatizes Tayler? He's never seen a woman or a man fully… you know."

"In some primitive tribes, the kids see nudity right away, and it's no big deal."

"We're not a primitive tribe! Where is your sense?" Her words shredded him. She'd lost all patience with him.

"We could go on ahead and check it out if you want," I offered, trying to keep the peace.

"What's the matter with you?" she repeated to him.

"Oh, I don't know," Nathan spat. "Having a wife who lies to me!"

"What?" she screeched, trying to keep quiet at the same time.

"You told me there wouldn't be a lot of people." He gestured out the door to the crowds swarming the streets. "They're everywhere!" He flailed his arms like a mental patient.

Receding hairline counter guy even took notice.

"Please," she replied. "I'm getting sick of trying to accommodate all your...stuff."

It was cold. It was unemotional. Of course my thoughts drifted back to me. I was a freak show of quirks. What if someday Ellie saw me that way, as someone whose "stuff" she had to accommodate?

Joanne tore out of the store and demanded we all head back in the other direction, where we met a very surprised Ellie on the sidewalk, holding a bag.

"What did you get?" I asked.

Ellie shoved it into her purse, not realizing I'd already seen it.

"What do you mean?" she asked nervously.

"I get it. I'm not supposed to know." I smiled to myself, imagining my future Christmas present. After all, my birthday was already past.

We headed back to the car, the kids out in front, anxiously awaiting the pool. We passed by an open bar where a TV was blaring some politician's speech about gay marriage "destroying the fabric of our society."

I exhaled painfully and took Ellie's hand.

"That must be hard," Joanne said.

"I'm used to it," I replied. "I love hearing that who I am is going to destroy society." I had a permanently painted on, sarcastic smirk. "That's the problem I have with gay marriage!"

Everyone stopped and stared at me.

"What?" I was confused. Why were they looking at me that way? "If Ellie and I were to do that, it still feels like a simulation of what's considered the 'norm.' And I want to be able to just be, you know? It should be romantic, not some debate on the news." I shook my head and kept walking, not noticing the loud silence behind me.

With each step, I took comfort in the rainbow flags waving from the upper balconies of shops and restaurants. I knew Ellie and I would always be welcome here.

Before moving to New England, I was used to having no rights in central Florida. When I filled out forms at the doctor's office, I had to check the "single" box even though I was with Valerie for twelve years. Where I grew up, nobody was gay, at least not out loud. When you never see or hear about something, it's as if it doesn't exist. And when I'd begun to realize I was different, I had no one except Boy George to relate to.

I thought about the Congresswoman who talked about invisibility, how if we don't speak out, we're agreeing to not exist. Inside me, there was a constant, restless contradiction. My conscience was always at odds with just how far I was willing to go to overturn the status quo. I was a coward who would suffer more than your average coward because I was so intensely aware of the injustices I was turning my back on. Sure I had my blog. But it was a forum where I could safely complain. When it came time to turn up the volume, my mouth was covered with duct tape. I wasn't proud of this. But I still preferred the Congresswoman to do the talking. I'd get too emotional and scramble all my words anyway, I'd rationalize.

When we returned to the cottage, there was a strange car parked in the driveway. We opened the door, and Mom rose from the couch with arms outstretched.

"Surprise!" she shouted.

I was shocked. Mom hated flying. How did she get here? Did she drive all the way up from Florida?

I gave her a big hug, then noticed Ellie. She was holding the doorframe to steady herself.

"I'm sorry," Mom said to Ellie. "I just couldn't spend the night in that seedy motel. Did I mess up everything?"

I looked at Mom, then Ellie, like a tennis match. "Mess what up?" I demanded.

Everyone was acting so weird. They all knew a secret, and I was the only one not in on it.

CHAPTER TWENTY-SEVEN

"Brotherly Love"

"What's going on?" I hollered. But no one would answer. My panic rose as they exchanged solemn glances.

Then the doorbell rang. It was Bryan, Ellie's brother, the one I hadn't met, holding a bouquet of flowers. He looked just like the photos I'd seen of him, tall and lanky with Elvis-black hair. He looked like he'd been adopted.

As if she could read my mind, Ellie quietly said, "My dad had dark hair."

"Oh." I nodded and smiled at him as he moved the bouquet up and down, not sure where to put it. Something about him reminded me of myself.

"Hi, all," he announced awkwardly. "I wasn't sure what to bring to a lesbian wedding, so I thought flowers? Or is that weird? Should I have brought tools?"

"Lesbian wedding?" All the blood rushed out of my body. "Whose wedding?"

Everyone stared blankly, as Ellie took the flowers from him.

"She doesn't know yet," Mom sighed.

"These are great, thanks," Ellie said softly, bringing Bryan inside and introducing him to everyone.

The Atlantic churned under a full, orange moon. We all sat on the back deck, sipping drinks, as the secret spilled out.

"I was going to surprise you," Ellie told me softly. "Tomorrow."

"*We're* the lesbian wedding?"

"I want to marry you."

My heart started doing cartwheels. Even though we'd already talked about this, even though she knew I didn't want to be one of those same-sex couples getting married on the local news, even though she knew I was still on the fence about being a mother...even though everything on my compass pointed in the opposite direction, she thought this was a good idea.

"Why? What? How...wh..." I began to babble like I'd taken an experimental drug.

I went inside to pop open another beer. I jumped at the sight of my sister suddenly right next to me.

"Just stay calm," she said. It was ironic coming from her.

"So this was the secret?"

"I'm sorry I was so obvious."

"Don't be. I didn't have a clue." I took a big swig, downing half the bottle.

"The woman you love is out there, scared to death you'd react like this, even more afraid you'll say no. Now you love her. So what's the problem?"

"What's the problem?" I repeated. "What's the problem?" My mind raced. I couldn't retrieve words fast enough. I rubbed my face.

"Is it Văldemort?"

"No." I couldn't explain. That was the truth. The whole gay marriage thing—it felt almost like being among the first African Americans to eat at a suddenly integrated diner where you knew the white patrons still didn't want you there. Somehow I can't imagine the food tasted all that great. "I love her. She loves me. Isn't that enough?"

Joanne considered this. "What's wrong with her wanting to celebrate that love with family and friends?"

She was right. "It's such a surprise," I breathed.

"It's romantic," Joanne replied. "The last romantic thing we did was put in a new bathroom floor."

"What about a marriage license?" I was looking for an escape.

"You can do that when you get home," Joanne said. "This was the only time Nathan and I could come up and Mom too. Ellie wanted us all to be here for you. I think she's really thoughtful and sweet."

"She was married to a man."

"Oh." There was a certain understanding on Joanne's face.

"That's what she did with him. For her, marriage makes it more official, I think. But not for me."

Joanne nodded. "You and Val never had that."

"We didn't need it."

"You think she doesn't take things seriously unless you have a ceremony?"

"I don't know."

"I know," Joanne said. "I can tell she takes your relationship just as seriously as you do. But this means something to her. You should be flattered."

I remembered Joanne's beautiful wedding. She had wanted it to be reminiscent of a romantic Masterpiece Theatre movie, minus the foggy English moors. Everything was perfect, except for the freshly cut flowers I had to hold that dripped all over the front of my dress. Everything else was perfect, though.

I made invisible shapes on the kitchen counter. "You do have a nice bathroom," I said. I was stalling.

Ellie looked through the sliding door, probably certain I was going to say no. As usual, I'd ruined everything. I was the one you could always count on to step in the cow pie at any party.

Joanne left the moment Ellie came in. Then it was just the two of us under the glaring lights of the kitchen. I was nervous and sweating, and I felt familiar rushes of heat running up and down my back.

"Your face is red," Ellie said. "You okay?"

"Yeah. We were just talking."

"I figured. A sister thing."

How could she be so understanding? I'd be upset if it were my surprise. "Sorry I wrecked your surprise."

"It doesn't have to be wrecked, unless you're saying no."

I watched her lower her eyes; she looked suddenly so vulnerable, dangling herself out there.

I had to know what I wanted. And I had to know in a matter of seconds. The pressure was too much. My stomach gurgled.

"We already live together," I said. "Why do you want to do this? You want to commit to me in front of the whole world?"

"Just a few friends and family."

"But I'm crazy! I'm insane! I have to wash my hands after touching doorknobs! I worry about my intestines every day."

She held me either to comfort me or to make me shut up. "I thought we could do a small ceremony on the beach," she said.

On a beach without bathrooms. The thought crashed down in a bolt of lightning, and I started pacing the white tiled floor. "Oh my God. A ceremony."

"Breathe. You need a paper bag?"

We were doing breathing exercises. That wasn't a good sign for a magical wedding weekend.

"I was thinking barefoot at sunset." She slid her arms around my waist to comfort me. By this time I was panting hard.

"How could you...why would you..." I screeched. "There are no...restrooms! What if I have to pee?"

"You can go in the ocean." She was unbelievably calm, holding on, silent minutes passing by, squeezing me tighter in the hopes I'd change my mind. It worked.

"If I was going to get married," I said slowly, "it would be to you."

"That's a start." Ellie was dangling off a cliff.

You know all those times in your life when you wish you had a do-over? My response to Ellie would likely be one of those times. Of course I loved her. I couldn't have handled two kids and all the stresses we dealt with every day with anyone else.

I took a deep breath. "Yes," I said. "I'll marry you on a beach without restrooms."

She screamed a joyful scream, lifted me off the floor and spun me around. I think I heard clapping from everyone else and maybe a few sighs of relief.

CHAPTER TWENTY-EIGHT

"Commitment or Committed"

"So everybody's happy now?" Joanne raised her glass tentatively.

I nodded, as Ellie led me back out to the deck, squeezing my hand.

"Thank God," Joanne said.

"Yeah, those plane tickets were non-refundable," Nathan added.

Joanne glared at him.

"Let's get the party started!" Bryan exclaimed, crossing his legs like a woman, his eyes fixed on Nathan.

"Once I get these done," Nathan said, flipping burgers like a madman.

Bryan came over to the grilling area. Ellie had forgotten to introduce him to Nathan.

"Are you married?" Bryan asked.

"Yeah, that's my wife." Nathan pointed to Joanne. "Because I'm straight, so…that's my wife."

"Of course she is. Lovely." Bryan sipped his drink. "I like the ladies too." He laughed impulsively as if someone had just tickled him from behind. "All kinds of ladies." His voice trickled off into the wind.

Nathan tried to hide his discomfort and started flipping the burgers he'd already flipped.

Cabbot presented Ellie with a smooth, brown stone he'd found on the shore. "For my new aunt."

I looked at my sister. Had she told him to do that? She shrugged to show me her cluelessness.

"Awww," everybody said.

Ellie turned the stone in her hand. "I'll keep it in a special place." She had such warmth, a real nurturing soul. Some people are born to be mothers. They know just what to say to encourage you or to make it all better when you fall out of your tree house and skin your knee. Ellie was one of those people.

Mom sat back and smiled proudly. "I wish your father could've seen this."

I thought about him. Looking up at all the stars, I wondered if he was among them, if he would approve. Mom could see the questions on my face.

"I'm sure now that he's an angel, he knows it's all right. Once they get on the other side there's no discrimination. That only exists among the assholes down here." Mom could say anything and still sound like Donna Reed. She sipped her wine daintily. Under her platinum perm and elegant façade, there was a whole other person none of us really knew.

Then a terrifying thought hit me. "When are we doing this?"

"In two days," Ellie answered.

"Longer than a weekend. What about the kids and the cat?"

"Greta's bringing the kids up for the ceremony and leaving Cookie at her place."

"Okay, right." I reminded myself that Cookie liked our neighbor. It took a while, but she'd eventually warmed up to Greta, only hissing at her once. The little fuzz ball preferred to stay at a place she knew, as long as her food bowl was full. And Greta had one of those cat jungle gyms that Cookie would likely stare at but never use.

Joanne laughed. "No offense, but everything freaks out that cat."

I scanned the deck. My family would be here for this occasion. "Anyone else coming?" I asked.

"Fran and Morgan," Ellie replied.

"Aw, really? I love them."

Mom was confused.

"Our friends in Vermont," I explained.

They were probably anxious to get out of their barn-like house where they rarely saw civilization.

"They're lesbians?" Nathan asked.

"Uh-huh," I said. "Their truck barely runs, but they came all the way to a Boston hospital just to be there for that muscle spasm scare Ellie had last year."

"Isn't that nice?" Mom marveled.

"They're natural-type, granola lesbians," I warned, fearful that anyone might make some insensitive comment, particularly Nathan. "They live off the land, growing their own vegetables and berries. They leave all their doors open when they sleep at night, and these giant horseflies get in, but nobody seems to care."

I remembered our last visit.

"They were nuclear-size flies," I told my sister, who winced in disgust. "And they didn't even shoo them!" As I remembered, they just kind of let them hang out, like additional guests. They'd swirl around our food, and I was flapping my hands all over the place while Ellie laughed at me.

Morgan had said, "If you leave them alone, they don't usually bite." *Usually*.

I knew Ellie didn't like it either, but as I told the story, she touched my leg to calm me down. "But did you see that view? They keep everything open because you're right against this mountain with this valley…"

"I don't care. You've got some big-ass flies you need to keep out." I gulped my beer. "When they get here, we're keeping that door closed." I pointed to the slider.

"Don't worry," Ellie said. "They're staying next door."

"Good," I said. "Don't get me wrong. They're wonderful people."

Mom seemed disturbed. I knew I'd gotten my feelings for the great outdoors from her. At least when you stayed in a hotel you could get cute little soaps and shampoos to take home. But staying in the woods your only souvenir might be a laceration from a hungry bear or a rash from peeing on leaves that you didn't know were poison ivy, because let's face it, who's really paying attention in biology class when they start talking about plants?

"What about clothes?" Different thoughts were shooting across my mind and scaring me.

"We'll be wearing some," Ellie joked. "It isn't that kind of wedding."

"Dang," Nathan joked.

"Get serious. I'm not wearing some bridal gown or a tux. Straight people think one has to be the man, the other is the woman." I turned to my sister and brother-in-law. "Not you guys. But a lot of people think that."

"I was imagining some dressy outfit with pants for both of us." Ellie reached for my hand again.

"Oh, really? Pants? On your special day?" Mom was liberal but stuck in the 1950s. She approved of her lesbian daughter's wedding, but she preferred we wear twirling dresses or poodle skirts.

"Well, it sure isn't going to be a dress," I snapped.

"You never did like girls' clothes," Mom muttered to herself.

"No," I said firmly. As a child, I'd always wanted a number shirt. I didn't know it was a football jersey. I was too young. I just called it a number shirt. That should've been the first clue.

"I liked baseball hats," Ellie added.

"So did I," Joanne argued. "That doesn't make me a lesbian."

"You say it like it's a bad thing," Ellie joked.

Nathan got a twinkle in his eye, looking at Joanne. "You sure there's something you're not telling me?"

Joanne shoved him hard in the ribs.

"Jesus, woman!" He gripped his middle.

"Don't be such a baby," Joanne barked. "It wasn't that hard."

"When are we getting these perfectly suited outfits I've never seen before?" I have to admit I was very cantankerous about the whole thing.

"I was going to tell you tonight, so we'd have a couple of days to go shopping."

I exhaled. I tried to keep my thoughts to myself. I looked like I was about to blow.

"What?" Ellie was on edge. Nothing had gone the way she'd envisioned.

"You know how hard my butt is to fit." I covered my face in shame.

Mom patted my shoulder. "Don't be so hard on yourself. We all have a pig in a blanket back there. It's hereditary. Just don't go to that dog collar shop I saw on the way in, unless you want a leather wedding."

I glanced at Cabbot and Tayler, who were still trying to make a sandcastle with this strange new sand that just wasn't sticking together. They were persistent. I envied them. They didn't have to buy a special outfit to be who they were. I resented the whole thing, but I didn't want to be an angry bride, or partner, or whatever I would now be called. That wouldn't look good in the wedding photos.

"Hey, y'all!" It was Penny, bursting through the front door.

"No one locked that?" Mom said in horror.

"No one read the invitations," Ellie said to herself.

"Penny!" I shouted, waving her outside. Everyone relaxed when they realized I knew her.

She swooped onto the deck with arms outstretched. "My little girl, gettin' married!"

Nathan stood up to shake her hand. "I know that accent."

"Tennessee," Penny said proudly.

"Georgia," Nathan countered.

Joanne squirmed. "She's a lesbian," she informed him, setting her empty drink in his hand. He was reluctant to refill it right away.

I enjoyed watching the exchange. Penny had a naturally flirty way about her, even though she played for our team.

"I wouldn't have missed it," she told me, taking a seat. "Course the prices up here are insane. I'm stayin' in a little rental shack down the road. It's got one window and a tiny TV. But what the hell!"

"How are things down in Connecticut?" I asked, handing her a beer.

"Oh, you know. Same old. I'm meeting someone next weekend."

"Great." I was grateful to think about something else.

"Yeah," Penny added. "She's flying in from Topeka."

"Another Kansas girl," I sighed.

"I'm the bride's mother." Mom shook Penny's hand.

"Oh, sorry," I gasped. "This is my sister, Joanne, Ellie's brother Bryan, of course you know Ellie. And out there, working on a doomed sandcastle are my nephews, Cabbot and Tayler."

"They're precious," Penny squealed. I could tell her excitement was once again built on the hope that only cyber love could bring her or the promise of it. She'd lost some weight since she last visited us in Massachusetts. She looked good.

"Is Maddie...?" I started to ask, but Ellie's face answered the question.

"She said she has to work," Ellie replied.

"Yeah." I drank my beer to hide my hurt. I finally gave up trying to call or email her. If she wasn't going to be happy for me, I figured she wasn't a real friend.

"I'm so glad your wedding is this weekend," Penny said. "In two weeks I have to fly to Atlanta for business."

"Ooh, you could meet someone there," I sang, starting to feel a slight buzz.

"Not if Ms. Topeka works out." Penny winked.

"Atlanta is a great city," Bryan boasted. "Gorgeous skyline at night and some cool gay neighborhoods." When he saw everyone looking at him, he added, "I got lost one night."

I wondered how he could not know he was gay.

"I'm still worried about my butt," I said.

"Get over it," Joanne groaned.

"What's with your butt?" Penny asked.

"Don't ask," everyone said.

"It's hard to fit," I replied. "That's why I hardly ever go pants shopping. It's painful and traumatic, like going to the gynecologist."

"Too much information." Nathan decided it was now time to fill Joanne's drink.

"We'll find something." Ellie touched my thigh. She was getting frustrated. And who could blame her?

That night, Ellie and I argued all the way to the bedroom.

As we changed into our nightclothes...

"Why are you so obsessed with your butt?" she asked.

"I'm not obsessed."

"I say I want to marry you and all you can talk about is your ass!"

"Shh! You want everyone to hear?"

"At this point, I'm not sure I care!"

I could see it now. We were becoming my sister and brother-in-law, or worse, Morgan and Fran. We were bickering like every married couple I knew. Everything between Ellie and me had been fine. Why did we have to ruin it with a wedding?

CHAPTER TWENTY-NINE

"Guess Who's Coming to the Cape?"

We got into bed, and no one said anything for a while. But I could tell by her breathing that she wasn't asleep.

"If you don't want to do this you don't have to," Ellie finally said.

"Why?"

"Who surprises someone with a wedding? I guess I thought if you didn't know by now, you'd never know." She sighed painfully. "I'm afraid you're going to look back on this as something else I controlled, and you'll hate me."

"I don't hate you," I whispered, giving her a soft kiss on the cheek. "I just thought I'd have more time to get used to the idea."

"I'm calling it off." She rolled over. Her back to me felt like a slap in the face.

"What! Don't! I want to go through with it."

"See how you said that? 'Go through with it,' like you're having a gallbladder operation." She turned, staring up at the ceiling. "I wanted this to be a happy memory we'd always have.

Now it's just gotten all gross and weird." A tear slid down her cheek. I could see it glisten in the moonlight.

"I'm sorry. Don't cry. Nothing's gross." I wiped away her tear and kissed her cheek over and over, until she turned her face. She kissed me, her velvety lips moving over mine as gentle caresses became more intense. Her hands slid under my shirt and we turned carefully, trying to quiet the squeaks of the bed, so no one could hear. Looking at her sad eyes in the moonlight, I stroked her hair and told her everything would be all right.

"Really?" Ellie whispered.

"Really." Moments passed, as the curtains blew. We couldn't even hear the ocean sounds in the distance.

At three in the morning, Ellie shook me awake. "I can't sleep! It's the damn waves! Constantly crashing. Jesus! They're too loud!"

I was half in a dream where a mystery woman was about to kiss me, though I'd never tell Ellie that. I drew her close, touched her hair and mumbled something about ignoring the waves, which later I found weird, because most people enjoy the sound of them. It's what you come to the Cape for.

"Just close your eyes," I said, "and think about what you want to wear to our wedding."

Wedding. The word felt clumsy and awkward on my tongue. Was it because it reminded me that she'd been married to a man? I didn't know where all of the weird feelings came from, but they were there.

* * *

The next morning I choked on my waffle.

"What? When is *she* coming?" I cried.

"Tomorrow," Mom said matter-of-factly. "Well, you wouldn't dream of doing this without your aunt Rita. She lives for this kind of thing."

"But she doesn't *know*…you know."

"It doesn't matter. When she heard her second niece was getting married, she said she wouldn't miss it for the world."

"That's because she thinks I'm marrying a man!" I yelled. "She's like eighty or ninety, and she watches Fox News. I'm screwed."

"We'll clear things up when she gets here. And she's only ten years older than I am, so that would make her…" Mom was doing air math, but it wasn't her strong suit. "Early seventyish."

"She's going to lecture me on going vegan again." I held my head. I couldn't eat. My stomach tumbled. I must have looked paler than usual with shoulders caving in. Aunt Rita and I had nothing in common. She always talked about growing up in 1950s Miami, getting candy for a nickel. She wore dresses voluntarily. Then she mentioned all the gays crowding into South Beach and showing their butts in thongs and how inappropriate that "lifestyle" was.

This was a nightmare.

Mom continued, "I'm picking her up in Boston. It'll be a drive, but I thought Nathan could help me navigate. I get so lost in Boston. If you take a wrong turn, you're immediately in a tunnel that goes on for miles, and when you come out, you're in New Jersey."

This couldn't get any worse. But if life has taught me anything, it's never to say that things couldn't get worse. They always can. Maybe in ways you never imagined—but they will get worse.

And they did. Shortly after breakfast, an older man with a white goatee, who was dressed in white from head to toe, straight out of the Civil War, appeared in the doorway.

"Dad?" Nathan slapped him on the back. So this was Owen Hutchins, Nathan's father and the richest man in Augusta, Georgia. I'd heard stories about him, but almost didn't believe he was real.

Mr. Hutchins removed his hat, unveiling his shiny, balding head. His face reminded me a little of Colonel Sanders. He winked at Joanne and said in a thick Southern accent, "I came just in case we got us a runner." He looked at his son.

Joanne smiled and nodded. "Thanks, but so far he's doing okay. Come on, sit down. Have some breakfast."

The deck was alive with breakfast food and odd conversation. Mr. Hutchins had changed into a pair of shorts he thought were in style and a Hawaiian shirt that was louder than his booming voice.

"So where are the gays!" he exclaimed, looking around.

Joanne was embarrassed. "This is my sister, Sydney, and her partner, Ellie."

We dutifully shook his hand.

"Y'all don't look it," he smiled, glancing us up and down. I believe he thought he was giving us a compliment.

"Well, I keep my tool belt in the car." I couldn't resist.

"Hey now, that's funny." He slapped me on the back. "You gals ever been down South?"

"I'm from Florida," I told him.

"No kiddin'. Whereabouts?"

"Orlando."

He seemed confused.

"Same as Joanne," I explained.

"I told you Joanne was from Florida," Nathan said, pouring his dad's coffee.

"I'm an old fart," Mr. Hutchins retorted. "You expect me to remember anything? Why you think I got other people runnin' my businesses? I need to retire." He looked out at the ocean with frustration in his eyes.

Years of wrinkles from the Southern sun and lines of stress from meetings and conference calls had left their mark all over what was once a handsome young man's face. I marveled at him for a moment—first, because he was willing to attend a lesbian wedding in order to help his son with his phobia, and second, because he'd lived in the same town his whole life.

I'd lived in many cities all over the country. I used to joke that I was working on getting a driver's license from every state. But the truth was, I'd followed different girlfriends to the places where they needed or wanted to be. My first girlfriend's job transferred her to Ohio, so I immediately bought a Cincinnati Bengals hoodie. Then another had a love of the great outdoors and the Old West, so the next thing I knew I was wearing a

Denver Broncos hoodie. Now I had a New England Patriots hoodie. I've been keeping the NFL successful for many years. But I wondered—had I molded myself to fit into the lives of each girlfriend? Was I doing the same with Ellie? No, this time it was different. It may have started out that way, with the New England Patriots bumper sticker, but as I'd gotten to know Megan and Matthew and remembered how much Ellie encouraged me with my work and my own identity—this time I knew it was real. I was no longer the refugee, the lost girl, traveling from city to city, trying to find herself in every skyline.

Later I'd learn that Mr. Hutchins was on his way to meet a woman in Nova Scotia and, realizing his son Nathan was here, decided to land his private plane for a few days first. He'd also invited Nathan's older brother, Harry. Mr. Hutchins thought his eldest son had never married because he was gay. When he'd gotten wind of the rumor that Bryan most likely was gay as well, he dialed up his son and had him flown in immediately.

Harry stood at the door, a distinguished-looking fortysomething with a strong build and tanned legs that ended in leather sandals. He held a bag and looked somewhat confused, as if he didn't really know what he was doing here.

"Hi." I gave him a hug. The last time I'd seen him was at Joanne's wedding.

Mr. Hutchins slapped Harry on the back and led him inside. "Harry, my boy, you're going to witness a lesbian wedding!"

Ellie and I cringed. We'd hoped to keep this an intimate event, not feel like we were in a fishbowl. It was becoming quite a tank now.

"Oh, how nice," Harry replied. What else was he going to say?

"I want you to sit right down there and have some waffles." Mr. Hutchins pointed to the space beside Bryan.

Ellie chuckled, realizing what was going on.

Joanne came out of the bedroom and seemed a little startled to see Harry.

"Hi, Harry." She set a bag down.

Harry stood up and gave her a quick, stiff hug.

"It's been forever," she said.

"Yeah. It has." He glanced away and took his seat beside Bryan again.

I wondered. Joanne had done some theater years ago, and she kept falling for gay co-stars. I thought maybe she'd fallen for Harry a long time ago but never told anyone. I'd have to get the scoop later.

"Here." Bryan slid two waffles off his plate. "They're whole wheat but sweet, not with that nasty aftertaste. I'm Bryan." He extended his hand.

"Harry." The disoriented brother looked around and when Nathan came out of the other bedroom, he immediately scrunched his brow at his dad.

"Hey," Nathan called to his brother. "What's up, Dad?" he asked.

"Oh, well, you know. We were on our way to Nova Scotia." Mr. Hutchins cleared his throat.

"*You* were," Harry muttered, drowning his waffles in syrup.

Bryan's eyes widened in disgust. "You might as well just slap the cellulite on your ass," he said.

Harry self-consciously set down the syrup.

CHAPTER THIRTY

"Lions and Tigers and…Aunt Rita!"

"I'm sorry," Ellie said as we walked down Commercial Street. Luckily everyone else had hung out at the pool, so we could be alone to shop and argue. "I didn't know about your aunt. When I told your mother, she said her sister would want to come, so I assumed she was cool."

"Aunt Rita is the opposite of cool. She's one of those women who says things like, 'You should act like a lady.'"

"Oh God." Then Ellie gave me an optimistic squeeze. "We won't let her ruin our day, okay?"

"Okay." I nodded.

Ellie had a reassuring smile that calmed me like gently falling rain. Of course, I mean a steady rain, not the beginning of a violent storm. That was my ex-girlfriend.

And she had such determination, so much beauty that she couldn't even see in herself. When I looked at her, I still had to catch my breath sometimes.

I managed a smile too. "How much worse could it be than a guy who's a hundred screaming, 'Where are the gays?'" We laughed until tears ran down our faces.

"I hope we'll look back at this and laugh," Ellie finally said. Then she got a strange expression. "That Mr. Hutchins is crazy."

"In which way?" I laughed.

"Well, it's obvious he's trying to set up my brother with Harry. But it's not like mating pandas. You put two of what you think are the same kind in a cage and they'll go for it. Besides, I think Bryan has a small crush on your brother-in-law."

"That's too bad," I replied.

"I know. He's like I used to be with straight women. It's a dead-end street."

Then she held my hand, and all of the drama floated away.

I saw the street laid out before us as we looked for a place to find our wedding attire. Unlike the day before with all the commotion, I could really take it all in.

In Provincetown everything that didn't make sense out in the real world made sense all mixed up together—straight, gay and undecided; every language around the globe; people with no fashion sense whatsoever mixed with those whose life was all about fashion; families and flamers; dog people and cat people silently duking it out in the park, trying to prove why their pet was better; and those still trying to answer the age-old question, lipstick lesbian versus leather-studded butch or neither—all while dodging kamikaze bicyclists determined to take out a small child or pet, like targets in a video game.

It was pure magic.

"I can't think of a place I'd rather do this," I told Ellie, my eyes tearing up. There was a Jimmy Somerville song playing in my head and it reached a crescendo that made me burst inside.

"Okay, get a hold of yourself." She wiped my eyes and looked around.

I held her hand in midair. "Nobody cares," I reminded her. There was a guy in an orange wig jumping on a pogo stick. "I'm having a moment here!"

After hours of being distracted by raunchy greeting cards and T-shirts that said "Cape Cod," we finally found what we wanted to wear to fit the occasion and still make us feel like ourselves. It was so obvious; it was pure inspiration.

The purple sunset peeked through our car windows as we drove back.

"Now I know why you packed so much food. And glassware."

"Yeah." She looked distractedly out the window at the glassy water of Truro Beach. Something was on her mind. "I'm surprised you never told your aunt. You've been out so long, I figured everybody knew."

Suddenly the serenity of sunset and the magic of Provincetown dissolved with a few small seagulls in the rearview mirror.

The truth was, there were people I chose to tell or not to tell, the criteria for which I'd detailed in my blog. Aunt Rita was on the "No Way in Hell" list. Some of my old friends from my small central Florida hometown were also on the list, though I did take a chance with a few of them occasionally and was often surprised by their reactions. Some I'd thought would start waving a Bible at me were the ones who said, "Good for you. It had to suck being in the closet." Wow.

Then, of course, were the ones who seemed like your friend, who seemed comfortable with who you are and your gay friends—until you find out they've been squirming under their skin the whole time. That was Debra. Luckily, she wasn't a surprise guest here.

"You'll be coming out for the rest of your life, Ellie."

She glanced at me, driving us back to the cottage. I knew it wasn't what she wanted to hear, but it was one part of being gay that would never be easy. Every time you started a new job and the conversation in the breakroom would go from business to what you did last night—you'd automatically know who was married to whom, who steals the covers in bed, things you didn't want to know. Then they'd all look at you. The question was always loud in the long, quiet pause. Is she asexual? Someone who doesn't have sex, like a Muppet? You'd be amazed how a topic people say they don't want shoved down their throats comes up constantly among *them*, even when you just go into the breakroom to innocently get your bologna sandwich. The truth is, everything gets back to sex, who's doing it how much, with whom. It's what people are most interested in no matter what they say.

"So how do you tell people?" Ellie asked. "I'm still a newbie."

"Don't call yourself that. Any woman with the guts to leave a marriage to live honestly is no newbie. You're braver than I am."

"But you were always out at work."

"Yeah. It gets a little easier, but not much. There's always that moment when your heart starts thumping hard in your chest, wondering what the reactions will be. And I don't mean what they'll say, because usually they'll always say something nice. It's what they're really thinking that you wonder about. There could be not one person you'd ever consider sleeping with where you work, but you worry if all the women now think you want them. I never do the dramatic, 'I'm gay' announcement. I try to make it no big deal, so they won't. I'd say, 'Oh, yeah, my partner and I took a trip there, and *she* got seasick.' See? It gets across, you know?"

Ellie smiled proudly at me. In those moments I could feel an admiration for me, whether or not deserved. But I could still feel it.

"When did you know?" she asked.

It was a long story, and the drive back to Truro wasn't long enough to tell it. The truth was, I'd known I was gay when I was in kindergarten, even if I didn't have the words for it. The teacher asked us to sit in a circle, and Bobby Goolsby kept trying to hold my hand. But I was trying to hold Katie Johnson's hand instead. That should have been clue number one. Katie was a dead ringer for Olivia Newton-John and I followed her everywhere, even scooting my chair closer to hers at snack time.

When I reached my teens, I had a new idol—Boy George. I watched Culture Club videos over and over again.

One afternoon, Dad looked up from his paper and saw the video. "Is that a man or a woman?" he asked.

"A man, duh. Geez."

Dad was horrified. "You like him?"

"He's beautiful!" I gushed. I figured I would definitely have to marry a man who wore eyeliner.

"Uh," Dad sighed. "I'm scared to see who you're going to bring home."

Years later, we laughed at that, although I still think he was uncomfortable with the whole thing.

I wished he could be here now to see that my life turned out okay, to see Ellie, to see how beautiful she was, how beautiful our life could be together.

CHAPTER THIRTY-ONE

"Straight People in Their Natural Habitat"

We stopped by the pool before going back to the house. Everyone was still there, talking at tables, kids splashing in the pool, and some in the Jacuzzi.

Bryan leapt out of the Jacuzzi and sat on the edge, whether it was to show off his pecs to Harry or free himself from the choking clouds of heat.

"So, real estate…" he kept repeating. I could hear echoes of their conversation.

"Not residential," Harry corrected. "I like to buy office buildings and resell them."

"Fascinating." Bryan was clearly not fascinated. He turned and watched Nathan, who was busy arguing with Joanne at a nearby table.

"I think he's doin' just fine!" Nathan's voice echoed throughout the pool house, making the towel attendant jump.

"He's too young." Then Joanne wanted me for backup. "Don't you think Tayler's too young to be in the pool without an adult? I think Nathan should go in there."

"He's had swimming lessons," Nathan added, trying to make his case stronger.

"I don't know." I took the easy way out. Then neither one would hate me at my wedding.

Nathan glanced at Joanne, and her look was all he needed to see. So he jumped up and went to the three-foot side of the pool to help his younger son kick.

Mom dangled her legs over the edge as she'd always done. She'd had an uncle who was struck by lightning in a bathtub, so she never trusted water. It's a wonder she ever went in the shower.

"I can't believe we have to fight over something so obvious." Joanne shook her head and flipped a page from a magazine she wasn't reading.

"You have great hair," Harry told Bryan.

Those of us who heard immediately turned to watch the soap opera.

"Thanks." Bryan ran his hand through it, definitely the mating sign of the gay male.

"Is Nathan close with his brother?" I asked Joanne.

"Not really. He never visits."

"Huh." I tried to figure out what the schism might be. Brothers were often competitive, but it seemed as though they were both successful. "Wonder why."

It wouldn't take long to find the answer. Amidst the bubbles and fog of the Jacuzzi, I heard Harry say, "Uh, Bryan, you seem really nice. But I'm not gay."

Bryan slid back into the water. "I'm not gay, either."

"Oh," Harry laughed. "For some reason I thought…"

"You know, I get that sometimes. I don't know why. I just haven't met the right one yet."

"Me neither." Harry laughed heartily, much like his dad.

Mr. Hutchins, who was obviously hard of hearing, came over to the hot tub. "Seems you two are getting along nicely."

"Dad," Harry said. "You didn't drag me up here because you think…Do you think I'm gay?"

"Well, son, I didn't want you to think it would change anything between us if you were a fudge guy."

"What?"

Mr. Hutchins stumbled over his words. "I heard some expression…now what was it? 'Fudge…'"

"'Fudge packer'?" Bryan bristled.

"Yeah, somethin' like that."

"That's a very derogatory term," Bryan said. Noticing their stares, he added, "I have a few friends."

"I'm not gay, Dad. I just have…bad luck." Harry glanced at Joanne, and all at once I knew. He'd had a crush on *her*. That was why he wasn't close to his brother!

I could see it all in that one glance where he seemed to look at her and at nothing at the same time.

"Did you ever like Harry?" I asked her later.

"No. A long time ago a group of us went to happy hour at that little bar, you know, Later, Gator. He introduced himself, but I don't remember a lot. I was too interested in his brother." She watched Nathan in the pool, remembering.

In a matter of seconds, Harry was out of the Jacuzzi, wiping off his trim body with a towel. Bryan hardly noticed; he was too busy watching Nathan with his son. All around I could see nothing but heartbreak. It struck me how the stars really have to line up just right for your biggest dream to come true.

Then I glanced at Penny, who had told me she was now doing a hundred laps a day in the pool. She was on number eighty-seven, just kicking and splashing back and forth. It seemed kind of boring. But that's how she was getting fit to meet her next possible star. I secretly hoped things would line up just right for her.

"It's okay, Dad," Harry said. "I know you meant well." He held up his hand to halt any further conversation. He had a kind face and a quiet way about him. Mr. Hutchins said a few words to him I couldn't hear. That night Harry took a private jet back to Georgia. He'd probably come up to see Joanne one more time before trying to move on. I'd later hear that was his intention.

But Bryan refused to say he was gay. Ellie's parents, who were both deceased, weren't going to pass judgment on him like my Aunt Rita. He really had nothing to lose. So maybe he just didn't like himself. He was a puzzle I wanted to figure out, although I thought I already had it solved.

Later that night, Nathan seemed right at home grilling steaks. There was an unspoken rule among straight people—the guy grills, the woman cooks.

"What did you get at the store?" Nathan asked.

"I hope Ellie got the T-shirt I wanted," Bryan said. "The light blue one that says 'Straight but Not Narrow.'"

"Uh, I think she did," I stammered. "This one's a surprise." I raised my bag secretively.

Cabbot tugged at my shorts. "Two women can't get married."

"Hush, Cab!" Nathan yelled.

"Who told you that?" I said, putting the bags down. I already knew the answer to the question.

Mom was silently chomping on a bag of chips, watching the drama play out nervously.

"You just can't," Cabbot said.

"Yes, we can." I stood tall, silently cursing my sister and brother-in-law for raising my nephews in a conservative neighborhood where they never saw anything different.

"Damn right." Bryan raised his glass. "If Kelly Ripa can have her own talk show, anyone can get married!"

"I've already told them there are different kinds of couples," Joanne insisted. "They just haven't seen…that…a lot."

"Of course not." I crossed my arms.

"The hell they haven't," Mr. Hutchins chimed in. "You can't turn on the news without hearing about the gays."

"Mr. Hutchins," I began in my polite-but-not-really-polite voice, "it's not *the gays*. That sounds like you're talking about a species—like the Tanzanian Beetle!"

"Calm down," Ellie urged.

"The gays sure are melodramatic," Mr. Hutchins said to my mom. "Though I'd have been proud if Harry had turned out to be, uh, a homo." He never could find the right language, and every time he reached for a word, the wrong one fell from his mouth.

"Give that man some new vowels," Bryan said to his drink.

"I can't calm down!" I shouted. "Cab and Tayler wouldn't see anything but straight bigots in Greenwood Downs." It was a gated place with cookie-cutter houses and a country club. The dues to join the club cost more than my car.

"I think we all need to calm down," Mom said.

"You could do a lot worse than Greenwood Downs," Mr. Hutchins muttered. He was sipping on a whiskey and sort of enjoying the arguing.

"Calm down? Meaning *me*." Furious, I stormed inside. Suddenly I preferred the company of little Tayler, who was talking to a toy truck that he was also slamming against the wall.

I leaned against the counter. What was I doing? Did I really want to celebrate the most important relationship of my life like this? It wasn't Cabbot's fault. His dad had called him a "little heartbreaker" and a "ladies' man" since he was six, just because he talked to some woman in a flower shop. He was sending his sons messages every day, just not knowing it.

Bryan came inside first and put his arm around me. "I know I just met you, but I love you."

"Thanks."

"Even though I don't understand this two-women thing, whatever, I think it's totally cool. And you should do what you want. Just don't drop your pants in public. There's a law against it."

I smiled a little, as he held my chin.

"Made you smile," he sang. "Fuck those straighties out there, except me. I'm a cool straighty."

"You sure about that?" My eyes locked on his.

He became a nervous fruit fly, darting toward the glass door. "Honey, I love me some ladies!"

"See, straight guys don't say that," I called to the door as it closed.

When Bryan left, Mom, the appointed family diplomat, was sent in by the rest of the gang to talk to me.

"It's an emotional time," she said. "Tensions are running high."

"All my life I've been hearing what a pretty girl I am, how I'd make someone a lucky guy. You can't turn on the TV without getting the message you have to be straight."

"And that's *our* fault?" Mom gestured outside.

"I know you grew up in a different world. You always said that. But I'm tired of always being the one who has to understand. For a couple of hours tomorrow, everyone else has to understand. And if you or Aunt Rita or anyone can't do that, then I don't want you to be here!"

"Why are you so angry?"

"Tell me something," I replied. "Will my wedding pictures be overflowing on your tables and walls for your bingo friends to see? Right alongside Joanne's wedding photos?"

"Of course they will!"

"Sorry." I searched the ceiling for the perfect words. I did get angry sometimes. "It's like you and Joanne and Dad were all on one side of this riverbank, and I was on the other side. And nothing I could do or feel or say would get me across the river. You know I used to make myself fantasize about Ricky Schroeder because we were the same age? I'd pretend he was my boyfriend."

"And?"

"Nothing." *Nada, zip.*

"When you were little," Mom said, "you'd play with the other children, but the teacher said you were just as content playing by yourself. You'd go over to this little playhouse and make up stories about all of the people who lived inside. You were different, but different in a good way."

I smiled in spite of myself, and she put her arms around me. With her warm, well-padded arms, Mom was the perfect hugger. And she always smelled like fresh air. And she was here. That *was* important.

"I'm glad you're here," I told her.

Joanne burst in with Cabbot at her side.

"He has something he wants to say." She squeezed his hand tighter.

"I'm sorry," he said on cue. "I'm happy you're getting married." He looked up at Joanne for approval. When she nodded, he ran back outside.

"Close the door all the way!" she screamed. "The bugs!"

Mom looked at the clock. "I'd better get some sleep. Have to get to Boston early."

"Wait," I blurted. "I don't know if that's a good idea."

"Aunt Rita is getting up there, you know. She'll probably be dead this time next year." With that, Mom gave me a goodnight kiss and headed off to bed.

"Huh," I muttered. "Can't argue with that."

Mom could win any disagreement by bringing up death. She used this power in most tricky family situations. I watched her stocky, determined little legs climb the ladder to the loft where she was staying. There was just enough room up there for a twin bed and a nightstand. I didn't even know it was there when we first arrived.

Joanne's face pitied me. I knew she didn't want Aunt Rita there either. She let out a heavy sigh.

"I'm sorry about Cabbot," she said.

"It's okay."

"Aren't you sorry for accusing me of being a bad parent?"

"I didn't accuse you of—"

"Is it my fault we're rich and our neighbors are white Republicans?" She tried to lower her voice with Mom in the loft.

"What's the deal with you?"

"Nothing." She was hunched over the counter like a kicked dog.

"What is it?"

"I love my kids. Don't get me wrong." Her voice was shaking.

I knew what was coming. Every few years Joanne would lament about the dream deferred, some path not taken, although she'd never say exactly where that path led. Until tonight.

"I wanted to be a gymnast. Mom knew it too. But she said you had the fatter thighs. No, wait, *muscular*, she said. So she didn't even consider it."

"It was your father!" Mom protested from above.

"I never took gymnastics," I replied defensively.

"I know." Joanne lowered her voice. "Mom never called the guy who taught it. Then it was too late. He moved out west to raise cattle. And that was it. Then I was too old to even start. They want you when you're like six, you know."

I was speechless. "How come you never told me?"

"It seems so stupid now, me on a balance beam. I get dizzy in elevators. But I loved the way they seemed so free on the floor exercises, leaping and jumping…"

"Huh." I was stunned. "That would explain the poster of Mary Lou Retton in your bedroom. I wondered if you had a crush on her."

Joanne laughed, shaking her head. "Sometimes when I look at Nathan, I think of how different my life would've been if I'd had an Olympic gold medal."

"The Olympics!" I was impressed; I'd always tried to keep my expectations low.

"I didn't tell anyone because what does it matter now?" She wiped her eyes. "And because you'd look at me like that!"

"Like what?"

"The pity pout!"

"No! I think it's cool you had that dream." I reached out to hug her. "You just have to make a new one."

She pulled back abruptly. "Easy for you to say."

"What does *that* mean?"

"You're always one step out the door."

My face flushed. "That's not fair. Uh, twelve-year relationship?"

"How many jobs have you had?"

I put my head down. "Hey, they weren't all my fault."

"I know." Joanne sounded a little tipsy. Then she got really close to my ear and said, "This one's a keeper. Don't run away."

"I'm not running—"

Then Joanne started crying—not crying, gushing. There weren't enough tissues in the house to catch all of the water streaming out of her. "The doctor said…" She couldn't finish.

My mind raced to the worst. She had some appointment and found out she had a disease.

"What?" I grabbed Joanne's shoulders.

"Quiet down there!" Mom leaned over the rail wearing an Elmo nightshirt. On most women her age, it might have looked odd. But not on Mom.

"I'm premenopausal!" Joanne cried harder.

I exhaled, relieved. "That's great! Just think, no more periods!"

She bawled uncontrollably.

"What? You *want* your periods?" In my world, this was a positive thing. I couldn't wait to be premenopausal. Then it hit me. I was talking to the Angel of Death. "Oh, you think you're closer to…"

"Just marching toward death!" she finished.

"I really think you should see a therapist about your death issues."

"Why…doesn't…everyone…have death issues? Doesn't it bother you?"

"I have bigger worries right now, like Aunt Rita."

She looked suddenly sympathetic, wiping her nose. "I had no idea about her. I swear."

Aunt Rita had been dying since she was fifty. She hadn't left Miami in forty years because she always wanted to be close to her doctors and her favorite hospital. The truth was, she'd probably outlive us all.

"I'm sorry." Joanne sniffed. "This isn't about me."

"Maybe some hormone pills will help." I patted her back.

"Oh, that's your answer for everything! Take a pill!"

Nathan came in. "So, Sydney, how you liking the violent mood swings?"

"What?" I was a little afraid.

"She'll be fine." He winked at me reassuringly and hugged Joanne until she could breathe normally again.

That was another thing about living so far away. I didn't know what was going on, and I wasn't the one who could help her like I used to. How was I to know she was in the midst of a hormonal tornado? Only Nathan knew what to do. It made me a little sad.

CHAPTER THIRTY-TWO

"Shut Up, Fran"

The doorbell rang, and Joanne pulled herself together in record time. She dabbed at her pink, swollen eyes and donned a plastic smile.

It was Morgan and Fran. They looked soggy and tired, but it wasn't raining out. I noticed the kayak on top of their car, which they took everywhere. They had moved from *Granolas Birkenstockius* to *Lesbius Action-Figurious* or something like that. Whenever we called, they were out hiking, biking or fighting off bears in the woods.

"Shut up, Fran," Morgan spat as soon as I opened the door. I think I startled them; they weren't ready to come in yet.

"Oh, hi," Morgan said, and then came the flurry of hugs.

"We're here for the big day," she announced robustly. "It's about damn time!" She scanned the place. "You must be the sister. You guys don't look a thing alike." She hugged Joanne so hard I thought I heard a bone crack.

"You're wet," I said.

"We snuck in a kayak ride," Fran said apologetically. "Morgan wanted to stop on the way or we would've been here sooner."

"Will you let it go?" Morgan barked.

"We missed dinner, I bet!" Fran hollered. Her eyes pleaded with me. She was wiry like a bird but could eat more than all of us.

"No, there's more out back," Nathan replied.

"I'm really glad you guys are here." I made all the introductions. "Joanne, Morgan and Fran. Ellie's out back, and Mom went to bed."

Then Mom, now with a green facial mask, leaned over the railing. "I'm not asleep. Nice to see you!" She waved.

"Hey, Ms. G," Morgan called, not the least bit rattled by Mom's appearance.

I took them in with one glance and imagined how Aunt Rita and Mr. Hutchins would see them—not as the loyal friends who left their horsefly-ridden barn house to be with us whenever we needed them or to come and pick apples with us last year just because it was fall and it seemed like the thing to do. No, they'd be squinting behind their trifocals, trying to figure out whether they were girls or boys. And Aunt Rita would say it aloud too. She might even call Morgan "sir" or something awful like that. They came all this way only to get their feelings hurt. I couldn't bear to think about it. I was worried. My stomach churned. It was a nightmare. I'd beg Ellie to call it all off if I didn't think it would kill her.

When they went outside to see Ellie, I gave Joanne a hug.

"Things will get better."

"What things?"

"The things you were crying about a second ago?"

"Oh, it's okay." Joanne waved me away, not wanting to share her pain in front of new people.

Ellie came in. "You joining the party?"

"Yeah." I was confused and worried. People were going to collide here, people who should never be in the same space under any circumstances.

Mr. Hutchins came in. "Nature calls," he announced.

He was followed by Bryan, who was getting more drinks.

"So you're not gay?" Mr. Hutchins repeated.

Bryan drifted into the kitchen. "Oh, no. I love the ladies. Love breasts and thighs…"

Mr. Hutchins squinted. "Are you talkin' about women or a bucket of chicken? All of a sudden, I'm hungry again." He laughed to himself as he made his way to the bathroom.

Outside, a storm was blowing in. *How appropriate.*

Everyone except Mom had settled in on lounge chairs. Bugs flew all around me, and I kept waving them away. I noticed no one else had this problem. Bugs always seemed to come to me; I was the Bug Whisperer.

"What did you do with your dog?" I asked Morgan and Fran. I could never remember its name, only that it was a hyperactive terrier of some sort.

"Had to board him." Morgan gave Fran a sideways glance. There had been an argument over this.

"We can only stay four days," Fran said. "I don't want him to get kettle cough."

"You mean *kennel*," Morgan corrected.

"Whatever."

"You know how to get to Logan?" Joanne asked Nathan.

"I'll figure it out." His calmness irritated her.

"It's great to see y'all again," Penny told Morgan and Fran.

"What is it with men and directions!" Joanne exclaimed.

"He can use my GPS," Ellie said.

"If he wants to go to Connecticut!" I shouted. "It doesn't work. When are you going to admit that it doesn't work?"

"Okay, blow my head off," Ellie mumbled. I'd done it. I could tell. She was getting her pouty lip.

"Sorry," I said. On second thought, maybe it wouldn't have been such a bad idea if Aunt Rita ended up in Connecticut. She'd be more at home there.

"Our GPS works," Fran offered.

"Shut up, Fran." Morgan crossed her arms.

"Say that to me one more time and I'm moving out!" Her spiked hair stood higher if that was possible.

"It's set to go back to Vermont. I don't know how to reset it."

"Really?" Fran was incredulous. "If you didn't insist on kayaking up and down the Eastern Seaboard, it might not be covered in rust."

"That's not why it doesn't work."

"I don't care!" Fran crossed her arms, unwilling to hear the exact technical cause of the malfunction.

"Whatever happened to maps?" I asked, trying to lighten the mood.

Everyone stared at me like I'd taken all my clothes off.

"I have trouble reading them," Morgan said. "All the little lines. I need two pairs of glasses to see the back roads."

Mr. Hutchins had returned from the bathroom.

"I got one of those larger print atlases," Mr. Hutchins replied, turning to Morgan and Fran. "Are y'all gay too?"

Everyone held their breath with awkward smiles.

"Uh, yeah," Morgan answered, shifting in her seat.

I stared intensely at her, trying to silently apologize. "Mr. Hutchins is Nathan's dad. We didn't know he was…coming."

She nodded, immediately understanding. "So what do you do?" Morgan asked comfortably.

"I'm a businessman. I own most of Augusta." He grinned broadly, taking a few chips. "What about yourself? I can't picture what a…young lady like yourself would be doing."

"I work for the post office," Morgan declared.

"Well, good for you. Yeah, that's a good thing. We need y'all. Can you get 'em to quit raisin' the price of stamps?"

"I'll see what I can do." Morgan smirked and gulped her drink. I could tell she disliked him.

Then he turned his attention to Fran. "How did you get your hair like that? Looks like you been plugged into a socket."

"Dad, come on," Nathan interrupted. Then to Fran, "He likes to joke."

"It was lightning actually," Fran replied. "It's never been the same since."

I smiled at Fran, so grateful for her warmth and humor. We certainly needed it tonight.

The waves had begun crashing harder, and the sky started to spit on us and the steak. As we took the party inside, I heard my therapist's words echoing in my head: "Breathe. You can't let worry in when you focus on your breathing."

Sometimes she was right.

CHAPTER THIRTY-THREE

"Ring Ring"

The next morning, I popped Tums and Xanax.

Ellie was like a little kid, excited to show me a secret. She pulled out a shopping bag from the closet and took out not one, but two boxes. I was confused.

Inside the box was a silver ring with two garnet stones embedded in the band. Garnet was my favorite stone, and Ellie knew that I didn't like rings with fat, protruding stones that can catch on your clothes or moving cars.

Before I could say anything, she opened the other box with an identical ring inside.

"I know how you feel about ring shopping," she said. "I wanted them to match."

I stared at them. "You did everything."

"Is that bad?" Her eyes were questioning and suddenly a little scared. "Is this a good surprise or a bad surprise? If you'd rather pick them out together, we could just use them for the wedding, then get different ones…"

I covered her mouth. "It's…great."

When your life is normal, so to speak, you tend to react to situations and events in a so-called normal way. But when you don't have a point of reference for the event taking place before you, you're kind of lost and confused and you don't react the way you're "supposed" to.

"We're not a man and a woman," I said carefully. "They have all these traditions, rules...the guy getting down on one knee, you know."

Ellie was already on the floor with me, so she lifted a knee. "Will you marry me?"

"Who said you were a guy?"

We laughed.

"It's just there are all these things, about rings, cakes, brides and grooms. I don't know what I'm supposed to do." I stared helplessly at her.

"Isn't that what you said was a good thing about being gay? You can make your own rules. There's no right or wrong way. Who cares who does what first? I got two women figurines for the cake. Isn't that cool? There's a shop here that sells stuff just like that."

"Oh."

"By the way, do you like the ring?"

I nodded. "A lot. But you knew I would." I smoothed out the carpet.

"What was that tone?" she asked.

"What tone?"

Ellie was vulnerable, a nerve ending of emotions. She leaned forward. "There was a tone. You do think I'm controlling everything."

"Well, no, just that I haven't had a say about the cake, the rings, the place, even the wedding itself."

"You do resent me!"

"No. You picked the same things I would have. And you're right. I have trouble doing more than two things at a time, so I doubt I could've pulled this off."

Her face fell to her knees. "I didn't do this because I don't think you're capable. I thought we felt the same about each other, and I wanted to be romantic for once in my life and surprise you."

"What do you mean, for once in your life?"

"Come on. I've ruined more romantic moments. You've told me! The first time you kissed me, I laughed."

"Yeah." I remembered.

"And the time you kissed my neck and I was watching TV over your shoulder and said that *House Hunters* was going to Costa Rica."

"Yeah, that was…yeah."

The door swung open. Mom, always a morning person, announced breakfast a little too cheerfully. "It's the big day!" she proclaimed.

So we came out into the living area, sporting our matching rings, and everyone applauded. I guess that's as normal as any reaction to the marriage of two women. Unbeknownst to them, I grew up in the same homophobic culture they did. And I felt strange. I admit it. It seemed like we were doing something totally wrong or, at the very least, weird. As far as I knew, we were just supposed to live together until we died.

We joined the others at the table. I had a thin piece of toast for breakfast.

Meanwhile, Nathan brought in grilled sausage and tried to slide it onto everyone's plates. He loved breakfast, especially breakfast meats. Ironically, my sister despised breakfast because it reminded her of going to school and the time she had a stack of pancakes and threw up on the school bus. This morning, she wandered out in her bathrobe, took one look at the sausages he was pushing and groaned, "Ugh, vomit."

"And you won't be having any," Nathan said casually, immediately retracting the offending spatula.

I held up my hand to show off my ring. Joanne's opinion was the most important. She took my finger and studied it. "Beautiful," she said. "It's very you."

Then she looked around. "Where's your dad?"

Nathan said, "He's staying a few places down, near Morgan and Fran's cottage."

"Oh, right. Well, good, everyone has a place." Joanne was so tense her shoulders were up near her ears.

Penny knocked tentatively on the door that was already open.

"Who keeps leaving the door unlocked?" Mom demanded. The mystery of where I'd gotten my OCD had been solved.

"I was hopin' I could join y'all for breakfast." Penny looked like she'd literally just rolled out of bed. "I can't do anything in that shack without touching a wall. It's smaller than my apartment!"

It was a shame. The sweet Penny I knew and loved would be cranky today. I had learned this from living with her. Without sleep, she would morph into a Southern Godzilla.

"Come on." Ellie touched my knee and nodded toward the beach.

"We'll be right back," I called, feeling rude, as if I had to keep everyone entertained.

We walked that morning for what seemed like miles but wasn't really that far, along the shore, looking out at the unusually gentle ocean and a lazy sunrise that I rarely got up early enough to see. Aside from sharp rocks shredding the bottoms of my feet, I felt a certain peace and comfort with my hand in Ellie's, as I always had. We didn't talk, especially not about the evening's event, and I felt a real happiness in the quietness.

"Remember when we watched *The Horse Whisperer* the other night?" I asked.

She nodded.

"And I was crying so much I used all the Kleenex," I continued. "Well, I was thinking…if I can't write something that good, that makes people feel what that story makes me feel…then there's no point in being a writer."

"You can do that," Ellie said without hesitation.

"Why are you so sure? Because you're totally blinded by your lust and admiration for me?"

She kicked some freezing water at me. "You know I don't like to read," she said finally.

"Yeah," I muttered ironically.

"You gave me your manuscript, and I finished it in one night. All two hundred pages."

"Yeah, well why can't you be a publisher?" I joked. She slid her hand back in mine, and all was right again. It amazed me the power she had to make the world rotate on its axis again just when I thought we were headed toward a black hole. Ellie didn't know it, but she could do things like that.

Back on the deck, Joanne was staring out at the motionless sea.

"Hey." I put my hand on her shoulder.

"Oh hey." She turned around. "I was meaning to talk to you before, you know."

"Sure." Suddenly I was transported to Tampa when we had our last talk as single sisters just before her wedding. I'd felt sad, like it was the end of a major chapter of our lives, but a necessary change at the same time.

"I want you to know something," Joanne said. "I know you hear me screaming at the kids and always looking for their fruit snacks so they won't get bored. It seems chaotic to you. But sometimes I look at their faces and think, 'Wow, we made that.' What I mean is, I wouldn't trade anything. And yeah, I was going through this phase where I didn't want Nathan to touch me, but I'm past that now."

"Good." I didn't know how to take back my wide eyes. "Well, I can tell there's real love between you, even now."

"Yeah?"

"Oh, yeah," I said. "Just the way he knows how to calm you down when you're having a hormonal crisis or how not to ever give you breakfast. He just knows. That's love." I smiled at her, and there was that unspoken sister understanding. I was lucky she was here, lucky she always accepted me, and grateful that had never changed.

Later that morning Aunt Rita burst into the cottage and before we knew it, there was a sweet-smelling powder filling every corner of the living room.

"Sydney! Come here!" she hollered in a raspy voice, arms outstretched.

I succumbed to the machine gun kisses she shot across both of my cheeks, then waited for her appraisal. This was the first time in six years that I'd seen her in person, and I was surprised at how much she looked the same. She still bleached her hair, had a small waist but pear-shaped, chunky body and none of the typical lines or age spots I'd expect for someone in her seventies or early eighties. She looked pretty compared to some of my relatives. Dad used to compare me to Aunt Ida, which offended me. He'd say, "What? She was quite a handsome woman in her day."

"Dad," I'd argue. "She has a mustache."

I missed him, especially today. Just thinking of him, I swallowed hard to rid myself of the lump in my throat. He never really approved of my orientation when he was alive. He never said it, but I knew it.

Then I braced myself for the explanation I knew I needed to provide Aunt Rita.

She glanced over at Ellie and reached out. "You must be Ellie," she said gently but with a devilish smile. Then she looked at me. "Your mother told me everything in the car. I'm so glad you found someone before I died."

Then she scooped up Ellie and I watched in awe.

Mom smiled knowingly in the corner.

I could picture my mom and her sister Rita growing up in 1940s and '50s Miami, where every car was aqua and no one had a decent refrigerator or hairstyle. Boys and girls shared straws at malt shops. Beaver Cleaver would never have been gay—even though he hung out with a guy whose nickname, Lumpy, was kind of peculiar. With that history, I just assumed there would be no way Aunt Rita could understand. Even my own mother sobbed when I first told her. She'd been brought up in Catholic school. But after many years, it was not only okay with her, but she'd send me cut-out newspaper articles about gay celebrities or anything having to do with coming out. I'd forgotten how supportive she'd become.

I did wonder, though, about Dad, with his Protestant leanings and his grim face when the subject was raised. When he'd first passed away, I used to wish he'd come to me in a dream and tell me it was all okay. But he never did. I'd see him in weird dreams, walking among irises, which he loved. But he never told me he was okay with me being gay. Mom would say, "Oh, he knows, and he's smiling on you." But that's a thing a mother would say. It's better than, "Oh, I don't know. He probably still thinks you'll burn in hell."

The day Dad died, we were all having lunch together in the sunroom of their house in Fort Lauderdale. It was the house they always wanted, right on a strip of water. We were having pork chops and talking about our dead-end jobs, Joanne and me, and I resented how they told her she didn't have to worry about working because she had Nathan to take care of her. Val was offended because we were seen differently as a couple— and because everything offended Val. Just as I was getting worried about Val ripping the tablecloth off or something along those lines since she was prone to fits of impulsiveness, Dad reached for his forehead. We all stopped talking and watched him holding his head. We watched helplessly as he collapsed forward onto his plate. Just like that. It happened in seconds. One minute he was there, advising us about the stock market, and the next, he was silent, heaped over his potatoes and green linen napkin and other insignificant details that I'd never forget for the rest of my life. It was so sudden it took our breath away. I lost all feeling on one side of my face for about two months. Every time I drove up a ramp, I'd imagine it suddenly collapsing. Every time I went to bed, I imagined not waking up the next day. Suddenly everything became fleeting and random, as his death had seemed. I'd always struggled with my faith, but now it was on major probation. Actually, I didn't feel like I had any left at all.

I was pulled away from my thoughts by Aunt Rita's thundering voice.

"I got shrapnel in my head from the war," she told Ellie, knocking on her skull.

"No," Mom explained quietly to everyone. "She was never in the war. There was an explosion in the textile factory where she worked."

Aunt Rita settled in with a whiskey sour at noon. She locked eyes on poor Ellie, who was too polite to leave the room.

"You know the Great Depression?" Aunt Rita continued. "Pretty bad. Folks jumping out of windows. I was smarter than that. I had the good sense to just become an alcoholic."

Ellie found my eyes, and I could see her surprise behind a cool exterior. We exchanged secret smiles.

Fran and Morgan came in around lunch, both looking tired again.

"Sorry," Fran said. "She dragged me down a bike trail."

"Shut up, Fran!" Morgan pulled leaves out of her hair. "If you had an inner tube around your belly and a cheesecake ass, you might want a little exercise too!"

"Are these the friends?" Aunt Rita finished sucking down another drink and rose unsteadily to greet them. "I'm the aunt who's been around since Jesus. Wanna drink?" She hugged Morgan hard, nearly choking her.

"Good to meet ya," Morgan answered politely.

"Yeah, yeah," Aunt Rita grunted. "I never had a thing for the ladies, although I heard Katherine Hepburn did. She was a cool lady, met her once in a department store. She liked to wear flannel. *A lot*."

Fran grinned warmly. "It's good you could come up all the way from Florida."

"I hate flying," Aunt Rita barked. "Hurling across the sky in a piece of tin. It's suicide. But my niece is worth it." She squeezed my cheeks, then noticed Mom putting out turkey and ham cold cuts for lunch. "You got anything that wasn't slaughtered in a cruel, inhumane way?"

All of our appetites came to a screeching halt.

Just then, Mr. Hutchins burst in, wearing a straw hat that he thought was tropical and a blob of sunscreen on his nose.

"Who's this pretty lady?" he asked, kissing Aunt Rita's hand.

"I'm Rita, from Miami," she replied, suddenly dainty.

"Don't tell me," he continued. "Are you a gay too?"

"No, but my niece is. She played a lot of softball as a child."

"Excuse me?" My face turned crimson, but Ellie grabbed my arm.

"Don't do it," she whispered.

CHAPTER THIRTY-FOUR

"The Ex Marks the Spot"

The doorbell rang and I jumped.

"Are we expecting anyone else?" I asked Ellie with trepidation all over my face.

"No," she said, going to the door. "My sister in Chicago would've been here, but she has jury duty."

When she opened the door, it was Marc, her ex-husband, with Megan and Matthew at his sides. With his smiling eyes and the jolly twinkle that was always in them, at least in the photos I saw, I could sometimes see what Ellie saw in him. He had dangerously thinning blond hair and some gold stubble clinging to his chin, which he kept to look extra manly. He was a testosterone-packed sort of guy. He seemed like the kind of guy you could have a beer with and then spit off a bridge or something equally manly.

"I, uh, offered to bring 'em," he mumbled, his bomber jacket crinkling.

Ellie stood frozen in disbelief. "Of course Greta said yes." She scowled. She knew her neighbor had always had a soft spot for him.

"I was in the area," he continued. "The ride gave us a little time to catch up."

Ellie whisked the kids inside, still staring at Marc. "Excuse me," she told everyone and went outside with him.

"Hey, guys," I welcomed them before Aunt Rita could scare them.

Megan had to be cool no matter what the situation, so she couldn't look too happy doing anything.

"Hey," she grunted.

"Is this your stepdaughter?" Mom asked, coming in for a hug. She hadn't met Ellie's kids before.

"Not exactly," I answered quickly. "Well, not yet, I guess."

I didn't know how much Megan and Matthew knew about the wedding. And Ellie would have killed me if I'd given away a surprise. I really didn't know what to say.

If anyone knew a secret about anything, it was Matthew, the future CIA operative.

"We know," Matthew assured me and hugged my mom.

"It's cool with us," Megan informed me, her mouth turned upward in an almost smile.

Aunt Rita strolled over, smelling like strong whiskey and now with bloodshot eyes. "You two are cute, the spitting image of Sydney!"

"We're not related," I told her.

"Then they look like *her*." She gestured toward Ellie outside and laughed at her own mistake, raising her glass to Nathan for a refill. He glanced at Mom for permission to pour one, and she nodded, overwhelmed.

Meanwhile, I didn't hear the conversation outside, which was gradually irritating me the longer it took place. Don't ask me why. There was no rational reason why each passing minute ticked me off more and more until finally Ellie came back inside. She donned her painted-on smile for the group of anxious onlookers, who pretended to not be watching.

Everyone continued their various conversations; Joanne eyed me curiously, the kids started pulling out their Wii controllers and taking over the TV. I motioned to Ellie to join me out on the deck where we could be alone.

"What took so long?" I asked before we were outside.

"What do you mean?" She closed the slider. I hated it when she acted like she didn't know what I was talking about.

"He flies through town, and all of a sudden, you have so much to catch up on?"

The belching and popping motor of his sports car out front was more annoying than any other sounds I'd heard, even more than screaming babies on a plane.

"He doesn't come by that often, and they are our kids." She always took a defensive position where Marc was concerned. Three years later, it still bothered me.

"He rides through town to spend some quality seconds with his kids?"

Her mouth tightened. "It's kind of a big deal for him to come all the way to the Cape, knowing I was planning to do this."

"Yeah, how big of him."

"What is it, Sydney? Really?"

"I guess when you have low expectations for someone, you're so much more impressed when they do something that would just be considered decent if anyone else did it." My eyes pierced her.

"True. I don't expect much. I never do. Still it was thoughtful to bring them down. He picked them up from Greta's to spend a few hours…"

I kicked away sand on the deck. "Yeah."

"It's always going to be an uneasy relationship with Marc. But he's still the father of my kids!"

"I know!" I shouted. "You never let me forget that! You think I need to be reminded again? Especially today." I laughed bitterly to myself. "On our wedding day."

"You don't want to go through with it."

I took a deep breath, searching for answers in the water. The sun was like diamonds on the ripples. Oceans seemed so spiritual; I always wanted to get important answers whenever I was there. If any place could give me a sign about whether or not I was going in the right direction in my life, it should be the ocean. But I got nothing. Just wave after wave crashed repetitiously, and I wondered if it was symbolic of human beings. We crash on the shore, over and over, expecting something to change. But it never does.

The right woman, the right job—how does anyone ever know? With women, I'd always listened to my heart. With jobs, I listened to my head. Usually, I never regretted the decisions I'd made with my heart, no matter how crazy they may have seemed. But I did regret plenty of decisions made with my head. I guess that was my answer. With Ellie, I was going with my heart but fighting it every step of the way.

"I don't know," I finally said. "Whenever he breezes in, we've changed our plans. Like Christmas Day."

"I know."

"I've seen how hard it is to be a parent. He's their father. Where is he? Where is he ever?" My voice was hoarse.

I could see the pain in her crystal blue eyes. I felt lower than crap for causing her to look that way. But I couldn't help it. Wasn't it too important a day to be anything but honest?

"Wow." She turned away from me. "I didn't realize he had such power to get between us."

"He doesn't," I replied. "It's me. Maybe I'm not strong enough. But the reminders are everywhere. You don't get it."

"I'm not constantly reminding you about him."

I put my hands on her shoulders. "You don't have to."

She couldn't understand. I was reminded that she'd slept with this man every time I saw her kids. Their school pictures lined the walls of our house. Photos of the kids with their dad in each of their bedrooms—I'd pick up the photos from time to time when I was dusting. I'd look at the happy expressions on their faces and realize that I was part of that happiness being broken. I knew our future was different and happy in a new way, but there it was again. The past. It was part of all of them but me. And my past was something they didn't share with me, either. This Marc in the photos, sometimes with a mustache, sometimes without, he was the one who shared these memories that I didn't. Sometimes he was posing at a school award ceremony, proudly, while a much younger Megan I never knew, was holding a math or reading trophy. He was in the soccer game photos, sharing a fiber bar with Ellie, as they watched their children together. And he was sticking bows on Matthew's head during their first Christmas. They were a family.

"I don't mean to drop a bomb on you," Ellie said quietly. "But he told me just now that he's planning to stay in Massachusetts. He's going to settle down, get a steady job and stay near enough to see the kids part of the week. He said the kids are excited."

"So that's what you talked about."

It would have been different if they had just split up the way I did with Văldemort. We didn't have children together. All we shared was a cat. When she turned into someone else, I never had to see her again or put Ellie in a position to see her. But Ellie had children with this man. He would be forever a part of my life, a man I never asked for or invited into my life when I met this beautiful woman online. So the question became, how much was I willing to accept? Could I adapt to this?

Ever since I'd met Ellie, I'd been adapting—from the way she had to load the silverware into the dishwasher to the way we had to shovel snow down a long driveway. This was manual labor I never wanted to experience, much like zip-lining through the Amazon. I had to adapt to waking up at six to help get the kids ready for school. I had to remember who liked crust on their sandwich bread and who didn't while Ellie fought with Matthew, telling him that if he wore shorts to school in thirty-degree weather they'd call Social Services on her. And sometimes all at once everyone would stop arguing to make a face at me to let me know my cat had just made a royal dump in the litter box. All of these details filled up so much of my days for the past three years. I had to adapt. I had to compromise.

But Ellie had had to compromise too. I knew I was neurotic and had enough explosive quirks to light up the sky on the Fourth of July.

But Marc—I suddenly imagined the three of us in bed together. I'd never asked for a relationship with two people. And while he had ridden off to Arizona to fulfill his boyhood fantasies of seeing the West and hitting the open road, he had two children who were growing up without him. Megan was struggling through the turbulent teen years without him. Matthew was starting to watch football games and asking where his dad was. But ever since Ellie divorced Marc, he had abdicated his role as a father or at least it looked like that. When she divorced him, she assured him it was nothing that he'd done; she was, in fact, a lesbian. It wouldn't have been fair to keep him locked in a marriage with a lesbian. But at the time, while he must have been loading his boxes into his beat-up Chevy, I'm sure he wasn't feeling like she was really doing him a favor. He was in pain and needed to get away for a while. But for three years? And he'd so obviously gotten his midlife crisis sports car, to boot.

Then I'd remember the photos in the bedrooms, and I'd think he must have been a great dad back then. So I suppose this was good news, at least for the kids.

I took a deep breath, inhaling the salt and wind. There was one immutable truth—I needed to decide if I could handle this man being part of the landscape of our life together. Marc would always be an awkward presence, reminding me of what had come before. And now he was going to be around every other week.

I looked at Ellie in the raspberry haze of a Cape Cod afternoon, the glow of the sun on her smooth, fair skin. I wanted to touch her cheek, to let her know that everything was going to be all right. But I wasn't sure of that now.

"He'll see them every other week," she said. "If you think about it, it'll give you and me more time to be alone together."

I knew she was trying to make it all okay.

"Ellie, what if you had to see Valerie every week as we transferred our cat from one house to another?"

"Why would you transfer a cat?"

"Sharing custody of the cat. What if we did that and she lived in the same state?"

"How do you share custody of a cat?"

I shoved her. This wasn't a time for jokes.

"It would probably be weird," she admitted.

"Wow," I breathed. "I'd thought about three-ways before, but not this kind."

"Shut up!" She shook her head, refusing to smile.

"I do love you," I said. "I do. It's just getting more complicated."

She threw her hands up in the air. "I've got tons of nice glassware, several pounds of crab and lobster meat, a band and a backyard here that's going to be transformed into a tiki hut party in about three hours. So if you can figure out what you can handle, do you think you could do it in the next three hours?"

"I don't give a crap how many pounds of lobster there are!"

Nathan stepped out on the deck, then went promptly back inside.

"This is a slightly bigger decision than lobster," I continued. "You've just sprung this thing on me, and I'm supposed to get on board quickly, like everything else!"

"Are we back to that?" Her eyes were shiny.

"I don't know. But you're not being fair, telling me how drastically our life is about to change right before we get married."

I could tell by her face she knew exactly what I meant. But she couldn't change it.

"He just told *me*. I wasn't trying to spring anything!" She smiled bitterly to herself. "You know what? I'm going to be right there." Ellie pointed to the shoreline in front of us. "Right there at sunset, ready to marry you for better or worse. I hope you'll be there."

She left me on the deck. The lump in my throat was swelling. I'd made so many mistakes. How could I be sure I wasn't about to make another?

CHAPTER THIRTY-FIVE

"A Rebel, A Loner"

"Whale watching? No, I'd puke." Joanne flipped through brochures at the Lighthouse gift shop. She had wanted to get me out of the cottage for a little while, and I welcomed the opportunity to clear my head. Her heavy Canon hung around her neck and reminded me of Ellie. They had similar perspectives through the lens. If there was a historical house, many would shoot it straight on, but Joanne and Ellie would shoot the old-fashioned iron door or a portion of the uneven wood fence. They seemed to revel in the imperfections, while I always took photos that I hoped would be perfect or I'd photoshop them later.

Joanne and I got to the top of the observatory where you could see for miles in every direction. The sun-kissed marshes, beaches and forests were the stuff of artists, like we'd stepped into a live painting. There was nothing like a Cape Cod afternoon.

After Joanne shot a few pictures from the balcony, she carefully screwed the lens cap back on.

"Are you getting cold feet?" she asked.

"I know I love her." I stuffed my hands into my pockets and let the wind smack my face.

"But you're worried about doing the wrong thing," Joanne said. "Who could blame you after that psycho? And the one before with the anger issues? You were like a loser magnet for a while. It's no wonder you want to be sure."

"Thanks, I think. But it's not that."

"You're sad about leaving Florida?"

"Hell, no," I laughed. "Seriously, I miss you guys. In the winter especially, I feel like I'm in Siberia. That's when I miss you most." I paused. "It's her ex-husband. I'm going to see him a lot more now. I just found out."

"Ugh." She said it all. "So a couple of hours before your wedding you've learned you'll be in a relationship with three people?"

"It doesn't have to be like that." I tried to convince myself if I just focused on Ellie all would be well.

Joanne found another shot, unscrewed the lens cap and started clicking again. "It's gorgeous here," she sighed. "The history, the seasons. I'm sorry about the ex." She put her camera away again. "You've never had a girlfriend who, you know, did it with a guy." Joanne tried to be delicate.

"Not just did it," I corrected. "But loved him. It was hard to get my head around that, but she explained it, and I got it. I'm still getting it, I guess."

"What did she say?" Joanne would always be the protective big sister.

"That something was missing from her marriage, that her life was somehow not whole. She had crushes on girls since she was five."

"That was you!" Joanne exclaimed. "Remember that girl in kindergarten?"

"I try not to," I laughed.

"Mom said you talked about her constantly. It was kind of cute."

"Cute," I repeated. It was funny how parents didn't care about sleepovers with other girls when you're growing up, but boys aren't allowed in your bedroom under any circumstances. If they only knew.

"So you know Marc's not a threat," Joanne said. "Then what's the problem?"

It was a good question. But there was a problem.

"Maybe I just can't be happy without having a problem with something."

"That's a family trait," Joanne responded with a distant gaze.

"Is that why Nathan's in the doghouse?"

She gripped the railing to steady herself. "He's not in the doghouse. I'm just trying to keep the spice in our marriage."

"Oh."

"After ten years, you have to work at it more. I tried all kinds of things. I got *Cosmo* and *Glamour* and *Ladies' Home Journal*. I even stooped to reading those online articles I swear I'd never read: 'Five Things He Won't Tell You He Wishes You'd Do in Bed.' Crap like that."

"And...no spice?"

"A little. I don't know. Maybe it's more about me feeling unfulfilled. I mean, c'mon, I don't want to be one of those rich wives who's so bored she ends up cheating with the pool boy."

"You don't have a pool boy."

"Not yet." Joanne winked in a devilish way. "I still think Nathan's cute. And don't you think the gray around his temples makes him look distinguished?"

"I guess."

"What?" She frowned. "You don't think he's handsome?"

"Yeah, I do. But you have to understand. Ever since I first met him, I'd think he was doing the nasty with my sister. I really don't want to picture it, okay? I'm sure you try not to think of Ellie and me."

Joanne laughed. "I don't know. She's so pretty I might do her."

I slapped her shoulder.

"Is anyone in her family coming besides Bryan?" Joanne asked.

"One sister has jury duty in Chicago, her brother in Napa has a winery to run, and the other sister in Texas thinks she's going to hell for breaking up her family and turning gay." I rolled my eyes. "She was turned by some evil woman."

Joanne put her arm around me. "It must hurt sometimes."

"It hurts all the time. You learn not to think about it all the time though, or you'd end up on antidepressants."

"Are you going through with it? Sydney?"

"I don't want to be anybody's wife."

"Then call yourself something else."

"Maybe." I went down the spiral stairs to the gift shop where Fran and Morgan were hanging out. They must have needed to get out of the cottage too.

"Hey, bride-to-be," Fran joked. She was dancing around in camouflage shorts. "Look, I'm going commando!"

"No, you're not," Morgan said quietly.

"Camouflage pants?" Fran replied.

Morgan pointed to Fran's clothes. "They're *shorts*, and commando is when you don't wear any underwear."

"Eew." Fran suddenly seemed embarrassed. "I thought it was military-type stuff." Then to the mixed crowd in the gift shop she shouted, "I am wearing underwear!"

The lady behind the counter looked relieved.

Morgan scooted us toward the corner. She had some serious news. "Ellie's acting weird," she announced. "We came to lend an ear if you want to purge, you know."

"Madame Zoe could help," Fran chimed in.

"I don't need Madame Zoe," I said. Then, "Who's Madame Zoe?"

"A palm reader right on Commercial Street. She told me when my chakras were out of alignment," Fran said happily.

"What if you just needed an oil change?" I asked. "Oh, come on. It's a joke. You sound like Ariel."

One major rule about some lesbians is that they take their psychics, Tarot readings and astrology very seriously. Once a woman refused to go out with me because she was a Gemini and her moon in Cancer collided with my insensitive Aries ram, making it likely that we'd kill each other within the year, she said.

"Oh," I'd told her. "So I guess going for pizza is out of the question then."

Joanne followed me down the stairs and saw my friends.

"She's under a lot of stress," Joanne said protectively.

"Maybe a pre-wedding massage?" Fran persisted. She was like a constantly enthusiastic Chihuahua who had too much coffee.

"Shut up, Fran," Morgan said. "She doesn't want to be asleep at the ceremony."

"Stop saying that to me, or I'll drop-kick you, I swear!"

"You guys," I laughed. "You do sound like Ariel."

There was a brief silence. Nobody talked a lot about Ariel anymore. She'd met up with some other chakra-loving women who owned some farmland. No one had seen or heard from her in two years. One of the conditions of her new living arrangement was that she get rid of all electronics, including cell phones, I guess. But let's face it. If everything had to be natural, the only way we'd hear from her would be smoke signals, and we'd never read them because we'd just think it was smoke from a chimney. So we feared that Ariel was lost to us but didn't want to open that can of chakras at this time.

"Why did you guys get married?" I asked. "You were already living together."

They were both quiet.

"I don't really know," Fran answered.

"Yeah," Morgan agreed. "We didn't need to simulate a straight ceremony to prove we're committed to each other. I kinda thought not being married gave more meaning to our relationship. But it became legal in Vermont. Everybody got excited. So we said what the hell."

I stared blankly at both of them. The air was sucked right out of my balloon.

"That's it? I thought there was some romantic reason, you know, a *good* reason."

"You dumb ass!" Fran whispered loudly to Morgan. "Did you have to say it like that?"

"First of all, don't call me that." Morgan was miffed, yet again. "I guess it feels more official now. And we have more rights and benefits."

Before I could ask...

"Don't ask me what they are 'cause I'm not sure. One thing I am sure of, it's nice to come home to that same someone you can count on, the one who will always be there." It was Morgan's soft underbelly showing, a rare side reserved for a very few. I was honored.

There were some people who needed to be married, to wake up each morning to someone pouring them coffee. Then there were people like me, more likely to have a TV dinner while watching sitcom reruns and go to bed alone. Maybe I was a loner. I didn't even sleep with my cat after I heard it could cause a disease.

"I'm something you count on?" Fran was about to skewer the soft underbelly. "Like a pair of good shoes or a pet?"

"I never said that!"

While they bickered in the corner, Joanne gave me a hug.

"How long have those two been together?" she asked.

"Ten years," I answered. "Fighting the whole time and Fran always threatening to leave. It works for them."

The sun had begun its slow descent toward the water. I had to know what I was going to do. There wasn't much time left.

CHAPTER THIRTY-SIX

"Riding the Roller Coaster"

White lights strung around the cottage could be seen for miles down the road. I entered beside my sister, noticing the blinding light over the front door too. It reminded me of the time Joanne had convinced me to ride a roller coaster, The Monster of Regret—not the real name, but how I'd always remember it—and we'd walked up the stairs while the loudspeaker woman reminded anyone who was pregnant or had a heart condition not to ride it. At this moment, with each step forward, I felt about as certain as I did back then.

"Where's Ellie?" I panted. "I need to talk to—"

"She's in the bathroom," Mom answered. "Getting ready. Looks like you should too. You don't want to be all sweaty at your wedding."

"We'll be outside!"

"But still." She made a face. "And we're all...dressed. Are you sure you want everyone to be so casual?"

"It's at the beach!" I stormed toward the kitchen, looking for the bar that Bryan had surely set up by now.

I noticed everyone in white shorts and nice tops. Then Bryan joined me in his flip-flops.

"Hey there, pretty," he said. "Do you have something borrowed and something blue?"

"I haven't even thought of that." I cried for Joanne. "See? I'm not ready! I don't have something borrowed or blue!" I downed a shot of vodka. Then another.

"Oh, Lord," Penny said. "She's comin' apart."

In the corner I could see Aunt Rita wiping some sunblock off Mr. Hutchins's nose. "Sun's gone down," she giggled.

Oh God. What if those two were becoming an item? I wondered, then tried to shake off the mental picture.

"Just calm down." Joanne grabbed my arms. "You can wear this." She took off her necklace and strung it around my neck. She fought with the clasp. "It's just so damn tiny."

"Here." Bryan was able to click it in place.

They both stared at me.

"It works," Bryan decided. "Very Rita Hayworth."

"Yeah," Joanne agreed. "Just don't lose it because Nathan got it for me."

I touched the gold thing lying on my chest. Who was I? Whose life was I living? I'd begun asking myself all kinds of strange questions.

"What about something blue?" I was panicking. I took another straight shot of vodka. It warmed my internal organs. I poured another.

"The blue," Bryan replied as if he were reciting poetry, "is the water." He gestured out to the nighttime sea.

"Looks more black to me," I muttered. My head had begun to feel lighter.

Then came the final straw. Nathan opened the back door with spatula in hand.

"Hey," he exclaimed. "I heard you ladies like *seafood!*"

"What!" I shouted.

Fran, Morgan and Penny turned around, concerned, as they viewed the train wreck that was suddenly me.

"That's so typical!" I exploded.

"Sydney…" Joanne tried to stop me, but it was too late. The runaway train was now off the tracks.

"Us ladies? Seafood?" I sneered. "Really, Nathan? Such class. Oh yes, we all know lesbians like fish!" I grabbed my crotch.

"I need my inhaler," Aunt Rita squeaked.

Morgan and Fran cleared their throats. If they were trying to tell me something, I wasn't listening.

"Why don't you just call us beavers, too? Oh yeah, we like us some beaver!" I strutted like a bowlegged cowboy.

Morgan chuckled, and Fran slapped her.

Mom stared at me, her jaw dropped so low you could see her dental work.

"What else do you call us?" I persisted.

Before I could storm out in a grand exit, Nathan held up a shrimp kabob. "I meant the seafood buffet was ready," he said weakly.

That was the last thing I heard as I slammed the door behind me. It was just as well, I rationalized. If I was ever going to consider something as serious as marriage, it would have to be legal in all states and not shared with some who could barely swallow their contempt for the whole thing.

I took the shuttle from Truro into Provincetown. Through the dark window, I pictured Mr. Hutchins's patronizing smile and his "little lady" attitude. I loathed them all. I'd become Godzilla that night. Everything was ugly and wrong. Then there was Aunt Rita, who pretended to be happy for us, but God forbid we talk too much about it or kiss in front of her. I knew they'd all be much more comfortable in Yuppieville with my sister and Nathan hosting them. So I wished everyone would leave. And even more I wished Ellie would never bring it up again. Ellie. I wasn't even sure I wanted to be with her anymore.

* * *

The harsh morning light hit me in the face. I woke up under a dune at Head of the Meadow Beach with sand caked all over my legs and in my underwear. There was an empty thermos beside me of what smelled like strong rum. Then I remembered. I was throwing back rum runners with a gay guy named Joel, and we were talking about how unnatural it was to commit to one person for the rest of your life. At first I thought he was calling me "unnatural" for being gay, and I told him to suck it. Then he took a seat and explained what he meant, and we became fast friends for a few hours.

Then it really hit me. I'd abandoned Ellie, who had probably been standing there at sunset with everyone…waiting. The white lights lining the cottage, the non-gender specific minister from the nondenominational church presiding over a non-ceremony…

It was all my fault! There was no place to put all the guilt welling up inside of me.

"Sydney! Sydney!" The shrieking came from over the hill.

I stood up and saw Mom braving the windy, uphill sand path. She wore a zip-up sweatshirt with a pointed hood and dark sunglasses. She sort of looked like an alien.

I held up my hands in surrender. "Please, don't! I can't handle it."

"I don't care what you can handle! You're going to listen to me!" She took a few more breathless steps, grabbed my shoulders and shook me like a rag doll. "I finally see you with someone who isn't crazy, and you leave her standing at the altar?"

"There was no church."

"You're darn right there wasn't. I raised you to be a good Catholic girl and you couldn't even find a decent church to marry your lesbian lover! How is Jesus going to hear you outside with all that ocean noise?"

"He didn't hear anything anyway."

"Darn right he didn't. Ellie sent Carlissa home." She kept putting her hands on her hips.

"Carlissa?"

"The woman minister. At least I think she was a woman."

"How bad was it? Was Ellie standing alone on the sand?" I couldn't bear the image of her lonely silhouette at sunset. I wanted to shoot myself.

"No," Mom answered, taking a seat beside me in the fluffy dune.

"What do you mean?"

"She didn't even get dressed up. She must've known you weren't coming back."

"Wow." I stared at the tiny grains of sand between my toes. "Really?"

"Yeah, all she had on was this Cape Cod tourist T-shirt."

The lump in my throat settled into my stomach. That was the plan. We were going to wear matching souvenir T-shirts to solve the clothing problem. She *was* dressed. I didn't think I could feel any lower.

"No one understood all the fish references," Mom said.

"Sometimes gay men call us, *women*, fish. It pisses me off."

"Nathan's not gay."

"I know."

"He had shrimp kabobs."

"I know, I know."

"I almost called the police," Mom continued. "But Ellie told me you weren't missing. She told me this was your favorite beach." Moments passed. "Ellie said you'd never get past Marc. I hate to ask, but is Marc an old boyfriend of yours?"

After all these years, I could see Mom still had hope in her eyes, the hope of me getting impregnated by a masculine manly man.

"Her ex-husband," I corrected.

"Oh, right." A long pause followed. "What's the problem?"

"It's complicated. It doesn't make sense."

Mom leaned closer. "It doesn't make sense that your aunt Rita is still alive, but there it is. Life doesn't make sense. So tell me. I deserve to know the truth after driving around this island for hours, finding only sculptures of naked women."

I didn't know what to say.

"You can't just get rid of the kids," Mom said. "They're part of the package."

"Not the kids! Her and me and her ex-husband. It's a little too crowded. You wouldn't understand."

"Oh, wouldn't I?" Mom responded. "When I first met your father he was still pining for his ex-girlfriend from college. Lorraine was her name. Lorraine and her double D's."

"Eew." That mental picture was worth at least five weeks of therapy right there.

"Oh yeah, I had to hear all about Lorraine this and Lorraine that for the first two years of our marriage."

"Seriously?"

"I almost walked out. If we'd had Facebook back then, he would've looked her up. So…Ellie still has the hots for Marc?"

"No."

"Oh, he does for her."

"No."

She eyed me curiously. "So what's the problem?"

"He existed." There, I said it. I slumped back into the sand.

"I did raise a couple of crazies, didn't I?" She sighed.

"I know it's stupid and irrational."

"Yes," she agreed. "Those are the worst kind of problems, because there's no fixing them. Kind of like voices in your head."

"I know it's irrational," I whined.

"I'll just get my oracle from the car and change the past for you," she teased.

"Ha ha."

Mom faced me squarely. "You have to stop this. You're forty-one years old! You're not a child. Stop pouting because things haven't gone exactly as you planned. Welcome to the real world."

I wouldn't correct my age for her. I liked being forty-one again. I tried to sit up a little, but she held me down.

"Sydney," she continued, "you can't just run away whenever things get to be too much for you. Sometimes you have to stay and face it. It's time to stop running away. Now you go back there."

"But—"

"But nothing! You can't change the past," she said. "All you can do is the now. Who is Ellie here for *now*?"

I hung my head. "I'm sorry I wasted everyone's time."

"No you didn't. Joanne and Nathan used the minister to renew their vows on the beach. It was quite romantic. Then everyone had cake. It was strange, though. There were two little women dolls on top of it."

"So Ellie's still waiting for me?" I asked.

Mom thought a moment. "Actually, no. She took the kids and left. Come on back. We have waffles." She waddled back to her car.

I rolled over, face down in the sand. My insides were on fire. What had I done? How stupid could I be? I told Mom I needed some time by myself. I just traced doodles in the sand, feeling numb. Certain the guilt would kill me anyway, I decided to die right there at the beach. No food. No water. Just lie there and die, face down. Then I saw a bike beside me, half buried in the sand, slowly being uncovered like a fossil in the wind. I must have ridden it last night, though I didn't remember.

When I looked up, I saw something farther down the beach. Too afraid of death to kill myself, I got up and went to see what was going on. It looked like some kind of gathering.

When I got closer, I saw that it was a couple of men dressed in tuxedos, sweating like crazy, getting married at sunrise. Local news crews were trying to stay a respectful distance back, but eventually the helicopters started swirling around. I doubt they could even hear their vows with the propeller noise overhead.

Yes, I noticed the irony of helicopters swirling around when I was trying to stay out of the spotlight on this issue. Then I realized something. For so long, I'd tried to keep Ellie and me an "us" and that political issue just a far-off thing I'd heard about on the news. But with all the struggle to keep us as "us," it didn't work. We still found ourselves colliding with that ugly political thing. And that thing was noisy with blue lights and loud propeller noise and wind. It was like the end of the world, only worse.

Crowds had begun to gather in the dunes, watching the couple from a distance. I was dismayed that these guys couldn't celebrate their union in peace. I ran alongside my bicycle, right through the crowd.

"Jellyfish alert!" I called. Watching everyone scatter, I was pleased with myself.

CHAPTER THIRTY-SEVEN

"Unnatural Acts"

"She's not here." Joanne pulled back the bedroom door to prove it.

I scanned our room. The closet was cleaned out, along with the giant cooler.

"And I think Aunt Rita slept with Nathan's dad!" Joanne whispered, like that was the most exciting news of the day.

"Gross. And they call *us* unnatural." I rubbed my head and slumped on the bed. "When did she go?" I asked.

"While Nathan and I were having cake. I tried to tell her you were just insecure and it was nothing personal, but I may have sounded a tad drunk."

The skies opened up. Lightning and blackness and Charlton Heston in a beard appeared overhead. It was over. The world as I'd known it was over.

"I'm such an idiot! I blew it!" I crumpled up on the bed with my hands over my face. "No, wait." I shot back up. "You're the one who always says everything happens for a reason."

Joanne replied, "That's only what I tell myself to keep from feeling like shit."

"It's for the best."

"How can you say that?" she squeaked. "You guys were perfect for each other."

"What the hell happened?" Morgan burst in and assumed her usual aggressively inquisitive stance. Were we at war?

"She needs her space," Joanne said, dripping with irritation and sunblock.

"No, she needs to talk about it," Morgan argued. "I've been taking a class on 'opening up.' At first I thought it was something sexual, but it's about communication, and I kinda like it."

"I'm her sister and I know what she needs!" Joanne pushed Morgan backward. It was definitely war.

"Please stop!" I cried. "Morgan, you're a wonderful, loyal friend, but I need my sister right now."

"Fine. Fran and I got the truck packed up. You want us to haul it out or hang around?"

"I don't know what's going to happen."

"Well, let me tell you something," Morgan shouted. "You guys were my rock couple. If you can't make it there's no hope for me and Fran."

"What're you talking about? You've been together nine years!"

"She's been talking about couples counseling." I hadn't seen Morgan look this frightened since she had to wear a lacy pink dress in her sister's wedding. She'd looked like a bad drag queen named Peppi Bismol.

"Really?" I sat there with my mouth hanging open.

"Yeah." Morgan's voice was unsteady. "You all know 'couples counseling' is just the first exit on the breakup highway."

"Not necessarily," I lied. "You might try easing up on the 'shut up, Fran' stuff. You kinda say it a lot."

"I'm going to take advice from someone who walked out on her wedding?" Morgan closed her eyes. "Sorry. I'm working on my impulsiveness issues, too." She left.

"These people are your *friends*?" Joanne sat at the edge of the bed.

"She's in a bad place," I replied. "And you're one to talk, living in Republicanville."

"Not all of them are homophobes. You'd be surprised. Some are liberal on social issues but believe in different ways to fix the economy."

"Wow, did somebody just turn on CNN?"

Joanne rolled her eyes. "What's with you? Why did you go off on Nathan last night? He was staring at that kabob for hours, wondering if it was a phallic thing. Wait. Don't tell me. I think you really didn't want to get married, so you were just looking for an excuse."

"Right, Sherlock. But I did kind of misunderstand him."

"So what about the wedding? Ellie can never get on with her life just because she married a man once?"

Tears rushed to my eyes. "Mom's right. You're right. But it's not as easy as it seems, Jo. It's every day. When he's on the road, he calls the kids. His voice, his presence, is always there. They even got the house together. So I'm living in a haunted house with a ghost who won't go away. Even the master bedroom is painted this awful tan color that *he* picked out! Now that he'll be around more, we'll have to see him at school concerts, everything. He'll *always* be in our lives!"

Joanne considered the situation thoughtfully. "It's a good point. I can see how that could drive you nuts."

"If I wanted a guy in my life forever, I'd be straight."

Joanne smiled. "The question is, do you love her enough to deal with it?" She stared at me intensely.

"I do," I said softly.

"Well, don't say it to me, say it to her! You were supposed to say it last night!"

When I came out of the bedroom, everyone was looking at me like I was the victim of an accident. It was an odd mixture of encouragement and pity.

"So you don't like the ladies anymore?" Aunt Rita swung her arm around my shoulders and put a drink in my hand. "As that Kinsey said, 'Sexuality is fluid.'"

Mom was surprised at her sister's knowledge.

"She still loves Ellie," Mom told her.

"Is Ellie that sad little girl who was standing in the ocean last night?" Mr. Hutchins asked.

"She's a *woman*," I corrected. Something about him brought out my claws.

"Then why the hell didn't you marry her?" Aunt Rita exclaimed, then laughed. "Wait, right. Two chicks can't get married."

"Yes, we can…in Massachusetts," I replied.

"So, let me get this straight, so to speak," Aunt Rita continued. "Say you get married here. Then one of you gets a job in Florida or Texas. Not married anymore?"

"It's dumb, isn't it?" I flopped on the couch. "I'm wondering if it is just a big joke."

"Telling someone you love them and want to commit to them for life is never a joke!" Joanne cried.

"But it doesn't fully count," I said. "Not like you and Nathan. We're still second-class citizens."

Nathan said, "Nah, you're second-class citizens because you're women." He looked around to see how many of us he'd offended. "It's a joke! I thought we could lighten it up a little!"

"I'm sorry, Nathan." I nearly choked on the words.

"It's okay." He winked just like his father and patted me on the back.

Aunt Rita slapped her leg. "Sydney, you missed one hell of a party last night. Course the kids were bored, so they played this game on TV where they shot people's heads off."

"I told them not to bring that," Joanne moaned.

"The next generation is not gonna know how to type or spell," Aunt Rita said. "But they'll sure know how to shoot the hell out of people and become first-class terrorists." With that, she made her way into the bathroom.

"Guess I better not tell her how many guns I own." Mr. Hutchins gave his son a playful shove.

"What's going on?" Cabbot asked me. His wide, round eyes were so innocent and confused. And he shamed me most of all.

"Just adults making things complicated," I replied. "We like to do that."

"Why?"

Good question.

CHAPTER THIRTY-EIGHT

"The One That's Getting Away"

"Flight leaves at four!" Nathan yelled, frantically packing.

"The boys will starve," Joanne said. "I'm making them ham sandwiches!"

"You're putting an innocent pig between two slices of bread!" Aunt Rita called, as she soaked in the view on the deck with her vodka on the rocks.

Seated beside her was Mom, who kept slapping at her legs. "These little bugs," she complained.

Then Mr. Hutchins came out to refresh Aunt Rita's drink.

"We could stay a little longer if you'd like," he told her. "No sense in all of us leaving."

Bryan came out and hugged me immediately. I wasn't sure if he was just sensitive or had a little too much wine.

"It's going to be okay," he said softly. "She loves you." Then he took a seat and stared at the tumbling water.

"He's right." Aunt Rita grabbed my leg.

"I don't know." I was lost in thought, not sure what to do. How could Ellie ever forgive me?

I vaguely heard the chatter around me but couldn't get out of my mood.

"So, Bryan," Mr. Hutchins began. "What's keepin' you from settling down?"

Bryan stirred uncomfortably in his seat. "I don't know. Haven't found the right one, I guess."

"The right one," Aunt Rita repeated. "It's all because of TV and movies. They give you this image of what a perfect woman should be like. It's a lie, I tell you! Real women have cellulite! And rolls of fat." She displayed her lower belly, which wasn't fat, and jiggled her sagging skin for emphasis.

"Tell me your ideal woman," Mr. Hutchins insisted.

"Well," Bryan said. "She'd have to have hair like Cher, eyes like Julia Ormond, legs like Tina Turner…"

Mr. Hutchins sat back. "You ain't one of them creepy fellas with body parts in your basement?"

Bryan laughed. "No, all my basement's used for is step aerobics." He rolled up his shirt as Aunt Rita had done. Not an ounce of body fat on him anywhere.

Mr. Hutchins and Aunt Rita both squinted, trying to understand him.

"What do you think of the gays?" Mr. Hutchins persisted.

"Oh, I'm not political," Bryan replied. "I always thought the right to bear arms was just about wanting to go sleeveless."

I gave Bryan a knowing glance and went inside.

Cabbot was commanding a fleet of navy ships in his video game and apparently had annihilated his brother, Tayler, who was crying again.

"Enough of that game!" Joanne hollered. "Turn it off, Cabbot. It's upsetting your brother."

"'Cause he's a sore loser," Cabbot teased.

"I missed you guys so much," I said, grabbing their squishy little bodies and squeezing them.

"We were going to stay longer," Nathan said. "At your place, but…"

"You don't know if you should go back there," I finished.

He nodded with a slight smile.

"I don't know, either. I guess she went back today." I looked around like a lost puppy. Then Fran came over quietly and showed me a text message.

It wasn't too late after all.

"You go get her," Penny whispered.

"Everybody stay where you are!" I announced, running out the door.

"Wait," Fran called. "You saw what she said. You think it's a good idea?"

"Yes." With that, I ran down the road toward Falcon's Roost, a small hotel just a few blocks from the cottage. I knew Ellie was staying there. Memories flashed before my eyes, and I'd begun to walk faster until I was doing a slight jog.

Suddenly all of the things I loved most about her came tumbling into my mind like the waves. I loved the way she'd dance with me in the kitchen early in the morning, even though she was tired and had to wake the kids. I loved the way she always lost her keys and her phone every morning. I even loved the way she yelled that the floor needed sweeping, yelling just because she was tired and later apologizing. I loved how she tried to eat potato chips in bed and sneak her arm as quietly as possible into the noisy bag while we were watching TV. And most of all, I loved the way I could slide into her arms at the end of the day and feel like everything was going to be all right.

Then I thought of all the things I'd started to love about our emerging family—how Matthew yelled "Sandwich!" and hugged us together. I loved how Megan would call from her bedroom, "Sydney! I have a grammar thing to ask you." I felt needed. I remembered how, on my birthday, there were hushed sounds and whispering outside the bedroom as the kids worked on homemade cards for me. And I loved how we'd be watching a movie in the family room and Cookie would jump up in between me and Ellie, so she could steal a piece of each of our laps. That was the stuff life was made of.

Surely after all the good times and all of the snow I'd shoveled for her, Ellie could find room in her heart to forgive me.

Seriously out of shape, I started sucking the air. When I looked up, I saw the perfect thing. The thing that was going to change everything. I begged the woman who was driving to let me climb inside for just a moment. I gave her careful instructions, and when she parked, I jumped out and ran up the stairs to room 206.

I pounded on the door. "Please! I was an idiot. You're all that matters! I want to marry you!"

A couple from Indiana had just pulled up and was taking bags out of their station wagon. They looked shyly at me.

"I hope he says yes," the man said with his thumb up. And they disappeared behind another door.

Ellie finally opened her door and I stretched out my arms, with the UPS truck behind me in full view. "You're still my UPS!" I cried.

"Don't make a scene." She yanked me inside as I waved goodbye to the UPS driver.

"You *do* care."

I followed her out to the back deck.

Matthew's eyes were big saucers watching our every move, while Megan pretended not to care. She looked up at me occasionally, while banging the remote control on the bed. It wasn't working, and she was no doubt missing an important show.

Ellie closed the slider to the back patio.

"Last night I blamed myself," she said. "For surprising you. I should've given you however much time you needed. People don't do surprise weddings. It's never a good idea."

"But it is! I *am* ready! What I was...worried about...it doesn't matter now."

Matthew was pressed against the glass, trying to hear every word.

"Please give me another chance?" My eyes were blind with tears, and I squeezed her hands as hard as I could. She pulled away fast.

"Ow, you dislocated my thumb." She made her pouty face. She grumbled and sighed. What was the verdict? I was on trial for my life. I didn't realize how serious until it became obvious she wasn't going to answer me right away. "You want to know the real truth? Why I brought you here to surprise you? I picked a place that meant something to us. But I made it all a surprise because I didn't...I didn't think you'd ever ask me. I heard all the things you said about marriage, gay marriage."

I didn't say anything.

Tears streamed down her face. "Would you have asked me?"

"I don't know. Maybe eventually." *Wrong answer.*

"See? I didn't want to wait anymore. But my biggest fear was that you'd say no. I never, ever thought you'd run out over some stupid thing Nathan said. And then I thought for sure you'd come back. But you didn't come back. That was the worst. I'm not sure I can forgive you. God, I felt like such an idiot!"

Sadly, Ellie was realizing a side of me I tried to push way, way down—the flaky side. Mom was right. She knew I liked to run away and give up when things got hard. In high school I was in a play. But I had trouble remembering my lines. So on opening night, I quit. The director told me I was more of a failure to quit than to go out and try to do the lines. He thought he was inspiring me to stay. But I took the safe route. And I had felt like a failure ever since.

"I'm so sorry," I said. But it was one of those times when "sorry" just doesn't mean anything. "It wasn't because of what Nathan said. Not really. But what it was doesn't matter now!" After a long pause, watching her wipe her face, I finally said, "Okay, I'll tell you what. I'll be there tonight, at the cottage. I told everyone to stay one more night. If you decide you don't want to marry me, take the kids and go home. I'll get the message and come for my things tomorrow. If you do decide to marry me, please get the kids and show up at the cottage at seven. And I'll have a minister from...somewhere. Okay?"

She was expressionless. "When things get hard, you run away."

"Not this time. I promise." I took one more look back at her sad blue eyes before leaving. My heart was pounding. I could only imagine how she must have felt last night. I wouldn't blame her if she wanted to put me through the same pain. But there was really no more to say.

As I headed back to the cottage, I did feel hopeful that she hadn't left the Cape completely after last night. Since she'd gotten a place nearby, it seemed as though she was still holding out hope for me, which gave me hope. I would know soon enough.

CHAPTER THIRTY-NINE

"Maddie as Hell"

When I came back to the cottage, I saw a strange SUV in the driveway. Standing in the living room was Maddie. I wanted to cry.

"You're a day late," I joked.

"From what I hear, I might be on time," she said. She came over to me and gave me a big bear hug. "I'm so sorry."

She didn't look much older, just a little tired around her eyes and the same full cheeks. She'd been experimenting with blond streaks in her hair. She looked good. She wore a cream sweater and a leather jacket. Everyone watched us.

"What made you come up?" I asked.

"Penny told me you guys were getting married."

There was an awkwardness between us, like just getting to know each other again.

"I was an idiot," she blurted. "A jealous idiot." She hugged me again.

"Is there gonna be a wedding?" Nathan called. "We canceled our flight."

"I don't know yet," I answered. I went for a walk outside with Maddie. We ended up at a convenience store that was always closed. We stood on each side of an old ice machine.

"Why the Cold War?" I finally said. "You were jealous?"

"I've always been a little mad at anyone who was happier than I was," she admitted.

"But you're never happy."

She laughed ironically. "I was once. See, about twenty years ago, I moved to New York to be a dancer. I'd gotten a callback for a Broadway show. I was so excited that I ran through the street. I couldn't wait to get to my one-room apartment and call my family back home. I ran right into the middle of the street and got hit by a taxi. It messed up my knee and no more dancing."

Wow. This was the secret I'd never known. I was flattered she chose to tell me.

"I've always kind of resented anyone who got to follow their dream. When I went into medicine, it was because I knew I'd have steady work, not 'cause I wanted to help people. And shouldn't that be the reason you do it?"

"Yeah," I answered. "I think so."

"And there's another thing." Maddie looked down. Whatever she had to say, this was going to be the hardest part. "I knew you'd leave when you and Ellie got together. The thing is, I've always liked someone for years, but it's never worked out. And it's not going to work out. I think it all just reminded me of that."

"Who? Who do you like?"

"It's tough to say. We've been friends for years, but I've never had the guts to tell her."

Heat spread up my spine. It couldn't be. Whomever it was, I didn't want to know. "Some things are better left unsaid." I covered her mouth with my hand.

"Not you, you arrogant jackass!"

I was so relieved and a little insulted at the same time. "Well, who? You can tell me."

"No, I can't. She's someone you know. You have to keep a secret."

"Oh, come on! Now I have to know."

Maddie was dying to spill it, to release her burden. "Penny," she said.

"Really?" I screamed. "Why haven't you done anything about it!"

"Why do you think I'm always teasing her, making fun of the online girlfriends and telling her she's not smart?"

"Maddie, that's what guys do. They pull a girl's pigtails on the playground when they like her. Why can't you just be nice to her?"

"Have you ever been in a routine with someone so long it would be weird to change it?"

I could see her point. "You should tell her, though, before she meets—"

"Miss Topeka, I know." She kicked at the crunchy, stone-filled ground. "She's always been there, you know? I thought she was so cute I couldn't figure out how to tell her the moment it went from friendship to this scary shit. And now she thinks I'm some old curmudgeon, so she probably wouldn't want me anyway."

"Stop it right there. Don't assume anything. She may like you too but doesn't think you could like anyone since Holly. You have done a good job convincing everyone of that."

"I know she likes me, Syd. I just don't know if she could *like* me, you know?"

I put an arm around her shoulder. "It's so nice to see this side of you."

"Keep it to yourself, okay?"

"I'm glad you came."

"Me too. Forgive me?"

"Yeah, but you better come visit. We have a great house. Well, Ellie does."

"So what the hell happened last night?"

"Nothing," I replied. "Cold feet. I just hope she shows tonight."

"She won't stay mad at you. I couldn't." Maddie gave me a smile as we headed back.

I watched the purple sun fading away and felt the eyes of my family on my back. If Ellie didn't come, I'd be the biggest jerk in the history of my family. My feet started sinking into the sand, along with my self-esteem. Joanne stood beside me, clutching the blowing, nearly withered flowers she'd been holding for half an hour. There was pity painted all over her face.

"You want to go in?" she asked softly.

"No!"

"I need a drink," Aunt Rita grumbled behind me.

"You have to wait!" Mom scolded her.

The only thing worse than Joanne's pity was the face of the preacher I got at the last minute. Ryan Aldrich, a gay minister from the same nondenominational church, had shown up bright and bubbly in his rainbow bowtie and sunny disposition. As the minutes ticked away, his brightness had begun to fade just like the actual sun, and I'd begun to feel like I'd just wasted his time.

"Women are notoriously late," he said, still trying to be cheerful. He kept fussing with a lock of unruly hair that fell into his eyes from the wind. He was getting more annoyed with that than the lack of a wedding ceremony. "Dammit! I wish I had my hairspray."

"I have some," Bryan offered.

Ryan studied his hair like a scientist. "No, sweetie, I have a special salon-strength kind. You can't get it in stores."

"So do I." He'd met his match.

Ryan raised an eyebrow.

Great. I was hoping to get married today, not be caught in the middle of *Hair Wars*, the lesser-known, gay version of *Star Wars*. They began talking. Bryan might meet his true love tonight, I thought. At least some good might come out of this.

CHAPTER FORTY

"The Great Beyond"

When it grew dark, Ryan politely excused himself, and Joanne escorted him to the door. But I refused to leave my spot. Call it hope, blind faith or just not wanting to look stupid, I held my spot.

Suddenly, there was a figure moving down the beach.

That's what I need, I thought sarcastically. A strolling couple will punctuate my final humiliation. But as I looked closer, it was one person. Still embarrassing.

As the figure emerged from darkness, there was something so familiar about the person's walk. It was a man. He flipped a few stubborn strands of hair left on his head back with his hand, just like my dad used to.

We had home movies with Dad swimming laps, and when he'd reach the edge of the pool, he'd flip his thinning hair back.

"Dad?"

He looked younger, the way I remembered him from childhood.

I immediately turned around to see if anyone else was seeing this, but they were still muttering amongst themselves, trying not to look at me.

"Mom! Look! It's Dad!" I shouted.

But she wouldn't look at me. She was too busy arguing about Aunt Rita's drinking.

"She can't hear you," Dad said calmly. And that was the strangest thing. Dad was never calm. Ever. He never spoke calmly or had this aura of peace about him that he did tonight.

"What…wh…how are you here?" I tried to move to him, to hug him as hard as I could. But the way he put up his hands stopped me.

"No, Sydney, I'm sorry."

He took a few steps closer.

"I had to come," he told me. "I have so much to tell you, but these damn afterlife rules…"

He looked around at or for something; I couldn't tell.

"Remember that box your mother gave you?" he asked.

I nodded, knowing exactly what he meant. Shortly after he died, Mom gave me a box of birthday and Father's Day cards he'd saved. I didn't want them back. I wanted to think they went out into the cosmos and would reach him somehow.

"I still have them." He smiled.

By this time, I was flooded with so many tears I couldn't see or appreciate the moment.

"Stop crying!" he hollered just like he used to when he was ordering us to change the TV channel.

"Joanne!" I screamed. "Are you seeing this?"

But she was talking to Nathan; they were all in some kind of weird bubble, or I was. It was like a science fiction movie.

"I don't have a lot of time, so listen to me."

Why did apparitions always say they didn't have much time? Was there a mother ship docked somewhere, waiting to take him home?

He laughed to himself.

"You're laughing," I shouted incredulously. "Don't you miss me? Isn't this hard for you?"

"I never left," he said. "That's the big cosmic joke. I've been with you through everything you thought I was missing, even your last job when you got laid off."

I put my head down. "Oh," I mumbled. "You saw that one."

"Listen to me," he repeated. "If I knew what I do now, I wouldn't have wasted so much goddamn time worrying…always waiting for the worst. My own wedding…my mind was all over the place when all I wanted to do was look at your beautiful mother."

He took my hands in his rugged, furry, always larger hands.

"Don't waste your time," he warned. He was so intense, like he used to be when he was talking about the "idiots in Washington," only more so. "Don't indulge your anxiety. It's meaningless. It blocks life from getting in." He gestured to his heart. "Listen to music and really hear it. When your friends talk, really listen. Don't let the troubles wander in."

But there was a question I had to know the answer to. He must have sensed it because he smiled and said, "Dammit, almost forgot the reason I came here."

He looked around again.

"Your wedding," he continued. "It's okay by me."

He started to turn away.

"Wait!" I called. "Really? You aren't upset that she's a woman?"

"She's a nice-looking woman."

"But Dad—"

"I never told you or your mother," he said, "but when I was in the army there was a guy named Frank. We all kind of knew he was, you know. He was the kindest, bravest guy I ever knew. Everyone thought a lot of him." There were tears in his eyes. "When you get over on this side," he said, "you understand that all the crap everyone fights about doesn't matter. It has no place here. When there's love, it's never wrong." He was looking at Mom.

He touched my shoulder. "Love is beautiful. The rest is crap." Then he touched my head like when I was a child and turned away, walking down the beach but toward the stars at the same time.

"Dad! Wait!" There was never enough time to say all that needed to be said, it seemed.

Then he was gone.

Remembering his words, a rare calmness came over me.

It wasn't long before the sky was completely black with only a few stars still hanging on. I turned around, seeing that most of my family was dozing off anyway. I was wearing a Cape Cod tourist-type T-shirt, one of the ones Ellie and I had planned to wear together. Joanne noticed it when I first came out with it on.

"That's why Mom thought Ellie hadn't dressed up," she'd said.

It was time for me to put everyone out of their misery.

"Well, guess this means lots of shrimp for everyone!" I clapped my hands, and everyone woke up. Buckets of chilled shrimp and gallons of cocktail sauce were all ready to be consumed.

I had to face the fact that I'd blown it, destroyed something beautiful with the most beautiful person I'd ever known.

CHAPTER FORTY-ONE

"Left of Center"

As everyone except Aunt Rita made their way to the seafood snack bar we'd set up, I had no idea that Ellie was back in her motel room ordering the kids to pack to go home. Later I'd learn that she'd changed the channel to catch the weather before they left. She wasn't coming back to the cottage.

"Mom!" Matthew whined. After all, he was missing a SpongeBob episode that he'd seen only seven times.

"I have to check the weather," Ellie said firmly.

At the same time, a reporter from a local news channel approached me behind the cottage. A bright camera light assaulted my face. "You're the author of that blog, *The Comfortable Shoe Diaries*?" he asked.

"Yes," I answered tentatively.

"Are you getting married tonight?" he asked.

"Not anymore," I said sadly.

"What do you think about gay marriage?" The reporter, a young guy in his twenties, thrust the microphone at me. I could tell that he hoped for a contrary answer to make things interesting. But knowing my blog, he probably wasn't expecting it.

"I don't believe in it," I answered.

The reporter was shocked.

That was the live news that Ellie saw. She sat on the bed, completely broken. "Change it! I don't want to see any more!" She threw the remote across the bed at Megan and resumed packing.

The reporter got excited, the microphone was shaking under my chin. "Really? Why's that?"

"I don't believe in gay or straight marriage, just marriage. When you love someone, you love them. Love isn't an issue to be argued over. It should be a right for everyone. I can't even believe we're having this conversation." With that, I trudged through the sand back to my guests.

Mom confronted the reporter. "This is a private party," she declared.

He took his cue to get off the premises.

"Well done," Maddie said. "I always knew you were a romantic."

"You could learn from her," Penny said.

"How do you know I'm not one?" Maddie asked.

I overheard Mr. Hutchins asking Nathan about what the reporter had said.

"I do an online blog," I explained.

"You write about bein' gay?" Mr. Hutchins asked.

"Different experiences. What it's like from this side of the fence." I shrugged, trying not to make a big deal out of it.

"So you're tellin' everyone on the Internet you're gay?" He couldn't get past that.

"There's lots of blogs like that, Dad," Nathan said, trying to change the subject.

Joanne put her arm around me. "I'm sorry it didn't work out."

"I deserved it. I should've trusted my heart sooner. Then none of this would've happened. I'm an idiot."

"No, I'm an idiot." The crowd parted as she pushed her way through the center. It was Ellie. What I didn't realize was that my interview had been live on TV.

"I'm the idiot," I repeated.

"You're both idiots!" Aunt Rita shouted. "Get married or go home."

"I heard what you said," Ellie told me softly. "Thanks to a broken remote I couldn't change the channel fast enough to miss the best part."

My mind raced trying to remember what I'd said.

"I think I understand you a lot better." She threw her arms around me tightly.

Whatever I said, I was so happy that I'd said it. Whatever it was.

"It's like watching *Gays of Our Lives*," Bryan sighed.

Aunt Rita put her arms around me and Ellie. "The trouble with young people," she stammered. "You all want guarantees on everything, like when you shop for a blouse. The material they use is crap, so you know the damn thing's gonna tear. You can't get a guarantee. You pick it up off the rack, get a feel for it, and it either grabs you or it doesn't. If it does, go with it. Don't think too much. Just get it and take it home."

Her drunken logic made sense.

"I'm sorry, Ellie," I whispered. "The minister's gone."

"Your Aunt Rita used to be a notary," Mom said. "She can do it."

Aunt Rita looked suddenly scared. "Only in Florida."

"Oh, come on," Joanne said. "Better a member of the family than someone we don't know."

Aunt Rita said, "I've married people, sure. Of course, with two women, I don't understand it. But I can do it."

Mom hesitated. "But Rita, haven't you had a bit too much?"

"Not nearly enough," Aunt Rita muttered to herself.

Then Mr. Hutchins followed closely behind Aunt Rita, holding her arm to steady her. As each new wave crashed over her feet, she let out a little cry at the sudden bursts of cold. The tide was coming in, getting closer and closer to the back deck. We really had to do it now or never.

My sister stood beside me, a little emotional because she could finally do something like this for me. Matthew, Megan and Bryan stood beside Ellie. She needed the support; it must have been bittersweet, knowing that a portion of her family believed she was going to hell. Matthew was dressed up in a nice suit, holding up the rings and grinning. Megan held a small bouquet and gave me a nod of approval that, for me, was worth a million dollars.

"Are you guys okay?" Ellie asked her kids.

"Uh-huh," Megan said. "Just hurry up. Mosquitoes." She waved her hand around.

"Yes!" Matthew replied emphatically.

"You like Sydney, don't you?" Joanne asked.

"Yes," Matthew answered. "But it's better if they get married because we'll get three Christmases now. At Mom's house, then Dad's, then Uncle Bryan's."

Bryan laughed. Apparently, his holiday parties were legendary. It was too bad he couldn't remember most of them.

Aunt Rita, with Mr. Hutchins holding her up, balanced in the rushing water, still screaming as the freezing water nipped at her ankles. Family and friends kept shooing the nighttime bugs that were attracted to the tiki torches we had set up on the back porch.

Penny touched Maddie's leg. Maddie jumped, thinking her intentions might have been different. But she was only smacking a bug on Maddie's thigh.

"I now pronounce you..." Aunt Rita stammered. "What do I pronounce you?"

"Married!" Ellie exclaimed. And we shared a kiss that lasted forever. I lost all track of time and place. She'd given me a kiss that really made me see the stars.

I glanced out at the beaming crowd. Mom was emotional. Maddie put her jacket around Penny's shoulders. Morgan and Fran held hands tightly. Bryan dabbed at his eyes, while Nathan tried to sneak a crab leg. My nephews didn't understand the meaning of this, but they were happy to be involved in any kind of party that involved food.

Shortly after, Mr. Hutchins approached us. "I didn't know what to get folks like y'all," he said. "I asked around town, and I got a lot of the same answer. I don't know if they were just jokin'."

I could see that he was earnest, really trying. So I patted his arm to let him know I appreciated it.

He reached into his shorts pocket and pulled out a gift certificate to Home Depot. Ellie and I started laughing. Then Fran and Morgan came over and laughed too.

"So they *were* kiddin' me," Mr. Hutchins said.

"Oh no," Fran replied. "That's right on the money!"

"Thank you, Mr. Hutchins," I said. "We'll use it for sure."

"We need a new toilet," Ellie declared.

"You're so romantic," I laughed, hanging on to her arm.

Mr. Hutchins turned to everyone. "They just got married and they want a toilet for a weddin' gift? Y'all are weird."

"You have no idea," Maddie said with a smile.

It wasn't exactly as I'd imagined it. Or as Ellie had imagined it. But then again, nothing in our lives had been planned so far. Many things had happened that no one ever expected. And that was okay. Part of learning to relax, for me, meant letting go of whatever I thought was supposed to happen and just letting it be.

Once again, my heart had shown me the way. And it was right.

Bella Books, Inc.

Women. Books. Even Better Together.

P.O. Box 10543
Tallahassee, FL 32302

Phone: 800-729-4992
www.bellabooks.com